SUNWING

KENNETH OPPEL

Aladdin Paperbacks
New York London Toronto Sydney Singapore

ALADDIN PAPERBACKS
An imprint of Simon & Schuster Children's Publishing Division
1230 Avenue of the Americas, New York, New York 10020
First Aladdin Paperbacks edition September 2001. Copyright ©
2000 by Kenneth Oppel. All rights reserved including the right
of reproduction in whole or in part in any form. Also available in
a SIMON & SCHUSTER BOOKS FOR YOUNG READERS hardcover edition.
Book design by Paul Zakris. The text for this book is set in 10-
Point Stone Serif. Printed and bound in the United States of
America
10 9

The Library of Congress has cataloged the hardcover edition as
follows:
Oppel, Kenneth.
Sunwing / Kenneth Oppel.—1st ed.
p. cm.
Sequel to: Silverwing.
Summary: Continues the adventures of Shade, a young bat, as he
searches for his father and struggles to prevent the evil jungle bat
Goth from wiping out the sun.
ISBN: 0-689-82674-5 (hc.)
1. Bats Juvenile fiction. [1. Bats Fiction. 2. Fathers and sons
Fiction.] I. Title.
PZ10.3.O555Su 2000
[Fic]—dc21
99-25322
CIP
ISBN: 0-689-83287-7 (Aladdin pbk.)

FOR NATHANIEL

PART ONE

DEAD OF WINTER

Wings trimmed tight, Shade sailed through the forest. The naked elms, maples, and oaks blazed in the moon's glow, their branches spiked with icicles. Beneath him, trees lay toppled like the skeletons of giant beasts. The groans of freezing wood filled the air, and in the distance Shade heard a mighty crack as yet another branch snapped and fell.

He shivered. Even though he'd been flying for hours, he was still cold, the wind chiseling through his sleek black fur into his bones. Wistfully, he thought of the other Silverwings, roosting snugly back at Hibernaculum. Even though their bodies would now be glistening with frost, they were warm in a deep winter's sleep that would take them through to spring. They hadn't wanted to come with him: It was too cold, too dangerous, they said. They didn't care enough to make the journey. Let them sleep, Shade thought, squinting against a sudden blast of wind. They had no curiosity, no sense of adventure.

He was going to find his father.

And it wasn't as if he was alone. Weaving through the forest alongside him were more than a dozen Silverwings. He could see Chinook, skimming over a heavy fir bough, knocking off snow. Up ahead was Shade's mother, Ariel, speaking softly with Frieda, the chief elder of their colony. There was another bat in the vanguard too, a male called Icarus, who was acting as guide. Shade hoped he knew where he was going. But after all he'd been through recently, he was happy to let someone else blaze the trail for a change.

"Cold?" he heard Marina ask beside him.

"Me?" Shade shook his head, trying not to let his teeth chatter. "You?"

She wrinkled her neat, pointy nose, as if the very idea was laughable. "No. But I'm pretty sure I saw you shiver."

"Not me," he said, and returned her suspicious look. "Anyway, you've got more fur. Look at all that fur!"

"Well, I am older than you," she pointed out.

Shade grunted. As if she ever let him forget!

"And Brightwings have better fur," she added matter-of-factly. "Just the way it is, Shade."

"Better fur!" he spluttered indignantly. "I've heard it all now! Just because it's thicker doesn't mean it's better."

"Sure is warm, though," Marina said with a grin.

Shade couldn't help grinning back. Of all the bats traveling with him, Marina was the only one who wasn't a Silverwing. Her fur was much thicker and brighter than his own, radiant in the moon's glow. Her wings were narrower, and she had elegant, shell-shaped ears. He'd met her last autumn, after getting lost on his first ever migration. She'd helped him catch up with his colony at Hibernaculum. She was an infuriating know-it-all but, he had to admit, she'd saved his life, once or twice.

A dollop of snow hit him on the back, and Shade looked up sharply to see Chinook swinging lower with a triumphant grin.

"Oh, sorry, Shade, did I get you?"

"You're hilarious, Chinook. Really." He shook the snow off before it melted. When they were newborns back at Tree Haven—and it wasn't so long ago—Chinook had treated him with about as much respect as a mulched-up leaf. After all, Chinook had been the most promising hunter and flyer, and Shade just the runt of the colony. But now, after all Shade's adventures, Chinook had decided he might be worth talking to.

"Chinook, that's no way to treat a hero," Marina said, her eyes flashing gleefully.

Shade sniffed. Hero? He sure didn't feel like a hero. Maybe the first night or two after he'd gotten back to Hibernaculum, and everyone listened to his stories. But after that, somehow, things went pretty much back to normal. He ate, drank, and slept like everyone else, and felt the same as he always had. Frankly, he'd expected better. What did he have to do to get some respect? He'd escaped from pigeons and rats, from owls and cannibal bats. He'd tunneled beneath the earth and soared through lightning storms. He'd flown in the blazing light of day!

And now he got snow dumped on his head.

Heroes did not get snow dumped on their heads.

With a grimace, he watched as Chinook swooped down beside Marina. Chinook liked her company, that was obvious. Over the past few nights he'd gone out of his way to fly beside her, and roost near her during the day. The amazing thing was, Marina didn't seem to mind. The snow was probably his way of impressing her, Shade fumed, and it seemed to have worked. Look at her, still smiling about it! Sometimes, watching from a distance, Shade would actually hear her laughing at something Chinook said—a kind of tinkly laugh he'd never heard before. She sure didn't laugh like that with him. It drove him crazy. What could Chinook possibly come up with that was so funny? He wasn't *smart* enough to be funny. Were they laughing at him?

"I've been thinking about those two cannibal bats," Chinook said. "Goth and Throbb."

"Uh-huh," said Shade.

"And I figure I could've fought them."

Shade's ears twitched indignantly. "No, Chinook. They would've eaten you." How many times did he have to go through this? Chinook just never quite believed he himself couldn't have beaten them in battle. "They were *huge*," Shade told him.

Chinook flared his nostrils carelessly. "How huge?"

"About *this* huge," said Shade wickedly, and he sang sound right into Chinook's ears and drew an echo picture in his head of Goth lunging, snout cracking open to show twin mountain ranges of dripping teeth, his three-foot wings slick with sweat, billowing . . .

The sound picture blazed in Chinook's mind only a fraction of a second, but was so sudden and so horrifying that he cried out and careened into a fir bough, dousing himself with snow.

"Was that really necessary?" Marina asked Shade.

"Oh, I think so."

"Nice trick," grumbled Chinook, shaking the snow from his shoulders.

"Still think you could fight them?" Shade asked.

"Well, we could've fought them back at Hibernaculum. There're thousands of us there."

"No," said Marina. "They would've waited until you were all asleep, and eaten you one by one through the whole winter. That was their plan. And they really would've gone straight for you, Chinook. Lots of flesh on those bones."

"Well, it's muscle," said Chinook proudly, "not fat," and then he frowned at the idea of being a meal. "I still think I could've—"

"Well, they're dead, so you'll never know," Shade said impatiently.

"Throbb, anyway," said Marina. "We saw him turn to ash. But we only saw Goth get *hit* by the lightning."

"There's no way he could've lived through that," said Shade, and he was surprised at the urgency in his voice; he wanted so much for it to be true. He could clearly see Goth's body spinning down through the thunderhead, charred. He doubted he would ever forget the two canni- bals, and they still haunted his dreams. Goth would pin him to the ground, and Shade could feel his weight crushing his chest, smell his rank breath. Then Goth would lower his head to Shade's and whisper things in his ear, terrible things that he never remembered upon waking at twilight. And for that, he was grateful.

"He's got to be dead," he muttered.

"Hope you're right, that's all I can say," said Marina. She looked at the scar Goth's jaws had left on her wrist. Shade too had been wounded, his wing slashed in two places. Though the rips had healed over, they still burned coldly as he flew. And he often caught himself glancing back over his wing, half-expecting to see Goth's monstrous silhouette.

"Not much farther now."

It was Icarus up ahead.

"We should come out onto grassland soon. And then it's not more than an hour's flying. That's what Cassiel said."

Shade's ears pricked at his father's name. Last spring, before Shade was even born, Cassiel had gone searching for a strange Human building, not far from Hibernaculum, and he'd never come back. Killed by owls: That's what everyone thought. But last fall, while flying south with Marina, Shade met an albino bat called Zephyr, who could listen to the past, present, and future.

And he'd said Cassiel was alive.

Shade didn't know much about his father. Only that he'd been banded by the Humans—and he'd wanted desperately to know what it all meant. He must've thought he'd get the answers at the building. And Shade was certain this was where he would at last find him, the father he'd never known.

Suddenly up ahead, he saw Frieda flare her left wing in silent warning, and he instantly veered toward the nearest tree with Marina. Digging his claws into icy bark, he flipped upside down, folded his wings tight, and tried to look like an icicle. Below him, he could hear the others quickly finding roosts, then silence.

"You see anything?" he whispered to Marina.

She shook her head. Carefully he swept the trees with sound, watching as the returning echoes drew pictures before his mind's eye.

There.

With its white plumage, the owl was so well camouflaged against the snowy branches, Shade might easily have passed over it with his eyes. But caught in his echo vision, the owl gleamed like quicksilver. It was a winged giant, easily four times his size: a deadly bundle of feather, muscle, and claw, its huge, moonlike eyes unhooded. Fifty more wingbeats and he would've flown straight into it. He should've been paying more attention.

The mere sight of the owl filled him with loathing. For millions of years, the owls had patrolled the skies at dusk and dawn, making sure the bats never saw the sun. By law, if a bat was sighted during the light of day, he could be hunted down and killed.

Just like they'd nearly killed *him* last fall. He could remember that dawn so clearly, how he'd waited, hidden, for just a glimpse of the rising sun. He *had* to see it. And he *did*, a blazing sliver of it that still burned gloriously in his memory. But what happened afterward was far from glorious. In revenge, the owls burned down Tree Haven, his colony's age-old nursery roost. He winced at the memory: the smoldering, buckled ruins of his home. That was the price he'd made everyone pay for his peek at the sun.

He glared at the owl. Now not even the *night* skies were safe anymore. Only months ago, the owls had declared war on them, convinced they were murdering birds. The only bats Shade knew who killed birds were Goth and Throbb, but the owls would never believe that.

"What's it doing out here?" he whispered to Marina.

It was, after all, the middle of winter, and this owl should be hibernating. Like us, Shade thought with a pang of guilt. It had been his idea to set out for his father in the dead of winter. But he hadn't realized how agonizing it would be to fight the sleep, how cold it would be. Even Frieda, though, had agreed that at least the skies would be free of owls.

And now here was this one, blocking their way through the forest.

Fly away, Shade thought angrily. Get lost.

But it wasn't going anywhere. Nor was it alone. A mournful hoot emanated from deep in the trees, and Shade's heart skipped. The first owl returned the call, and began a slow swivel with its huge head.

One owl might be unlucky; two was definitely suspicious.

"Sentries?" Shade whispered.

"In the middle of winter?" Marina said.

"Maybe we're near a garrison, or hibernation site."

"They don't usually put guards out in winter. Could be they're just looking for us," she added grimly. "You don't break hibernation for nothing."

He shuddered. If these two owls were awake, how many others were there, and what were they planning?

"Above the tree line," suggested Shade. "We could fly over them."

"No. Look." Shade followed her gaze, and through the naked branches caught the silhouette of an owl circling tightly against the moon.

"We'll go around," said Shade. "They can't have picketed the whole forest."

His feet, buried in the icy crust of the branch, were starting to go numb. He shifted his claws slightly and then watched in horror as a crazy spiderweb of cracks spread out along the branch. A long husk of ice suddenly broke free, carrying a dozen icicles with it. Down they all fell, clattering through the branches. Shade scrambled to regain his grip, and his eyes shot back to the owl.

Its head swiveled around sharply.

"Don't even blink," Marina hissed at him.

Shade could hear the owl's own search echoes striking him, bouncing off, and he tried to make his body stiff as an icicle. It was a horrible feeling, being probed by this raptor, almost feeling its blunt sonic blows against his fur.

Shade waited, hoping fervently the owl would turn

away, dismiss the noise as falling ice. You idiot, he raged at himself. Why couldn't you just stay still? But no, you had to squirm and make a miniature avalanche!

With two strokes of its powerful wings, the owl lifted from its roost and was over the tree. It landed on their branch, its mighty four-taloned foot crunching into the wood just inches from Shade's tail. His whole body urged him to bolt, but he knew that if he did, the owl would snatch him up in its hooked beak in a second.

He gazed at Marina, and together they locked each other in place with their eyes. The other Silverwings were scattered on the lower branches, and he hoped they too had the sense to stay still.

Suddenly the owl hopped down to the next branch, landing hard, and shaking free a deadly rain of icicles. It knows we're here, Shade thought in horror. He knew what the owl was doing: trying to flush them out, or impale them in the process. The owl paused, cocking its head. It hopped down another branch. More ice fell. Then the owl ducked its head so that it could look *beneath* the branch. It was only a matter of time before it spotted the others.

Then Shade noticed the icicle. It hung on his branch, farther in, and it was much larger than most, fed by a number of twigs. It hung directly over the owl's head. Quickly he made some calculations.

He caught Marina's eye and nodded at the icicle.

"Drop it," he mouthed.

She frowned. How? she asked with her eyes.

There was no time to explain. He picked a frequency

the owl wouldn't hear and focused all his attention on the base of the icicle. Over the past few nights, he'd realized he could not only see things with sound, and sing sound pictures into other bats' heads—but he could also *move* things with sound. During the day, he practiced on leaves. He wasn't very good at it yet. He could shift light things, just a little. But an icicle . . .

He pelted it with sound, his whole body tensed, his eyes clamped shut. Sweat prickled his fur. In his mind's eye he saw the base of the icicle wiggle. He took a ragged breath, and checked on the owl.

It had hopped down even lower. Shade knew that beneath the next branch, his mother was roosting with Frieda and Chinook. He didn't have much time. With all his energy he lashed out at the base of the icicle. It wobbled. He heard a faint click, but still it held.

He tried to catch his breath. Maybe once more. But before he could stop her, Marina was scuttling down the branch at full speed toward the icicle. Bark crackled beneath her claws, and Shade saw the owl look up, its eyes impaling them with rage. It flared its wings and shrieked at the same moment Marina slammed herself against the icicle.

It plummeted, spinning onto its side, and clubbed the owl soundly on the head. The giant bird teetered for a moment and then plunged unconscious to the forest floor, tangled in its own wings.

"Fly," came Frieda's shout from below, and at once they were all back in the air. Marina at his side, Shade flew after the others, wings pounding, skidding through the forest, grazing whippy branches and blazing a trail of snow and mist behind him. He knew it wouldn't be long before the other owls came to investigate.

Suddenly he broke from the cover of trees and was soaring over open grassland. He felt afraid—they were so exposed out here, all that open sky weighing down on them. Instinctively he dropped lower, wings nearly grazing the tall blades of grass. He risked a backward glance: Circling high in the sky were half a dozen owls, but their shrieks sounded far away. Maybe they hadn't spotted them after all.

For a thousand more wingbeats they all flew without speaking, intent only on putting more distance between themselves and the owls.

He glanced at Marina. "Thanks for your help."

"You're welcome."

After a moment he added, "You know, I could've done it by myself."

She looked at him with that pleasantly amused expression she put on just to torment him. "Of course," she said.

"I almost had it!"

"We didn't have much time, Shade."

He knew she was right, but he was still angry at himself for failing. "Well, you try dropping an icicle with just sound!"

He knew she couldn't, which was why he said it. At first, he'd thought all bats could move things with sound. But it wasn't so, Frieda had told him. It was a kind of gift, a rare skill. She herself could just barely flutter a blade of grass, and not from very far away. Still, his own last effort had hardly been impressive. He'd nearly passed out trying to snap that stupid icicle.

"Look," said Marina, swiveling her ears dismissively, "you've got all your fancy sound tricks. I just do the boring stuff. Like making sure the icicle falls and hits the owl on the head."

"Well, who noticed that icicle in the first place?"

"Who squirmed and got us into that mess in the first place?"

Shade sucked in his breath, scrambling for a reply, then saw Frieda circling back toward them.

"That was quick thinking," the Silverwing elder told them. "Well done, you two."

"Couldn't have done it without her," Shade said generously.

"Oh, it was his idea," cooed Marina. "I just helped."

Frieda smiled faintly. "So humble, both of you. It's touching." And she soared back ahead to the front.

Shade felt a wing jostle against his own, and turned to see Chinook inserting himself right between him and Marina. He sighed inwardly, moving over to make space for the bigger bat.

"Well, that was exciting," said Chinook. "But you know, I could've fought that owl."

"Go lick an icicle, Chinook," Shade said, and pulled ahead. It wasn't just that he wanted a break from

Chinook—and Marina's tinkly laugh—he really wanted to listen in on what Frieda, Icarus, and his mother were talking about. He could take someone else leading the way for a change, but he couldn't stand the idea of being left out of anything important.

He nodded at Plato and Isis as he passed: He envied Chinook having both his mother and father with him. Sometimes he caught himself watching the three of them together during the day, huddled close, talking. Still, he was grateful his own mother wasn't always circling back, asking if he was cold or hungry, or if his wing hurt—but secretly he had to admit he liked always being able to *see* her up ahead, just a few wingbeats away. Hanging back, he flared his ears, concentrating.

" . . . for the owls to break their hibernation, it's worrying," he heard Frieda saying.

"They're awfully close to Hibernaculum," Ariel said softly. "Do you think . . ." She trailed off, as if she couldn't bring herself to finish her thought. What? Shade wondered anxiously. Did she think they'd *attack* Hibernaculum? But it was a secret place, wasn't it? And not even the owls could attack a colony of sleeping bats. It was too cowardly. . . .

"I fear they may be massing for war," said Frieda gravely. "And if they choose to attack in winter, we're all in terrible danger."

"Bloodthirsty brutes." Icarus's voice was savage. "The Humans will help us fight them. That's the promise of the bands. Nocturna's Promise."

Shade listened attentively, heart slamming against his ribs. Back at Tree Haven, Frieda had told him about Nocturna, the Winged Spirit of the night. Deep beneath the earth, in the echo chamber, Shade had seen the stories of the Great Battle of the Birds and the Beasts, and how the bats were banished to the night skies for refusing to fight. But Nocturna promised that one day they'd be allowed back into the sunlight, and wouldn't have to fear the owls anymore. And the Human bands were a sign of that Promise: perfect, gleaming circles like the sun itself. That's what Frieda and Cassiel believed, anyway. And Shade too.

"If the owls are making war," said Icarus, "the Humans are our only hope. Cassiel knew it. That's why he wanted to find this building."

"When we get there," Shade heard his mother ask carefully, "what is it we'll find?"

"What do you think, Shade?"

He jolted in surprise as Frieda glanced back at him over her wing: She'd known he was there all along.

"I was wondering when you'd join us," said his mother with a wry smile.

"Come forward," Frieda said. "Cassiel's your father, and we might not be on this journey if it weren't for you. Or you, Marina."

Shade turned to see Marina, keeping pace just behind him. So she'd been listening in too! Typical, not wanting him to know anything she didn't! At first he felt a flash of annoyance, but was quickly ashamed. After everything she'd already done for him, she still wanted to help him find his father. And she wanted to know the secret of the bands as badly as he did. After all, he thought enviously, she'd once had one, before Goth had torn it from her forearm.

"What if Cassiel's not there?" Ariel asked.

Shade looked at his mother, aghast. Of course the same dark thought sometimes glinted in his own mind, but he always smothered it. Hearing his mother say it, he felt a current of panic go through him.

"But he's got to be there," he said, wanting to be reassured. "He has to be. . . ." He saw Marina's kind smile and stopped, feeling childish. All he knew was that his father was alive. Somewhere. It was only gut instinct that told him he'd be in the Human building.

"We should be prepared for disappointment," said Frieda, "but let us hope for the best."

A whisper of sound grazed Shade's face, and he pricked up his ears, straining. "You hear that?" he said.

"Just the wind," Marina said.

"No, it sounded like—"

"I hear it too," breathed Frieda. "Yes. Voices."

Shade twitched his tall ears and banked sharply to the right, trying to chase the sound. It was definitely bat voices, but so faint, he couldn't make out words. It was like being back in the echo chamber all over again, hearing those ancient currents of sound and trying to lock on before they slipped away.

"I've got it now too!" Marina said.

"And me!" That was his mother.

"Silverwings, follow," he heard Frieda call out.

Shade shut out the rest of the world and followed the voices. They were a little stronger now, all running together like an airborne river.

"Look!" he heard Icarus say.

Before them, the grassland fell away in a slow curve, and spread out on the valley floor was a dazzling pool of light and sound. All at once, the bat voices seemed to well up from this place, soaring through the air toward them—a mysterious chorus, confusing, but melodious and irresistibly beckoning.

"What're they saying?" Marina asked in awe.

Shade shook his head. It was impossible to tell. What did it matter? "They want us to come," he said excitedly. "That must be the Human building down there! Come on!"

Down into the valley he plunged, and now he could make out walls, a roofline soaring with glittering metal towers. The music of bat voices was so overwhelming now that it all seemed less like a building than something woven from dazzling sound itself. It was the most beautiful thing he'd ever seen or heard.

This is what my father was searching for! There were answers here, Shade was certain now. Inside. That's where the voices were coming from. And where his father was! So how do I get inside? The voices would lead him. He locked on, and let them pull him in closer.

With Marina at his wing tip, he skimmed over the vast roof. From its smooth, dark sheen he guessed it was glass, yet he could see nothing through it, not even a smudge of movement or glimmer of light.

Still, the voices pulled him on, to the far edge of the roof, and there the sound was so intense, it created a halo of blazing light in his mind's eye.

"It's here!" he called out to the others.

Just under the roofline, high in the wall, was a round opening, and it was from here the bats' voices were emanating. Without hesitating, he flew for it, braked, and landed inside. It was some kind of tunnel, and he was already hurrying down it on all fours.

"Shade, maybe we should wait. . . ."

It was Marina, landing behind him.

"Come on, they're all in here!" They wanted him to come, it was so obvious. He was supposed to come inside!

He scrambled down the tunnel, and then he felt the floor give way beneath him. The chorus of beautiful, melodious voices was abruptly extinguished. There was a powerful blast of warm air in his ears, and he tumbled straight down. Before he could even open his wings, or dig in with his claws, he was propelled through another opening. In a second his wings were unfurled, and he was circling, staring in amazement at what greeted him.

A VOICE FROM THE CAVE

Goth limped through the sky.

For two nights he'd flown south, his lightning-scarred wings shrieking with every stroke. But at least there was no more wretched snow on the ground, and each night the air was slightly warmer. The landscape too was changing, flat and marshy. And now for the first time, he saw some familiar stars on the far horizon, bits of constellations he had grown up with in the jungle. His heart leaped. It wouldn't be long now before he was back home among the other Vampyrum Spectrum. In the sacred temple, he would pray to Cama Zotz, and be healed.

For now, his mangled wings made him slow, clumsy, and much of his prey escaped him. Still, he managed to catch enough to survive: a dopey but well-fed mouse; a nesting sparrow hidden beneath a canopy of branches. One night he'd been so hungry, he'd even eaten a few insects, and nearly gagged in disgust. It was bats he craved, as always, but he'd seen very few, and he didn't

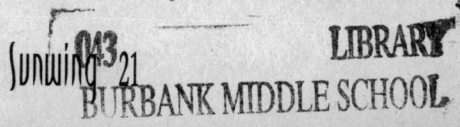

know if he was fast enough to catch them in his weakened state.

He was wary now in the night skies, and he hated that. Before being struck by lightning he was fearless, a master of the night; but now he was a crippled creature. He didn't relish the prospect of having to fight an owl right now.

And he was even more worried about the Humans.

They'd been looking for him. Once before, they'd tracked him down in their flying machine, and shot at him with sleeping darts. And just a few nights ago, he'd thought he'd heard the rhythmic chopping of their machine, and he'd waited breathlessly, deep in a tree, until the sound had passed.

Shade and Marina, those two puny northern bats— they had brought this calamity upon him. They probably thought he was dead, like Throbb. If anyone deserved to be incinerated by lightning, it was Throbb. At least Goth wouldn't have to listen to his whining anymore.

The eastern sky was starting to brighten, and Goth swept the landscape with sound, looking for shelter. In a rocky hill, he found a crevice and gratefully flew for it. Inside, using his echo vision, he saw he was in a vast network of caves. Delighted, he flew deeper, and rather than getting colder, the air warmed, until a delicious tropical heat surrounded him. It was coming, he could tell, from vents in the stone floor, as if from the earth's core. How long it had been since he'd felt this warm!

He probed the roof of the caves with sound—strange

that there were no bats roosting here. It seemed a natural place for them. He'd been hoping for a good meal. But he was too warm to feel very disappointed.

He wanted to go deeper into the caves, deeper and lower, lured by the warmth—and something else that beckoned at the very fringes of his mind. What was it, this sense of being drawn? His eyes were so heavy, he wanted sleep, and yet he flew on. Would it take him to the very Underworld?

It was so dark here, and he flew by sound alone, eyes drooping shut. Finally he reached a large, round cave with no other passages leading from it, and he hung, exhausted, from the wall, sleep taking him instantly in its silken wings.

"Goth."

The whisper coiled around his head.

"Goth."

"Here I am," he said drowsily. Was he asleep or awake? Then he stiffened. Who was there? Just the voice of sleep, maybe. But cold electricity coursed through his body, and his fur lifted. His eyes were open but saw nothing. In the impenetrable blackness of the cave, everything was sound—the corrugated rock walls and ceiling glimmering silver in his head. But there was something else he was seeing now with his mind's eye, a kind of current that swirled slowly, hypnotically through the cave. A current of pure sound.

He watched in awe as it filled the cave, swirling, never still. His heart thundered.

"Where are you going?" the voice whispered.

"Home," he said. "To the jungle."

Sound pictures were painting themselves on the walls and roof like moving hieroglyphs. A jaguar, a feathered serpent, a pair of unblinking eyes without pupils.

"Who am I?" the voice asked, grazing his ears.

Goth's body felt icy. He knew, yet he wanted to be sure. He wanted proof. "Show me," he said boldly.

Laughter rumbled through the room. "Not until the sun is dead, Goth, then you will see me in my full glory."

"The sun, dead?" he asked in confusion.

"Who am I, Goth?"

"I know you," he said, and faltered, suddenly afraid to utter the name, now that he was in his very presence.

"Tell me."

He swallowed. "Cama Zotz."

"Yesssss," came the slithery reply. "The Humans are chasing you."

"I know. But they won't catch me."

"Let them."

"But they are our enemies, Lord Zotz. They treated me like a slave; they mock you."

"They think they are using you, but you will be using them."

"I don't understand."

"You will."

Goth said nothing for a moment.

"Are you my servant, Goth?" The voice, no longer soothing, cut into his ears, slashing light through his head.

"Yes, Lord Zotz."

"Do my bidding, then, and you will be king."

And then it was as if all the sound was suddenly sucked out of the cave, all the silvery echoes dissolved, and Zotz was gone. Goth was alone. His breathing calmed. The silence was so total, he wondered if he had only dreamed his conversation.

Let himself be caught by Humans—it made no sense! These were the Humans who had trapped him in his homeland and brought him north to their artificial jungle and imprisoned him. The Man, always watching him, stabbing him with his darts. Was he to return to that? What good could it do?

He shook his head, and cast echoes around the empty cave. He'd had dreams before, and visions too. But none so vivid, none where he'd felt Zotz's breath on his face, seen the very swirls of his presence. Could Zotz really find him so far north? Maybe it was nothing but a confused dream. Already it seemed unreal.

He could fight sleep no longer. He plunged down into blazing dreams of the jungle, so real that he could smell the soil, the damp stone of the royal pyramid. All around him soared the Vampyrum, but they looked smaller somehow, leaner, and there was something wrong with the jungle too, the trees and creepers and fronds all charred and smoking.

He bobbed in and out of sleep, wrapped in his dreams. He lost all sense of time. He heard his own voice crying out in pain, and was aware of angrily ripping off the Human bands that festooned his forearms. Or was he just dreaming it? All but one of the bands tore free, and that was the one the Man had put on him back in the artificial jungle. That one he could not tear free.

Dreaming again: And this time, Shade was caught in his claws, pinned to the ground. "I will eat your beating heart," Goth told him. He opened his jaws wide and lunged.

He woke. And this time he knew he was fully and truly awake. How long had he slept? A second, a day? He couldn't even guess. He shifted his wings and noticed instantly how different they felt. He cast a wash of sound over them, and looked.

All the Human bands, but one, were gone.

And his wings were healed.

Goth flew from the cave and cut tight circles in the air, scanning the horizon. South. The jungle, his home. His whole being pulled him back there.

But Zotz's words echoed in his head.

He must be obedient. He was a prince of the royal family, the Vampyrum Spectrum, and must follow the orders of the bat god. And what of this promise to be king?

He opened his wings, testing them. Incredible. Before, they'd been scarred and seared, the skin melted away from the bone in places. He'd thought he'd never be whole again.

Now healed.

Only Zotz could have performed such a miracle.

Zotz gave him his strength back so he would do his bidding. Zotz had always looked over him: in the artificial jungle; in the thunderhead when lightning struck.

He angled his wings and flew north.

He knew it wouldn't be long before the Humans caught him.

PARADISE

It was summer.

Forest stretched as far as Shade's eyes and ears could see. Not the icebound forest he'd just left behind, but forest in full leaf: maple, elm, beech, oak, hemlock, their foliage creating a lush canopy. Wildflowers twined themselves through the branches, and Shade could smell ripening fruit. Far below, he heard the ripple of a stream. The air was silky and warm, fragrant with bark and soil, and absolutely teeming with insects. Just hearing them made his mouth water. But how could it be so warm in the middle of winter? Where was he? In confusion he looked overhead. The familiar stars glittered in a brightening sky.

But you're not *outside,* he had to tell himself. You're *inside.* He realized he was seeing the night sky through a glass roof—the same roof that, outside, had bounced back his echo vision, as hard as stone.

He swirled in midair as Marina shot through the same portal he'd come through. Then, in twos and threes, the other Silverwings burst into the forest, and Shade noticed there was some kind of metal flap that automatically opened and then snapped shut behind them. Soon, the whole group had arrived and was circling in amazement above the forest canopy.

"Is it real?" Marina breathed, flying alongside him.

"Smells real," Shade said, and cautiously dipped toward a treetop, batting a leaf with his wing tip, and then settling on a branch. He dug his claws into wood. "Feels real too."

It was incredible, a living forest inside a building! After the fierce winter cold, he felt his bones begin to thaw; he felt lighter.

Suddenly a tiger moth flashed past his nose, setting his ears alight, and he couldn't resist.

"Shade!" he heard his mother call behind him, but he was already off, spinning down into the trees after his prey. Jubilantly he homed in, ignoring the barrage of echoes the tiger moth sprayed out to confuse him. Closer, closer, and he braked, scooping the moth up with his tail and volleying it into his open mouth. After weeks of snow fleas and caterpillar cocoons, it tasted so good, he almost passed out.

He swooped low over a swift, bubbling stream, delighted to see water that wasn't frozen solid. Outside he'd gotten used to drinking by gobbling snow and wincing in pain as it melted against his teeth. Now he skimmed the stream, dragging his mouth along the water's surface and letting it spray deliciously down his throat.

And then, pulling up, he noticed the hundreds of bats swirling curiously all around him. Graywings and Brightwings and Silverwings, staring at him intently. There were Small-foots, Fringes, Long-ears, and other kinds of bats he'd never even seen before.

"Welcome!" they called out. "Newcomer, welcome!"

"Was it a long journey?"

"So late in winter!"

"Didn't expect any more newcomers till spring!"

Then he felt as if he were swept up in their wings and carried higher, back through the dense forest canopy to Marina and Ariel and the others. There were even more bats here—easily thousands—wheeling around them, barraging them with questions. Some, he noticed instantly, were banded, but most were not. They all looked so friendly, and so genuinely glad to see them.

"What is this place?" called out Frieda.

"Paradise."

The voice came from a Hoary bat, flying up to meet them. She was an older bat, Shade could see, though not nearly as old as Frieda. Her fur was a mottled gray, with rivulets of silver running across her chest and back. She had a short, pale beard that ended in a sharp point, and her black eyes were flecked with white, making her gaze fiercely penetrating. On her left forearm blazed a Human band.

"My name is Arcadia."

"I am Frieda Silverwing; we've come from Hibernaculum, two nights' journey from the east."

"We're so glad you've arrived," said Arcadia. "Now come and roost with me, and let me explain everything." She led them to a maple with an abundance of interlacing branches, and the Silverwings gathered around Arcadia. Shade landed beside Marina, suppressing a groan as Chinook found a place on her other side.

"I hope this doesn't take long," he heard Chinook whisper. "I'm hungry."

Shade's eyes were on Arcadia as she rustled her wings and folded them neatly. She turned her head to take them all in, meeting their eyes in turn, and Shade couldn't suppress a slight tremor when that gaze came to rest on him. They were intelligent, even beautiful, eyes but there was also something hard about them; maybe it was just those flecks of white, like sparks of mica in stone.

"There's no need to be anxious," Arcadia said, smiling. "All of us here remember how confusing it was at first. The suddenness of it, the unexpectedness of it. But you can shed all your worries. Your journey is over. As you can see, the Humans have created the perfect home for us. The trees never lose their leaves; the stream never freezes. It's forever warm as a summer night, with as many insects as you could ever hope to eat."

"How many are here?" Frieda asked.

"Several thousand at least, from all different colonies."

Shade caught his mother's eye, and knew what she was thinking. Thousands of bats, and one of them must be Cassiel. He wanted to break from the tree at once and soar across the forest to find him. His claws clenched restlessly in the bark. It was torture knowing his father was here and not being able to go to him at once.

"We came from roosts a million wingbeats apart, from east to west," Arcadia was saying. "But we had two things in common. We believed in the secret of the bands. And we heard the call."

"The call," said Frieda. "You mean the voices outside the building?"

"Yes. To summon us. My group was the first to arrive, some two months ago." There was a hint of pride in her voice. "The forest was empty, waiting for us, as if Nocturna had just created it."

Shade frowned. "But where did the voices come from then?" he blurted out. The way Arcadia turned her eyes on him, he could tell she disapproved of such a young bat asking questions. He looked at his claws, uncomfortable. He'd never been very good at holding his tongue. "I mean, if the forest was empty, how could you hear bats?"

"That," said Arcadia, "is a mystery." And she said it in such a way that there could be no more discussion of it.

"And there were no other birds or beasts here?" Frieda wanted to know.

Shade was suddenly aware of the sky brightening above them. In any other forest, the dawn meant owls would soon be patrolling the sky, birds rousing themselves in their nests, beasts snuffling for food. But Arcadia didn't seem at all concerned. She smiled again.

"Of course not," she replied. "The Humans made a

perfect haven for us. There are no owls, or any other bird, for that matter. Nor are there beasts. Only bats."

The words were out of Shade's mouth before he could stop himself. "But why?" he asked. "Why have they built this place for us?"

"To fulfill Nocturna's Promise," said Arcadia simply. "Come and see."

Arcadia led the way to the topmost branches of the tree, and there Shade could see the sky paling, and a stronger band of light across the eastern horizon. As if drawn, the other bats of the forest were sailing up through the foliage to gather near the roof, some finding roosts on high trees, others circling excitedly, watching. The thrum and creak of wings filled the air.

"Watch!" they whispered in fevered anticipation. "Look!"

It was the dawn. Shade stared, transfixed, as a bright sliver of sun curved above the distant horizon. And his thoughts flew back, months ago, to the northern forests, when he was just a newborn, and he'd risked his life for such a sight. The memory of the owl that had tried to hunt him down—the smell and sound of it—fluttered so strongly through his head that he couldn't help glancing over his shoulder, just to make sure he was safe. He could see the same mixture of anxiety and awe on the faces of the other bats from his colony, even Frieda's.

Millions of years without the sun, and now they were watching it rise with regal grace, trailing streams of mist from the horizon. Shade had once flown in the full blaze of day, but he'd never seen the sun break free from the horizon. The bats had fallen into a silent reverie as the sun assumed its full glory, a blazing disc of light in the sky.

Shade looked around at all the ecstatic, upturned faces, their fur bathed in the sun's light, their eyes sparkling. And he sensed that this must be a ritual for them, gathering to see the dawn.

He looked at Marina, and it was as if he were seeing her for the first time, her fur so luminous. And so soft. Every sleek hair glittered. She seemed like some new kind of creature, spun out of light. She turned her bright eyes on him, a miniature sun in each one, and smiled, and he smiled weakly back and looked away, surprised and awkward.

The sun seemed to transform everything, to pick out details he'd never noticed: the veins of leaves, the shadows in the bark. He wanted to touch everything all over again. The world seemed *more.* He looked back at the sun itself and was surprised to realize he was only squinting a little. He frowned. "It's brighter than that," he muttered to Marina.

She nodded. "I remember."

When they'd flown under its full glare to escape Goth and Throbb, he couldn't even turn his gaze on it fully without powerful twin stabs of pain through his eye sockets.

"The roof must dull it somehow," he said, and he remembered its dark sheen from the outside.

Arcadia rose into the air and circled above them, eyes gleaming with light. "You see," she said. "The Promise has been fulfilled! Here is the sun! And we're able to look at it. We're able to fly in its light, and fear nothing. There are no owls, no beasts to hunt us. Do you see? The sun is ours again! Our banishment is over!"

Always Shade had thought there would be a war with the owls. How else to end their banishment, to win the right to fly in the sun? Never had he imagined it would be like this—a perfect world created for them by Humans.

"And the bands?" said Frieda. "What is their significance?"

"After I was banded I wondered about that a great deal," said Arcadia, "as many of us have, I'm sure. But these bands aren't magical objects in themselves. They don't single out good bats from bad. We share no common language with the Humans, so they are a way of linking us. They are a sign of friendship, a symbol of the Promise. They tell us that Humans have a part to play in the coming of the day. Nocturna made the Promise; the Humans have delivered it!"

Across the treetops Shade met his mother's eyes and smiled.

"Let's go find your father," she called to him.

His heart pounded. Somewhere in this vast forest was his father, he could feel it.

"We've come looking for someone," Ariel said to Arcadia. "A banded Silverwing named Cassiel."

Arcadia settled on a branch and looked thoughtful. "Cassiel. So many have come, let me try to . . ." She raised her voice and called out across the treetops: "Is there a Cassiel Silverwing among us? Send out the word!"

Shade's fur lifted in excitement as he heard his father's name racing out through the forest like a ripple through water. He couldn't keep still; he had to be aloft. Up to the very rooftop he flew, listening.

"Cassiel! Cassiel Silverwing! Is he here? Cassiel . . . Cassiel . . . Cassiel . . ." until the voices became softer and softer, fading away into silence. Shade felt the blood booming in his ears. He sought out his mother, her face so still, her ears pricked hopefully, waiting for the return call.

It didn't come.

After a few agonizing moments, Arcadia said gently, "I'm sorry."

"Thank you," Ariel said, her ears slowly folding back against her head.

Shade heard sympathetic voices around him, telling him and his mother they were sorry, so sorry, but they were just noise to him. He looked at Arcadia.

"No, he's got to be here," he insisted, and his own voice sounded deafening to him. "He came here late last spring. He knew about this place! He must have come here—before anyone else, even. He's here!"

"When my group arrived, we were the first," said Arcadia firmly. "There were no other bats in the forest, and I don't remember a banded Silverwing by that name. I'm sorry to have to tell you unhappy news. But you must try to be grateful for the Paradise you have found here."

Shade looked at her angrily and flew off, his eyes blinded with tears. He hurtled himself deep into the branches, roosted, and tried to think clearly. He would not cry, would not. He'd scour the forest himself to make sure. That stupid bearded bat didn't know everything. She probably wasn't even an elder, just some self-important old crone. . . .

When his mother came to roost beside him, he couldn't turn to look at her. If he saw her eyes reflecting back his own sorrow, he knew he would sob.

"He's alive," Shade said through gritted teeth. "Zephyr said so."

"Maybe Zephyr was wrong. We can't spend our lives looking for him."

"Why not?"

"You're so restless, so like him," she said. "Every journey has to end somewhere, Shade."

"You're giving up?" he asked, amazed.

"Giving up." She sighed. "Is that what it is? Plenty of us have lost mates. It's one of those cruel things that's unavoidable."

He hated how sensible she sounded. How could she think so sensibly?

"I'm not so unlucky," she said. "I've got you. And I'm not too old to have more newborns."

Shade stared at her, shocked. "You can't."

She laughed gently, but Shade felt his face burn beneath his fur, as if he were a child again and had just said something ridiculous.

"How do you know your father's not done the same, somewhere else?"

"He wouldn't."

His mother said nothing. She's right, he thought miserably. What do I know? I don't know anything about my father, really. Never met him. Maybe never will. And suddenly he was angry.

"He's always just a little bit ahead of me. Why doesn't he slow down and help a little, give us a sign, leave us a message! A million wingbeats I've come for this, and he can't even . . ."

He trailed off, knowing he wasn't making sense, but he couldn't hold back the frustration and disappointment inside him any longer. If he knew his father was dead he could try to get over it, and at least there would be a sense of finishing with something, nothing more to be done, no more work or worry. He wondered if his father even wanted to be found. Too selfish to even think about his mate and son? Doesn't *he* want to find *me?* he thought in despair.

"He might never have reached this place," Ariel pointed out. "The owls might have caught him on the way; he might have gone"—she sighed and looked away—"elsewhere."

"I just don't see how you can give up," he said.

"I think it's time to get on with other things now." She looked at him. "You've got to take care of Marina, you know."

He snorted bitterly. "Oh, I think she's pretty good at taking care of herself. She's already more popular than me. You should see the way Chinook hangs around—" He looked at his mother, startled. "What do you mean, *I've* got to take care of her? I don't think she even *likes* me half the time."

"It's hard for her. She's not a Silverwing, and I don't want her to feel like an outsider with us. She doesn't have anyone else."

Shade nodded uncomfortably. "I know, I know." When he'd first met Marina, she was living all by herself, expelled from her own colony because she'd been banded. They thought the bands were evil, and would bring bad luck on all of them. Even her own parents had shunned her—something Shade found unbelievably painful. After reaching Hibernaculum together, she'd thought about going back to her own colony, now that her band had been ripped off. But she hadn't. Shade smiled, remembering how glad he'd been when Marina had accepted Frieda's invitation to stay with them. Then he frowned.

"She's fitting in just fine," he muttered. Ariel treated her like her own daughter, and he could tell Marina liked the attention—the way she practically purred when she was combed. Chinook liked her, and she seemed to return the favor. And Shade hadn't missed the way some of the other young males looked at her admiringly—probably all that superior Brightwing fur, he thought with a sniff. True, the young females didn't seem that thrilled to have her in the colony, but so what? She didn't seem to be suffering.

"She's good at hiding things," said Ariel, as if reading his thoughts. "Look out for her, that's all I mean."

"Yeah. Sure," he said. She was making him feel like an ignorant newborn again, and he didn't like it. He didn't even know why they were talking about Marina right now. He wanted to talk about his father.

Ariel touched his cheek with her wing. "So restless," she said. "Be proud of the things you've done, Shade. Without you, we probably wouldn't have made it to this place. You brought us the sun, just like you wanted."

He nodded, remembering the promise he'd made himself long ago, but his heart felt leaden.

"We have to tell the others back at Hibernaculum," Frieda was saying. "They have a right to know what we've found here. My only concern is when. Do we go now, or wait until the spring?"

"By then the owls might've already attacked," Icarus pointed out grimly.

Shade roosted near the burbling stream with Marina and the other Silverwings from his colony, listening. But he was watching Arcadia's eyes; they were so unlike Frieda's. You could tell that Arcadia didn't want you asking questions; and she didn't want you answering back.

"I'm afraid it won't be possible for you to return to Hibernaculum," Arcadia said simply.

Shade felt a slap of indignation. Who was she to be telling them what they could or couldn't do?

"I don't understand," said Frieda calmly.

"The rest of your colony has already made its choice. They decided not to come with you."

"But when they hear about this place," Frieda said, "they may change their minds."

"I believe this place was meant for those who had the faith and courage to seek it."

"Do you think that's a bit severe?" Frieda's voice was still calm, but Shade could tell, by the sudden ripple of her folded wings, that she was annoyed.

"This was the way Nocturna wanted it. And it's already been decided for us. The door only opens one way."

"We're trapped?" Shade blurted out.

Arcadia looked at him mockingly. "One cannot be trapped in Paradise. This is your final destination. Come to accept that, young bat."

Shade bristled. Young bat. I've probably seen more things than you have, Beard Breath. But already he could hear a warning shrill of panic in his mind. The rest of his life, here in this one place? Forever? The notion was too big to even get a grip on. He'd never even liked the idea of hibernating, and that was only three months. How could he stay here—anywhere—forever?

"Got to be a way out," he muttered, impulsively flying

from the tree, back toward the roof. He soon found the opening and dug into the metal flap with his claws. It didn't budge, even when he slammed his shoulder against it. He scratched at the surrounding stone and metal without dislodging even a speck of dust.

"Marina, Chinook," he called out, "give me some help over here!"

"That's enough!" snapped Arcadia sternly, flying toward him. "Only Humans open those doors. I'm shocked at this appallingly ungrateful behavior. Look around you. What do you see? Forest as generous as any you could ever find. Who flees Paradise?"

"If it's Paradise, why isn't there a way out?" he demanded, his voice shaking.

"The door was designed to keep us safe, to keep out our enemies."

Shade could see Ariel and Marina and Frieda behind Arcadia now, and tried to read their faces. His mother, he thought, looked concerned, but did she share his fears, or think he was behaving poorly? Marina couldn't even meet his eye. Ashamed of him? Did she think he was cowardly, childish for wanting a way out?

"If the idea of living here troubles you," Arcadia said to Shade, fixing him with her cold, flashing eyes, "perhaps you were not meant to come."

Goth heard the Humans coming.

The sound of their flying machine throbbed in the air, and this time he locked on and flew headlong toward it.

It didn't take long before he could make out the machine's bulbous outline, dead ahead, rimmed in light.

His wingstrokes faltered, but only for a moment.

Zotz had made him strong again; Zotz was looking over him. More than that: Zotz needed him to fulfill his designs. He would be king of all the Vampyrum Spectrum, and he would fill his mouth and belly with Shade Silverwing's flesh.

The machine's nose reared before him, sliding sideways through the air. Behind the open window, he could see the Man. He knew it would be him, and he hated the sight of his mangy beard and drooped eyelid. A long weapon was held close to his face and shoulder.

Goth gritted his teeth, waiting.

He felt the dart bite into the side of his chest, and had to fight all his instincts not to rip at the feathered tip with his teeth, not to fly.

Then the horizon lurched crazily, and he fell.

A Way Out

Five nights in Paradise, and he was still trying to find a way out.

Every night Shade circled the entire forest, searching. Even now he had to admit it was wonderful, a mix of conifers and leafy trees, a soft floor of mosses, wildflowers, and grass. A pleasantly broad stream meandered through the whole length of the forest, but the water, he soon realized, had a hard, metallic edge to it. Craggy stone cliffs—it felt like real stone, he'd checked—bordered the forest on all sides, rising up to the glass roof high above the tree line. He'd discovered numerous small portals, just like the one he'd entered through, but they were all just as tightly closed and impossible to move.

But he wasn't about to give up. There had to be a way out. He wasn't sure he would use it yet, but he wanted to know it was there, anyway.

Now he skimmed beneath the roof, straining for a draft of cold air, anything that might lead him to a crevice, a vent, any possible exit. Nothing, as always. He looked across the forest. He knew it would take him months to scour all of it, and even then he could miss something.

If only he had help . . . but everyone else just wanted to sleep, and when they weren't sleeping, they were hunting lazily and combing their fur. Ariel would invite him to roost beside her, or hunt, but he stayed away. He had things to do, and it made him angry she didn't feel the same way as he did. She didn't say anything, but he knew. She was happy here, like everyone else. Even Frieda spent most of her time on a favorite stone by a pond, warming her old bones in the sun's path. Why wasn't she more upset about the others back at Hibernaculum? And what about the owls? She should've been trying to get out too!

Marina had made friends with a group of Brightwings, and when she wasn't with them, she was always with Chinook. It was unbelievable. When he heard that tinkly laugh of hers he wanted to bite through rock. At first she'd asked him to join them, but he always made excuses, and now she didn't even ask anymore, just gave him a quick, tight smile and flew off with the others.

All around him, everyone was happy, and he felt like a soggy leaf.

"Still looking?" Marina had flown up behind him.

"Hmm," grunted Shade. He glanced at her quickly, unsure whether she was just being friendly or quietly mocking him. But he was happy to see her, especially without Chinook trailing after her. He hadn't seen her alone in nights.

"So how're you enjoying Paradise?" he asked, unable to keep the sarcasm from his voice.

"It beats getting eaten by owls," she said with a smile. "Come on, Shade, take a rest. If anyone's earned it, you have. This place isn't so bad."

He wanted to believe her and, for a moment, felt himself relax. Maybe this was the end of the journey after all, and why shouldn't he fold his wings up and have a good, long sleep? It would be so easy. A tiger moth fluttered inches from his nose, and he frowned.

"You know where the bugs come from?" he said distractedly. "These tiny little holes in the cliffs. They're all over the place. Look, there's one right over here." He flew closer and jabbed with his wing tip. "Look at this. The bugs just shoot right out. Can you believe it?"

"Shade, what does it matter?"

"They don't even taste that great."

"You're complaining about the food? You'd rather be out scraping frozen fungus off a tree?"

"Admit it, Marina. The bugs don't taste normal, and they all taste the same. The beetles don't have the same crunch to them. You must've noticed that."

She scowled. "Maybe I have, but is it so bad?"

"Too easy to catch," he muttered. "Even the tiger moths are dopey. I haven't missed one yet. Tiger moths should put up a bit of a fight. . . ." He trailed off, feeling childish. Together they fluttered down to a tree and roosted side by side, saying nothing for a few moments.

"I'm sorry about your father," she said.

"I just don't understand how he can't be here. It makes me think, I don't know, this isn't the right place, that we made a mistake."

"Doesn't feel like a mistake to me," Marina said. "Why are you so suspicious? I see you flying around, looking for ways out. Why can't you just enjoy it?"

"I can't believe this is the right ending."

"Shade, everything fits. The light of day, free from owls, the Humans helping us. The whole Promise."

"I know, I know," he said testily. He'd thought it through himself, over and over, like chewing on a stone until it had worn away to dust, to nothing. "But even the sun's not the same. It's brighter than this. You saw it with me, you remember."

"It was too painful to look at outside. This way we get to enjoy it. Shade, why would the Humans go to all the trouble of making this place for us?"

"Come on," said Shade, "I'll show you something else I found."

He led her skimming over the treetops, and realized he felt happy for the first time in nights. He was so glad just to have her beside him, all to himself, the way it used to be, traveling somewhere together. The journey didn't last long, though. The forest, he'd realized when he'd first explored, was extremely long, but relatively narrow. Set into the cliff face, above the tree line, was a long window.

And behind the window were the Humans.

Shade roosted with Marina, just above the window so they could hang down and take a good look inside. There were five Humans: two standing, the others sitting. All of them wore white robes. Beyond the glass, they were only a few wingbeats away. He remembered seeing them, long ago, in the city cathedral, praying. He'd admired Humans so much, their size, their power. Here they seemed even more formidable.

The room was quite dark, and light washed over their faces and bodies from various gleaming metal surfaces. A couple were speaking to each other; Shade could see their mouths move. Even if he could hear them, their words would be meaningless to him. The others were looking out the window. Shade knew that from their high vantage point, most of the forest was within sight.

"They watch us," said Shade. "Maybe they study us."

"Maybe," said Marina, noncommittal. "So what?"

"That's the Man."

He jerked his head at the Human Male standing in the center of the room, tapping at some kind of machine. He was tall and gangly, with an untidy black beard, and one eye that always seemed half-closed.

"What do you mean, 'the Man'?" Marina was saying.

"Remember Goth telling us about him? When he and Throbb were in the fake jungle? He said there was a Man who watched them all the time and flashed lights in their eyes and stuck them with darts."

"You don't know it's the same one."

"No, but—"

"Okay, let's say he is. Any Human who tries to capture Goth and keep him locked up sounds good to me."

"They're keeping us locked up, Marina."

She was silent for a moment, and when she spoke, her voice was impatient. "Why do you even bother thinking about Goth? He was a liar; he wanted to destroy us and your whole colony. For all we know, he made the whole thing up. Maybe there was no fake jungle, no Man."

"Goth and Throbb were banded too. And the Humans came looking for them in their flying machine. I almost got hit by one of their darts, remember?"

"Of course I remember," she said, annoyed. She sighed. "They're not flashing lights in our faces, or sticking us with darts. Arcadia's been here two months, and nothing bad's happened to her. Everyone seems pretty happy, don't you think?"

"Very happy," he muttered. He looked at her intently. "Don't you feel like a prisoner at all?"

"You're so suspicious! Isn't it enough they've made this place for us?"

He felt ungrateful, but he couldn't help himself. "No, it's not. I want to know *why* they've done it."

"How's that going to happen? You want them to walk through that glass wall and talk to you?"

"That would be nice," Shade shot back. "If they're so smart, why don't they explain everything to us, once and for all? For all we know, maybe they're just collecting us. Maybe they want something from us."

"No one forced us here," Marina reminded him. "We

chose to come. We didn't have to fly inside. You went first, remember?"

"I thought I'd find my father."

She sighed. "I'm sorry, Shade, but I'm happy here. I've been an outcast for so long, I just want . . . look, I feel like I've got a home here, a family. Ariel's been really kind to me. And so have you."

"Let's not forget Chinook."

He regretted it the moment the words left his mouth.

She was looking at him carefully. "You don't approve of me spending time with Chinook?" she asked, with a faint but dangerous edge of anger in her voice.

"Forget it."

"It's not as if you've been around much, Shade. You're always off flying, looking for cracks in the walls. Or sulking."

"I don't sulk," said Shade.

"Whatever you call it, then."

"I'm thinking. I do that sometimes. Unlike Chinook."

"I'll admit, he's never going to be an elder. He's not *special*"—she gave the word contemptuous emphasis—"but I think he's got a good heart."

"Well, if you can't have a brain, it's great having a good heart." Beneath his fur, his face burned with jealousy and anger. "And let's not forget how hilarious he is. Why else would you spend so much time with him?"

"Well, he's also handsome," Marina said carelessly.

"Really?" Shade said, his anger giving way to genuine surprise. Chinook, handsome. He was certainly big;

strong, of course; a good flyer and hunter. But Shade had never thought of him as handsome.

Am I handsome? he wondered, and knew immediately he wasn't. He was too runty to ever be handsome. Sometimes, beside Marina, with her luxuriant fur and elegant face, he felt positively ugly.

"You're right," he told Marina coldly. "He's very handsome."

She looked at him strangely, then shook her head. "You know what? He likes you. He's jealous of you too. Surprised? Maybe you've been too busy to notice." There was a sharpness in her voice that surprised him. "You've been too busy for all of us."

"What d'you mean?" he asked, frowning.

"Take a break from being a hero, Shade. And guess what? You're not the only one who's lost a father."

And she flew off.

Shade hung from a low branch, angrily snapping off oak leaves with pellets of sound. He took aim at another stem, blasted it, and watched with satisfaction as the leaf snapped neatly off and fluttered downward. Still, a leaf was not an icicle. Too easy. He turned his attention to the ground and spotted a small stone, about seven feet away. But he couldn't concentrate.

You're not the only one who's lost a father.

He winced as the words echoed in his head. Marina was telling him to get over it, reminding him she'd lost a father too, *and* a mother, and life went on. Well, maybe she could live like that, but he couldn't. Cassiel might be lost, but Shade was going to find him. Was he supposed to apologize for that? Not giving up? Not wanting to float around here forever like a sun-stroked moth, eating bad bugs?

Take a break from being a hero. Now that really spiked his fur up! He was just doing what needed doing—since no one else seemed to be taking care of things. What about the other Silverwings back at Hibernaculum? What about the owls and their plans for war? What about the fact they were shut up in this artificial forest? If he didn't worry about these things, who would? Someone had to make things happen around here!

No wonder Marina liked Chinook better. He had both his parents, he never wondered about anything, never worried about anything. He was just so contented, he made Shade sick to his stomach. Must be great being Chinook.

He glared at the stone on the ground.

Move, he told it, and slammed it furiously with sound.

To his surprise, the stone flipped over on the grass. He tried again and managed to push it along a few more inches before he gave up, breathless.

"Very good," Frieda said, and Shade turned in surprise to see her hanging beside him. "You're getting better."

"Well, I've got lots of time to practice."

She smiled. Shade had always liked the way her gray fur crinkled around her eyes. There was something gently expectant about the way she was looking at him.

"Is there something wrong with me?" he asked the elder. "I mean, we've got the sun, lots of food, and summer even though it's really winter. No owls to worry about. And everyone seems so happy."

"Except you."

Shade nodded. "Except me."

"What troubles you?"

He didn't know where to start. "It's not like I imagined."

"Our imaginations are limited."

He nodded, feeling humbled.

"You sought the Humans," said Frieda, "we all did. We believed they were linked to us in some way, through Nocturna's Promise. We believed they would help us."

"I guess I just expected more."

"Some kind of marvelous transformation, perhaps? Or a war to defeat the owls and reign over the earth?"

He looked away, embarrassed, remembering how much he'd wanted to fight great battles and take his revenge on the owls. A big part of him still did.

"It seems the Humans have done so much for us here," Frieda said, watching him carefully. "And yet you're not content to trust them?"

"But it's like we're in a cage," Shade blurted out. "It's a nice, big cage and everything, but still, the bugs don't taste very good, and even the sun is all pale, and I just don't see the point."

"I agree."

Shade fell silent. He just looked at Frieda, feeling a smile soar across his face. "You do?"

"Yes."

He'd felt so alone since they'd arrived, thinking he was

the only one who didn't believe they'd found Paradise. And all along, Frieda had felt the same. His relief was boundless. "Then you'll help me find a way out!"

Now Frieda sighed. "There's not much journey left in these wings," she said. "I think, for me, this might be the last destination."

With a jolt, Shade saw her through new eyes, not as the elder of whom he'd always been in awe, but as an aging bat who'd flown countless summers and winters. She looked tired, her shoulders stooped, her fur listless. Only her dark eyes retained their brightness.

"I don't think this is the fulfillment of the Promise," she said.

"But I don't understand why—why didn't you say anything to the others? To Arcadia?"

"I'm not sure Arcadia would listen."

"But you're an elder!"

Frieda smiled. "Arcadia has already made up her mind, and I don't think I could persuade her. She has a strong hold on the bats here, that's obvious. They believe what they want. And I suspect this place is more powerful than my words. They think it's a Paradise, and in many ways it is. But not, I believe, what Nocturna meant for us."

"I've tried everywhere," said Shade wearily. "The walls, the roof. I'd crawl through those stupid insect pipes if I were smaller. . . ."

"You'll find a way," Frieda told him simply. "I know you will."

"How?" he said tiredly.

"Sound. It's the tool of all bats, but it's also your special gift. Remember, I always said you were a good listener, that you'd hear things no one else could. You'll listen your way out of here."

That night, his dreams were polluted with the sounds of Goth breathing, the beat of his heart, as if Shade were inside his belly. Silvery images, like sound pictures, flared in his sleeping mind, and they were somehow so familiar, he knew he must have dreamed them before. A two-headed serpent with feathers, a sleek jaguar, and then, most horrifying of all, two eyes without a face, just twin slits cut in the darkness, blazing blacker than any night.

He wanted to wake up, but he couldn't.

His dream was suddenly suffused with a strange smell, sweet and slightly sickening; he fought to open his eyes and maybe he did, because he thought he saw the forest, and through it moved tall, two-legged shapes. Humans? They had no faces. They slipped among the trees like specters, and he watched them in horror, unable, in his dream, to shift. They had arms, long skeletal arms that moved jerkily up into the air, into the branches of the trees, toward sleeping bats. . . .

And then he could keep his eyes open no longer, and a horrible darkness swallowed him up again.

He woke to the sound of anxious voices, all talking over one another.

" . . . can't find him anywhere . . ."

" . . . where've they gone?"

" . . . she's disappeared . . ."

His heart kicked up. Disappeared? He lit from his roost, flaring his ears wider. Bats were streaking through the forest in all directions, calling out names with increasing desperation.

"Daedalus . . . Hecuba . . . Miranda?"

He angled his wings, beating hard for the place he knew Ariel and Marina liked to roost. He felt strangely sluggish, his mouth dry and sour-tasting. A dull pain pulsed in the base of his skull.

"Gone . . . gone . . . gone." The word echoed through the trees, mingled with the sound of sobbing.

"What's going on?" he asked a frantic Graywing who was flapping toward him.

"Have you seen my Ursa?" she demanded.

"No, I—"

"I can't find her anywhere," moaned the Graywing mother. "She's gone, just like the others."

"What do you mean?"

"They're all gone!" And she flew on, calling out her daughter's name in her cracked voice.

Shade veered through the branches now, smashing through leaves, and darted out over a clearing. How stupid he'd been, staying away from them, quarreling with Marina. All the angry thoughts he'd had about both of them now seemed so childish and cruel.

"Marina? Mom?"

This was the place they usually slept—where were

they? He called out again, but there were so many other bats calling out names, it was hopeless, just a haze of noise. Nearly choking with breathlessness, he flew up through the forest canopy. A large, swirling crowd of bats had gathered above the tree line, and he could see Arcadia at its center.

"Shade!"

He turned and almost cried out in relief when he saw Marina and his mother flying toward him. "We were looking for you!"

"So was I."

They embraced briefly in midair, the three of them. Then Shade pulled back. "Frieda?"

"She's fine, but there're others missing. Icarus. Plato and Isis and . . ." His mother faltered.

"Chinook?" Shade said softly, and saw his mother nod. His head throbbed, and he felt sick—and guilty. He'd spent so much time wishing Chinook would just vanish, he couldn't help the crazy feeling he'd had something to do with it.

"How?" he said in confusion, his head still feeling muddy.

"What's happening?" the bats in the crowd were calling out in anguish. "Where have they all gone?"

"We do not know yet!" shouted Arcadia. "We must all of us be calm!"

"There're hundreds missing!" a Pallid bat cried out. "Where could they go?"

Shade suddenly understood. "The Humans," he

whispered, then louder: "The Humans!"

His voice only made it halfway into the crowd, but those closest to him heard and turned.

"The Humans took them?" they said, scowling in disbelief, but quickly this idea spread through the crowd until the words were on everyone's tongue.

"Are you sure?" Marina asked him.

"Who says this?" demanded Arcadia. "Who saw the Humans take the bats?"

A heavy silence fell over the crowd.

Shade swallowed. "They came while we slept," he said. "I saw them. At first I thought I was dreaming, but it makes sense. There were lots of them, moving among the trees and they were reaching up into the branches. . . ."

"Why did no one else see this?" snapped Arcadia.

For a few moments there was nothing but silence, then a few mumbled replies:

"Maybe I did . . ."

"I'm not sure . . ."

"Thought it was just a dream . . ."

"It was like I was drugged with a sleeping potion," Shade went on, remembering the berries Zephyr had crushed into his mouth once. "I couldn't keep my eyes open." More came back to him. "That smell! Did anyone else notice it?"

"Sweet," came a voice, "yes, I smelled that too. I thought it was part of the dream."

A few others muttered halfhearted agreement.

"They put us to sleep so they could take some of us," Shade said. He wondered if that explained the pulsing pain in his skull, the bad taste in his mouth.

Questions erupted from the crowd:

"Will they bring them back?"

"We have to find out where they've gone!"

"I want my children back!"

Shade watched as Arcadia pulled thoughtfully at her beard with a clawed thumb, her eyes coolly sweeping the bats' faces. He felt reassured by the sorrow around him, the confusion—he wanted their help in finding a way out of this place. He wanted answers.

But when Arcadia spoke, her powerful voice seemed to squash the others. "If the Humans did indeed come, and take some of us, it must be part of the plan."

"But what kind of plan is it?" Shade said, his heart beating furiously. "Nobody knows. We should try to find out!"

"Silence!" shouted Arcadia.

"You can't silence him, or anyone else," said Frieda calmly, and Shade turned gratefully to see her flying up from behind. "We all have a right to ask questions. Hundreds of bats have been plucked from the forest—it's right that we should worry about what's happened to them."

"No," said Arcadia with an icy smile. "We must trust in the Humans. They have taken care of us so far, and they will continue to do so. Perhaps we aren't intended to stay here forever."

"But I thought this was supposed to be our Paradise!" said Shade.

"Maybe these bats will return soon. Or maybe this place is just the first stage, to prepare us for something more. Something even more wonderful."

"Don't know how much more wonderful I can take," Shade muttered to himself.

"I don't know what the next stage is," Arcadia continued, "but I, for one, am willing to put my faith in Nocturna, and the Humans! If they've taken us somewhere, it is a place of miracles!"

"Yes! They've treated us well so far!" said a Fringed bat in the crowd.

"They know what's best for us!" said another.

"Yes!" said a Long-ear with growing conviction. "They'll take care of us."

Shade watched, amazed at how quickly the bats could move from crying over their lost mates and children to this excited fervor.

"The Humans will take care of us!"

"I'm sure," Arcadia said, her voice swelling with confidence, filling the forest, "that we will soon be reunited with those who were taken. Don't fear for those who have been taken. They are the lucky ones. They have gone on to an even better place. They have been chosen, as you will be chosen in time!"

"Chosen!" said the bats, and it became a chant. "Chosen! Chosen! The lucky ones! Chosen!"

"We must not allow ourselves to despair," said

Arcadia, and Shade saw her turn her powerful eyes on him, "or let ourselves be troubled by those few who are afraid of Nocturna's will."

You'll listen your way out of here.

That's what Frieda had told him. It seemed not very useful advice at the time. After all, hadn't he already scoured the roof and the walls for fissures and openings that might be a way out?

It was a few hours into daylight, and the forest was asleep. Hanging from his roost, he closed his eyes and swiveled his ears. He tried to breathe smoothly. He made his mind black, casting out no sound.

He listened.

What am I hearing? Everything. Too much. Insect wings, leaves rustling, bats breathing.

He tried to pick just one thing at a time, listen, discard it, and move on.

What good is this doing?

He opened his eyes. This was pointless. Listening wouldn't get him out of here. All he was doing was wasting time. He should be flying, looking with his eyes and ears.

Just one more try.

He listened again.

The spill of water.

That was the background of every other sound in the forest, the trickle of that stream over its rocky bed. His eyes snapped open. Of course: the stream.

That was the way out.

* * * *

Wing tips grazing water, Shade followed the stream as it snaked through the forest. Why hadn't he thought of it before? The stream came from somewhere, so it must *go* somewhere. He skimmed the water, dipping beneath foliage and long, whippy branches that blocked his path. Almost there.

The forest ended in a sheer, stony wall, and the stream narrowed and flowed right into it at the base. Shade flared his wings, braking, and settled on a low ledge for a closer look. The water disappeared into a smooth tunnel gouged into the stone, with only a sliver of air overhead. He wasn't even sure if it was enough space to breathe.

If he were to swim . . .

But if it was the only way, he would do it. He'd keep his nose high to catch whatever air was there, and hope the tunnel brought him out somewhere soon. Bats didn't do a lot of swimming. With a shudder, he remembered paddling clumsily in the sewers with Marina, vainly trying to escape rats. You couldn't really swim with wings.

He flew down to the bank of the stream and stared at the swift water, steeling himself.

"What're you doing?"

He looked up in surprise to see Marina fluttering down beside him.

"Just a little trip downstream," Shade replied.

"You're crazy! You can't even swim that well, and there's nothing to breathe!"

"It'll come out somewhere; it's got to."

"Sure, but when? You could drown before then."

"I've got the current," Shade reminded her.

"That's good going out, but what if you want to come back?"

Shade let out a big breath. He hadn't thought of that. He felt a twinge of fear, but irritation too. Poking holes in his plan, as usual.

"I'm not asking you to come," he said sharply.

"I wouldn't go, even if you begged," she returned, just as sharply. "I didn't come this far to drown."

"You're just like the others," Shade said. "Why don't you just go roost near one of those bug holes and keep your mouth open so you can eat without having to hunt. What a great way to spend the rest of your life!"

"At least I'd have one. Going down there, yours is going to be pretty short."

He almost smiled—and was that a twitch of laughter at the corner of her mouth? He was amazingly glad to see her, and be arguing with her again, just like they used to.

"There's more than this inside the building," he insisted.

"You don't know that."

"Remember how big it was from the outside? It's bigger than this forest, that's for sure. So what else is in here?"

"Maybe we'll find out if we wait."

"Like the bats who got taken today? How do you know it's a good thing, what happened to them?

Wouldn't you rather know before it happens to you?"

She was shaking her head. "Shade . . ."

"Don't you miss Chinook?" he asked tauntingly, and saw her ears flatten in anger.

"Of course I do," she said coolly. "He's my friend. Yours too, whether you like it or not."

He grunted. "Well, let's see, he's tormented me my entire life. Stolen my food, made fun of me. He used to call me 'Runt' all the time, did you know that?" He let out a deep breath. "I miss him too. Don't you want to make sure he's all right?"

He watched her carefully for her reaction. Just *how* friendly were they?

"Who says he's in danger?"

"So you believe Arcadia?" He was incredulous.

"Yes!" she said, a little too loudly.

"All right," said Shade, "that's fine. But I want to know why the Humans are doing this, why they built this place, what's it all for. Because I don't trust them. I don't think this is what's supposed to happen."

"You must really hate those bugs, huh?"

For a moment, Shade chuckled with her. "Remember what Zephyr said about hearing the stars if only you listened hard enough?"

Marina nodded.

"Well, we'll never hear the stars if we stay in here. We're cut off. We can't hear out, nobody can hear in. There're walls all around us. No sound gets through."

She said nothing.

"And what about the bats who don't come here, or don't find their way, or get lost? What happens to them? Are we supposed to forget about everyone else and just have our happy little lives? What about all the Silverwings back in Hibernaculum? What about your own colony of Brightwings?"

He regretted saying it right away. Stupid.

"They had no trouble leaving *me* behind," she said with a snort. "Why should I worry about them now? I like it here, Shade. Banded, unbanded, everyone who comes is welcome. You don't get shunned, or praised, because of some piece of metal on your forearm. That means something to me. Anyway, maybe the Humans built lots of places like this, enough for everybody."

Shade considered it. "Maybe, but we don't know that."

"You can't know everything," said Marina angrily. "What makes you think you're so special?"

His face burned with indignation. "You know what?" he said. "It's not easy being special! I'd just love to be like Chinook. I really would. I'd love to let someone else do all the thinking, and take care of things for a while!"

Marina stared at him and burst out laughing.

"What?" he snapped.

She was still breathless with laughter, wheezing out the words. "The idea . . . of you . . . letting someone else . . . take care of things. That's . . . I'm sorry, Shade, but . . . that's the funniest thing I've heard in ages." There were tears in her eyes. "You couldn't. It's impossible for you."

"You're the same," he said softly. "You always wanted to know as much as me. That was part of why you came with me from the very start. To find out what the bands really meant."

"Maybe I'm happy with the answer."

"Are you really?"

For a few moments neither of them said anything.

"There's something else too," he said. He'd been almost afraid to mention it, in case by speaking it aloud, the idea evaporated like mist. "If the Humans are taking bats away, maybe my father *was* here. Even before Arcadia and all the other bats. Maybe my father was here with lots of bats, and they took him away. So what's happened to him, Marina? Where is he now?"

Marina shook her head and stared at the stream disappearing into the cliff.

"I just can't believe you were going to do this alone. Without telling anyone. What about your mother? What about me?"

"You said you loved it here!"

"But if you're going somewhere . . ." She trailed off. "Listen, you'll just mess things up by yourself. I'm coming with you."

DOWNSTREAM

Shade looked again at the fast water and, before he could change his mind, dropped into it, shuddering as it took hold of him and seeped through his fur. Marina splashed in beside him, and together they shot toward the mouth of the tunnel.

It was much worse than he expected. There was scarcely a whisker of air overhead, and it was almost impossible to get at it, nose scraping against the tunnel roof, desperately sucking in more water than air.

"No good," Marina spluttered.

But without warning, the air was gone. Shade tried to find the surface, and there was no surface, only solid water. Submerged, he whipped around, eyes wide, seeing nothing but dark smudges. Was that Marina? He tried singing out, but his echoes bounced back sluggishly to his clogged ears, painting a senseless, tarry ooze in his head. Water streamed down his throat, and he clamped his mouth shut.

He didn't even know which way was up anymore.

He was blind, with only the current to guide him. He forced himself to stay still a moment and wait for the water's tug. This way. He didn't have much breath left, and all he could do was hope the current would bring him out somewhere soon. And that Marina was still close by.

His chest felt as if it might explode. He wanted air. He tried to row with his wings, but it was slowing him down more than helping. He felt his body start to panic. Air. He knocked his nose against the roof of the tunnel, hoping for a breath. His thoughts splintered and danced in his head. Air. Which way? Can't. Hurry, hurry, please.

Suddenly he was gasping and choking, his head above water. Rivulets streamed down his face, his fur plastered against his body. He turned clumsily, blinking water from his eyes, to see Marina splash up nearby, spluttering and sucking air hungrily.

"Another great idea from the master," she said sarcastically when she'd caught her breath. "Thank you, Shade."

They had spread their wings to keep themselves afloat and were drifting down a stream lined with willows. They were in another forest—so familiar-looking that for a moment, Shade wondered if by some trick the tunnel had simply returned them to the same place. Spreading around them was the same lush mix of conifers and leafy trees; far overhead the same glass roof, the same sun. They drifted lazily down the stream.

"Maybe this is where they take the bats," whispered Marina excitedly.

Impulsively Shade drew in breath to call out his father's name, but Marina smacked a wet wing across his mouth.

"Are you crazy? We don't even know what's in here yet!"

Shade scowled, but nodded. Cautiously, he swept the trees with sound, searching beneath branches for the telltale shape of roosting bats. Nothing so far . . . just leaves . . . more leaves . . . and then something moved, something much larger than what he'd been looking for. He'd been searching only for bats, his focus tight, but now he pulled back in alarm and saw a huge, feathered head with horned ears.

Heart hammering, his echo vision skittered along the branch, and then into nearby trees.

The forest was teeming with owls.

"Marina . . . " he breathed.

"I see them. Good thing you didn't call out."

He'd never seen so many owls in one place before, and he doubted any bat had, since the rebellion of fifteen years ago. He'd already counted three dozen. They were all sleeping, it seemed, and Shade wanted to keep it that way. But what were they doing here—in an identical forest right beside their own?

"We're going back," Marina said in a tight voice.

Shade nodded, but with a shock realized how far they'd already drifted down the stream. The tunnel mouth was out of sight around a bend. Stupid! He'd forgotten how fast the current was. He clumsily paddled with his wings, but wasn't doing much more than treading water.

"This is no good," hissed Marina. "It'll take too long."

"We're going to have to fly," Shade said.

Marina grimaced, and Shade didn't like the idea, either. To fly was to risk being spotted by a restless owl. But once airborne, they could probably make it back to the tunnel in less than a minute.

"This was a bad idea, wasn't it?"

"Definitely," said Marina. "Let's climb out."

Stealthily, they hauled themselves up onto the bank, quietly shaking water from their fur and wings. Shade knew they should really wait until they were dryer, but they didn't have the time. He just hoped they weren't too waterlogged. With a clumsy leap, he was airborne, heavy and flapping hard. With Marina, he flew low, streaking back through the forest to the stream's source. There it was.

They settled on the bank. The water burst from the tunnel, frothing at the sides. He hadn't realized how fast it was. They'd nearly drowned coming through, and that was *with* the current. There was no way he could imagine them getting back alive. His stomach shifted heavily. He looked at Marina. "I'm sorry," he said.

She was trembling with anger. "I can't believe I let you do this."

"You didn't have to—"

"Just start thinking, all right, because—"

"Bats!"

It was the legs Shade noticed first, those surprisingly long legs dangling as if boneless, but tipped with four-pronged claws, ready to slash. The owl dropped toward them like a huge, winged head, beak open, shrieking to wake the forest.

Shade veered up into a tight weave of branches with Marina, the owl plunging narrowly past her tail.

"Bats!" the owl screeched again.

Shade could see the owl was a young male, traces of down still clinging around his wings. But even so, it was a giant compared to him. In the center of his chest, the mottled feathers made a pattern of white lightning bolts.

All around them, owls were waking, and within seconds, the air was churning with wings. Even as he blurred through outstretched talons, between legs and over winged heads, Shade was desperately scanning the forest for a hiding place. It was only a matter of seconds before he would be snatched up and eaten whole. He spotted a knothole in a tree, too small for owls, just big enough for them—he hoped. There wasn't time to make a better measurement. He looked around anxiously for Marina.

"The tree!" he called out, and shot a flare of sound toward it so she could see. And then he hurled himself at the knothole, shooting through and almost knocking himself out against the inside. Dazed, he shifted out of the way as Marina half-flew, half-tumbled into the tree.

"Move back!" Shade cried, and she jerked away from the opening just as a she-owl's beak thrust through, snapping. Its hard, pointed tongue vibrated as she roared.

Huddled together at the bottom of the hollow, Shade watched the owl press her flat face against the knothole and glare down at them with one huge, luminous eye. "Why are we here?" she shrieked.

The question surprised him. "I . . . I don't know what you—"

"Are we to be prisoners until we die, is that your plan?"

"What do you mean, *our* plan?" Marina said.

The she-owl's eyes hooded dangerously. "Your plan with the Humans. Yes, we know all about it. You've asked them to fight alongside you, and now you trap us here in their building."

"How could we ask them?" said Shade in confusion. "We can't talk to them any more than you can."

"Tell us the way out!" the she-owl demanded.

"I don't know the way out!"

"Then how did you get in *here?*" said the she-owl slyly.

Should he tell her the Humans had trapped them too, that he was trying to find a way out, just like them? No, he wouldn't risk telling her there were thousands of bats just on the other side of the tunnel. Even if the owls could fight the current, the tunnel was too small for them, he was quite sure of that—but he wasn't about to take any chances.

"We had nothing to do with trapping you," he said.

"We can wait, little bats. We have patience." With that, the owl withdrew her head.

Shade looked at Marina. "We've been in worse trouble than this."

"Yeah," she said, without much conviction.

"We'll tunnel out."

Marina followed his lead and started searching the hollow for fissures in the bark. Even as he searched, he knew it was probably futile, but he had to stay busy to keep himself from shaking inside.

"What're the Humans doing?" he muttered angrily.

"Maybe the she-owl's right," whispered Marina. "Maybe this is part of the plan, just like Arcadia said. Get all the owls in here, and then they can release us back outside."

Shade faltered for a moment. He couldn't deny the idea was appealing. All the owls in the world out of the way? Sounded good. But a big job, wasn't it? There were a lot of owls out there.

"Here I was, happy with my life for the first time," Marina muttered, "but no, you had to come along with your big frown and big questions, and I was *stupid* enough to listen to you."

Shade winced. What if she was right, and the Humans were taking care of everything all along, and he just hadn't been able to accept it? He'd risked his own life, and even worse, Marina's, just to find out. She was right: He was vain, he was selfish.

"You find anything?" he asked her weakly.

"I think it's thinnest over here," she said.

Shade looked over with a surge of hope. "How long will it take to claw through?"

"About a week. Don't suppose you have any fancy echo tricks to get us out of this one."

"Look out!" he cried.

Marina lurched out of the way as a stone plummeted down from the knothole, almost braining her. Shade looked to see the owl's beak, pulling back. A moment later, another beak thrust in and dropped a second stone.

"Keep to the sides!" Shade cried. By plastering themselves against the bark, they managed to avoid the steady avalanche of stones the owls were now dumping from above.

"They're filling it up," said Marina dully.

Shade knew it wouldn't be long before they'd be forced out of the knothole, into the owls' waiting claws. He knew what they did to you. Swallowed you whole, alive sometimes, and spat out what they didn't want: the bones and fur matted together. He'd seen these gruesome pellets once before and they'd made him sick with fury. More rocks thudded down, and they had to scramble up onto them to keep from getting crushed underneath.

"They're not getting us," he said.

"What're you doing?" Marina said in alarm as he clambered up the bark toward the knothole.

"Get ready to fly."

He crouched flat, just below the knothole, waiting for the next beak to poke through; then, when it pulled back, he'd leap out and shriek an image of Goth so terrifying, it would scare them half to death. That would buy them enough time to get out, and after that—he'd worry about that later.

Shade waited, counting his furious heartbeats, sixty-seven, sixty-eight, sixty-nine, and still no beak came. The longer he waited, the more frightened he became, and that made him even angrier—and then he wrinkled his nose and frowned. "Smell that?" he whispered over his shoulder at Marina.

She took a quick breath. "Sweet."

"It's what they used to make us sleep!"

A huge, wheezing sigh passed through the forest. He could hear leaves fluttering, and then thumping footfalls, which he felt through the bark of the tree. Carefully, Shade inched up and peeked out the knothole. No owls were in sight, but the rhythmic thuds were louder now. He leaned out for a better angle and gasped.

Walking through the forest were the same faceless wraiths from his dream, but this time he knew they were Humans, cloaked in white, heads covered with thick hoods with only slits for eyes. They were tall and terrifying as they took their slow, heavy steps through the forest, fanning out among the trees.

The owls, Shade could see, had all collected in the highest branches, huddled near the trunks. But if they thought the Humans couldn't reach them, they were wrong. They all held long, metal sticks—in his dream he'd thought they were skeletal arms—with big nets at the end. And as they raised them, they grew even longer, stretching up and up into the trees.

He watched as the tip of one metal stick grazed an owl's belly. There was a sharp, crackling sound, and the owl slumped into the net at the stick's end.

Many of the owls seemed strangely lethargic—the sleeping gas, Shade knew—and the Humans netted them easily. Others had fight left in them, and began to shriek, flaring their plumage so they seemed to double in size. But the Humans' terrible sticks only had to nick their feathers, and the owls slumped, twitching, into the nets. The Humans carried on, steadily, deliberately. Shade could hear their voices: thunderous, low things.

His own eyes drooped, and he snapped his head back, fighting the heavy calm that oozed through his body. He looked down and saw Marina, her eyes glazed and serene.

"Wake up!" he shouted. "Now's our only chance. Come on! Move!"

He dropped down beside her, prodding her roughly toward the knothole, then after only a second's hesitation, nipped her tail.

"Hey!"

"Fly!"

He leaped after her and soared a tight circle to get his bearings. There, the stream. They couldn't go upstream, only farther down in the hopes it would bring them out somewhere safer.

"This is your fault!"

He turned sluggishly and saw the young owl with the lightning bolts emblazoned on his plumage. He too seemed dulled by the vapor in the forest, his wingstrokes slow and clumsy, so that he listed slightly as he flew. Still, he was coming at them head-on, claws extended for fight.

Shade and Marina flew. He looked back over his shoulder, and still, the owl was dogging them, and getting within striking distance. Shade tried to cast a sound illusion behind him, but he had no breath left in him, and the image melted before it was even out of his mouth.

He'd lost the stream, but then suddenly they were over it again, racing with it, as it came out of the trees and disappeared into a high stone wall. It would take them even farther away from their own forest, but what choice did they have now?

"Into the stream!" he shouted. He tucked his wings, and barely had time to suck in air before he cut the surface and shot into the tunnel. He was blind again, buried beneath the water, with only his own momentum and the current to guide him. He tried again to use his wings, and this time had more success: Keeping them bunched tight, he levered them up and down, and used his tail membrane as well to propel him forward. But it tired him out faster too, and what if there was no end, what if the tunnel kept going on and on under the earth, until his lungs were gorged with water?

He was through almost before he realized it, head

above the water, choking in air. Marina splashed up beside him.

Even as they grimly clambered out onto the bank, he noticed the heat—a fierce, soaking heat that hung in the air like mist. Overhead were trees he'd never seen before, with strange, broad leaves, and luxuriant fronds. It was drizzling; warm, soft drops of water falling gently.

He'd barely had time to catch his breath when Marina stiffened. "Look," she said.

In the stream, Shade saw a large shape darken the water before breaking the surface.

The owl had come too.

Shade couldn't decide if the owl looked less, or more, frightening wet. Certainly he looked skinnier, his usually voluminous feathers plastered against his body; but his head, with its matted plumage, looked ferociously gaunt, the eyes and beak even bigger and more vicious.

Frozen beside Marina, Shade watched as the owl lurched to the bank and wearily hauled himself out. Then his head swiveled, and he looked straight at them. They faced each other warily, no more than twenty wingbeats apart.

The young owl made a valiant attempt to flare his plumage, but only succeeded in shaking spray from his soggy wings. The piercing shriek that escaped his mouth was, however, more impressive.

Too exhausted to fly, Shade forced himself not to flinch.

The owl cocked his head, to the left, the right, laying it almost flat. It was a curious gesture, almost comical, but Shade knew the owl was just measuring the distance to them, preparing for a strike.

Instinctively, Shade and Marina bared their teeth and hissed, flaring their wings and tripling in size.

"Go back!" Shade yelled.

"I'm not afraid of you," said the owl, but Shade could hear a tremor of uncertainty in his deep voice. The bird glanced down at the mouth of the stream, as if hoping more owls would be coming soon.

"He's half feathers," Shade said loudly to Marina.

"You're right. There's nothing to him."

The owl rocked slowly from side to side.

The heat crawled through Shade's fur like worms. Even on the hottest summer day he could remember, it had never been like this. He stole a glance up at the broad leaves, mossy vines draped from branches. It was hard to breathe.

"Stupid bats." The owl looked at the water once more.

"No one's coming to help you," said Shade. "They're too big to fit through."

"You're in league with them, aren't you?" spat the owl. "The Humans. They came to help you back there. They helped you escape, and they killed those other owls."

"They're not dead," said Shade. "They were still moving."

He couldn't stop himself from feeling a pang of

sympathy for the owl. Before his dream-dazed eyes, he'd seen the Humans snatch and steal his fellow creatures. This owl had been trapped in a forest, just like Shade, wanting to get out, not knowing what was happening to them.

"They're doing it to us too," he said, looking quickly at Marina, not knowing if this was the right strategy.

"Liars. You bats have always been lawbreakers. You started this war by killing birds at night. The city pigeons, then owls, then—"

"That wasn't us," said Shade desperately.

"They were bats."

"No . . . well, yes, they were bats, but not northern bats. They came from the jungle. The Humans brought them up from the jungle, and they escaped and—"

"So the Humans *are* in league with you!"

"No!" He looked despairingly at Marina. How could he explain this?

"There were two of these jungle bats," said Marina. "And they ate birds. They ate beasts. And they ate bats. They nearly ate us, if that makes you feel any better. They were monsters."

"And they're dead now, anyway," said Shade, with a brief surge of hope. "So this whole thing, the whole war, it's a misunderstanding. We don't want a war."

But he could tell from the owl's rigid face he was far from convinced. Just more bat lies, that's what he was thinking.

The owl snorted. "This is stupid, talking to you. The enemy."

"I'm not your enemy."

"All bats are enemies. You kill birds."

"But I just told you . . . look, I've never killed any birds."

"Only because you can't."

Shade felt a stab of guilt. The owl was right. How often had he wished for the power to kill the owls? For so long, he'd harbored a hatred of them.

"Have you killed any bats?" Shade asked.

"Not yet."

"Then you're not my enemy, either."

"So why are you here, if you're not in league with the Humans?" the owl demanded.

"I told you. They're trapping us too," said Shade. "There're thousands of us here, and yesterday, they came and took some of us away, just like they did to you back there."

The owl seemed to consider this carefully. "Where do they take them?"

"I don't know," said Shade. "That's what we're trying to find out. How long have you been inside?"

"Several weeks. Just before winter set in hard. We were flying to our hibernation site and passed over this building. We heard owls, and went closer. There were openings in the wall, and it looked like it might be a barn, a good wintering site, so we went inside and found the forest. And once inside—"

"There was no way out."

The owl nodded.

"What do they feed you?" Shade asked.

The owl's great brows furrowed at the question. "Mice, mostly," he said hesitantly.

"I bet they're lousy, right? All taste the same?"

A quick, somewhat alarming, hoot came from the owl's throat, and Shade stiffened before realizing it was laughter.

"You should try the bugs they pump out for us," said Shade. "I had one today, nearly gagged!"

"Does the water have a strange taste to you?" the owl wanted to know.

"Yeah, like metal," Shade said.

"Yes, metal," said the owl with another short chuckle.

"Well, see how much we have in common?" said Marina.

The owl stared at them, some of his wariness coming back. "I won't be tricked by you."

"We don't have any tricks right now," said Shade. "We're as confused as you, believe me."

The owl swiveled his head to look at the huge trees and lush plants. "What is this place?"

Shade shook his head, listening. He heard nothing but the *drip-drip* of water from the leaves, and the occasional chirrup of some strange insect. It was disturbingly quiet.

"Has to be something inside," he said, "doesn't there?"

"Maybe they're waiting to fill it," said Marina.

"What kind of creature would fill a place like this?" the owl asked.

Fear tingled along Shade's bones. There was something terribly familiar about this place. Had he seen it in one of his dreams, maybe? Or had somebody described it to him, drawing it in words.

A vine rustled.

There was something watching them. Shade knew it with utter certainty. He tilted his head and peered with sound into the shadows of a fleshy tree. A narrow, spiky leaf shuddered, dislodging a rivulet of water.

It wasn't a leaf.

It was a nose, a high-flared nose that curved into a sharp, ridged point—and beneath the nose, a long, houndlike set of jaws that was splitting open to reveal twin rows of incisors. Shade saw the two huge, black, unblinking eyes; the high, pointed ears, the crest of bristly black fur between them.

He knew what it was.

In his mind, he said its name.

Goth.

The Place of Miracles

He'd always known.

He'd seen Goth ablaze with lightning, spiraling life-lessly down through the clouds—and somehow never doubted he'd survive. All those times he'd argued with Marina and insisted Goth was dead, he secretly knew he was lying. His dreams had known the truth all along.

"What is that?" he heard the owl say, in a choked voice.

"It's him," was all Shade managed.

With a violent snap, Goth unfurled himself, three feet of wing punching leaves. He plunged like something jagged torn from the night sky, and in the few seconds before he was upon them, Shade's mind blazed. Where were the metal bands that once festooned Goth's fore-arms? And how was it that his wings looked so undam-aged? They were taut and strong, completely unscarred. Had the Humans healed him somehow?

Shade flipped out of the way, but the stunned owl was not so quick. Goth knocked him over onto his back, pin-ning him with both rear claws. The owl beat at him with his wings, but Goth withstood the blows, head darting, waiting for an opening to tear in with his teeth.

"Let's go!" Shade heard Marina hiss.

But he couldn't rip his eyes away, transfixed by the fear in the owl's face; the sheer, unbelieving terror. It was too awful. Goth reared, his long snout opening.

Shade soared in front of Goth and threw an echo picture in his face—a skeletal Human hurtling toward him, face hooded, eye slits ablaze.

Goth reared back with a cry, and lost his grip on the owl.

"Fly now!" Shade screamed at the bird.

The owl needed no prompting: He was away in a feathery explosion of wings. Shade slammed air, veering over Goth's head as his sound illusion evaporated. He saw Marina in the distance, disappearing into a thick screen of leaves, and hunched his shoulders, beating furiously to catch up.

Behind him, he could hear Goth's roar of anger, but didn't turn to look. He burst through the thicket, and Marina was waiting on the other side. Wordlessly they buried themselves deeper in the luxuriant fronds, and finally roosted behind giant leaves with curved edges, hiding themselves almost entirely.

"More of them?" Marina whispered to him.

It was a horrifying thought—more creatures like Goth collected here, just as the owls and bats had been collected in the other forests. If the Humans had captured Goth and Throbb in their jungle, maybe they'd caught others, and brought them back. Right now, he wouldn't have been surprised to see Throbb too, all his charred ashes reassembled. If they could heal Goth's wings, what couldn't they do? Shade peered up through the dense foliage, listening, but all he could hear were the sounds of the cannibal bat thrashing through leaves, getting closer.

"It's about time they fed me some real food," Goth roared. "I'm to feast on you, Shade! I've seen it in my dreams, and my dreams always come true! I dreamed my wings were healed, and they were. And I dreamed I tasted your beating heart! And I will!"

Shade's legs trembled, and he tensed his exhausted muscles to still them. A drop of sweat snaked through his fur and into one eye. He tried to lie to himself, tell himself it was just another bad dream, but he knew this was real, and there'd be no easy escape by jerking himself out of sleep. He was horrifically awake.

There was sudden silence, stretching out long enough to make Shade hopeful, and just as he was turning to Marina to whisper, their screen of leaves was swept back by a dark wing, and Goth swung toward them, upside down.

Before Shade could even move, the owl had dropped onto Goth's back, driving them both down through the leaves. Shade lit with Marina as the owl and the cannibal bat fought on below them.

"No!" Shade cried out in dismay. "You can't beat him!"

He knew the owl would lose; it was only a matter of seconds. But there was no helping him now. Shade flew into a small clearing and nearly smacked into a Human.

Robed in white, the hooded Human ignored him and

Marina and moved into the heart of the thicket. In his hand was one of the long, netted sticks. Shade swirled to watch as the Human lifted the metal stick high in the air. There was a sharp crackle, and Goth slumped into the net. A second Human appeared from the far side of the thicket, poked the owl with his stick, and netted him as he dropped lifelessly.

He saw them put Goth into one cage, the owl into another. Then they paused, looking around the jungle.

They know we're here, thought Shade.

He heard a faint hiss of air, and turned to see a section of the stone wall swinging open to admit a third Human. And already the wall was starting to close behind him.

"Marina," he hissed, and led the way, pounding furiously toward the opening. The Human must have seen them, because it made a low, drawn-out moan of surprise, turning as they streaked past. The wall was almost sealed shut again, but Shade wasn't stopping. He'd flown through fissures in waterfalls and he could do this. He flipped sideways, sucked in his belly, and trimmed his wings and made it through, Marina almost clawing his tail as she shot after him. With a sucking noise, the wall sealed itself behind them, and they were out of the fake jungle.

He'd been inside a few Human buildings, but mostly in the high recesses where the Humans never went: cathedral spires, a clock tower, the attic of an abandoned mountain cabin.

Now, they were in a blazingly bright passageway, with lights running overhead. The walls were white; so white, they'd be spotted in a minute. Instinctively, they flew to the corners of the wall and ceiling, trying to drag themselves into the tiny smudges of shadow there.

For a moment they rested, and Shade could feel Marina trembling against him. Then he realized it was he who was trembling.

"He saved us, that owl."

Marina nodded. "Never thought I'd ever get help from an owl. Why did he . . . why did you help him?"

"I don't know. It just . . . seemed right."

"Did the Humans kill him with those metal sticks?"

"I thought both of them were still moving, only kind of stunned."

"Good thing for the owl the Humans came, or he'd be dead. What's Goth doing here?"

"Must've caught him again, but the bands—"

"Gone, I know," she said. "And his wings, did you see his wings?"

"No scars."

Marina nodded miserably. "Maybe you're right, Shade, maybe they're just studying us for something. We've got to tell the others."

Shade wanted to get farther away from the door: It probably wouldn't be long before the Humans came back out, and they'd almost certainly be looking for them. Which way, though?

The passageway seemed to stretch on forever in both

directions, doorways on both sides. Shade closed his eyes and quickly regained his sense of direction.

"Okay, maybe this passage runs behind all the forests: Goth's, then the owls', then ours. It's how the Humans get inside."

Marina was nodding. "We follow it back to our own forest?"

"All these doors on the right open into them, right?" He looked at her, hoping for reassurance. "We wait for the Humans to open a door, and slip back in."

"We could wait a long time. What about these?" she asked, nodding at the doorways on the left side of the passage.

Shade shrugged. "Maybe they go deeper into the building, or to other forests—or else outside," he added hopefully.

Suddenly there was the sound of footsteps, and a Human Female, her head unhooded, was approaching. Shade held his breath as she passed beneath them. The ceilings were high, but she had one of those sticks; she could easily reach up and poke them. Luckily she never looked up.

"Follow that one," Marina said.

Sticking to the high shadows, they followed the Female down the tunnel, keeping to a safe distance. After a minute, she came to a door in the left wall, tapped at it, and pulled it open.

A horrible tide of weeping washed out, mingled with shouts of pain and fear—and then was instantly erased as the door sealed itself with a hiss. The passageway buzzed quietly, but Shade's ears still sang with those terrible cries.

They were the cries of bats.

"They're in there," Shade said, his mouth parched.

Marina was shaking her head, eyes wide with panic. "I don't want to go in there, Shade. It's going to be something really, really bad."

"That's where they take us. We've got to," he said hoarsely. He wasn't thinking too clearly, his thoughts surging uselessly in all directions. "We've got to see what's inside."

More footsteps sounded along the passageway, and Shade could see three more Humans coming, two of them carrying cages. Goth and the owl. They stopped before the same door and poked at a cluster of metal buttons.

Shade looked at Marina, and she shook her head anxiously.

"What if my father's in there?" he whispered. He saw her look away, then give a quick, resigned nod.

The door hissed open. Shade dropped down from the ceiling with Marina and landed on the back of the Human bringing up the rear. He clung delicately to the loose folds of the white robe, claws just pricking the fabric, afraid of poking through. Above him, between the Human's shoulder blades, he saw Marina holding on tight. He could feel the Human's energy conducted through the swing of the robe. The Human hesitated for a split second. He feels it, Shade worried, the extra weight—but then the Human hurried after his companions.

Inside the doorway, they dropped off instantly, soaring straight for the high ceiling. A mournful tide of cries rose up with them. Only when he'd reached the very top did Shade turn and look down.

He squinted. The room hurt his eyes, brighter even than the passageway. It had a smell too, a horrible smell of sweating, panicking bodies, of mouths stale with fear.

Running the length of the room were two raised troughs, as thick as great, fallen trees. They looked to Shade like they were made of metal and, straining with his echo vision, he saw that the tops were covered by some sort of glass, pricked with tiny holes.

All along the length of each metal trough, Humans hunched over the glass. Their hands were shoved through numerous openings on either side of the troughs. They seemed to be handling things.

Bats.

Shade caught his first glimpse of the familiar shapes beneath the glass, spread out in a long, single line, but each separated by little dividing walls. The space was enough for the bat to lie flat, wings spread. Shade frowned. Without moving, the bats seemed to be gliding along the inside of the trough, stopping whenever Humans were stationed outside.

In went the hands, and Shade couldn't see what the Humans were doing to the bats, because the hands blocked his view.

But he could hear their voices, shrill in the humid air.

"Please!"

"No! No . . ."

"Why are you doing this?"

And worst of all, he could hear them calling out names, calling out to each other across the room, trying to find out where they were, what was happening to them.

The Humans worked in silence, cold and efficient. He saw Males and Females, their hair tied back, doing this work, and he remembered when he'd seen Humans in the cathedral, in the city, standing and praying. They were silent then too, but he'd thought differently of them. He'd been in awe of their size and strength. Now he was terrified of them.

"I can't see," he whispered to Marina. "I've got to go closer."

"Don't."

But he couldn't stop himself. He had to find out what they were doing. He dropped down, hugging the wall for cover, watching the Humans. They were all so intent on their ghastly work, they never looked up. They wouldn't notice him.

"Shade!" Marina was following him, clutching at him with her claws. "Come back up. We've got to get out of here. We've got to tell the others."

He shook her loose and continued to drop down in quick, tight curves.

Set out beside the Humans were small, high platforms

covered with metal instruments, which glinted harshly in the light. Some were sharp, the sight of them making a stab of pain in Shade's stomach. The Humans picked up their instruments, and pushed their gloved hands through a pair of round portals in the side of the trough. Shade heard the bats cry out.

Not since the owls burned down Tree Haven had he been so angry. Fury roared in his ears, and for a moment he couldn't see. Closer he flew, his eyes filled with tears of rage. This was not the Promise.

"Shade!"

He heard Marina's shout, and almost at the same instant, a horrible jolt went through him. He tilted crazily, all his limbs numb. He saw bits of things as he fell. The point of a metal stick, a Human face, the mesh of a net closing around him.

He was in a metal trough.

Like living things, a pair of fat, gloved hands surged toward him and took hold of him deftly, flipping him over onto his back and pinning him. The hands were cold, and had a pungent smell. From the other side of the trough, a second pair of gloves ballooned around him. Metal glinted sharply. Before he could even cry out in alarm, a blade sliced across his stomach, shaving off a neat patch of his fur. He stared at his pinkish flesh. Like a newborn, furless and weak.

The hands pulled back, and with a whirring noise the floor of the trough moved. Through the glass top, he watched the two Humans slide away, and then two more Humans were sliding toward him.

His heart was a gallop of fear. The floor stopped. He leaped to his feet and clawed desperately at the glass. He didn't even leave scratches. With some difficulty he turned and faced the little walls that hemmed him in on either side. He slammed against them, and pain hammered through his shoulder. The barrier didn't even shift.

"Marina!" he called out. "Marina!"

There was no answer. He hoped she'd escaped, and maybe was still hovering near the ceiling, watching helplessly.

Gloved fingers closed around him, and he cried out in alarm. A second hand plunged toward him, and this one clutched a long, wickedly sharp dart, longer than a pine needle, long enough to pierce him through. Again he was pushed over onto his back. Even as he struggled he knew how futile it was: These hands that contained him could crush his bones if they wanted to; he could feel their blunt strength in every finger. He cried out as he saw the needle coming. Its tip bit into the bare patch on his stomach, but went no further. With relief, Shade watched it withdraw. The hands released him.

He looked at his stomach, a tiny welt bubbling up from the needle's prick. He touched the place with his wing, and it felt strangely thick and numb, as if it weren't a part of him at all.

He was moving again. Wearily, he rolled back onto his

stomach, wings held tight to stop the shaking. He shook, anyway. He watched the Humans sliding toward him, their faces disturbingly warped by the glass. They did not meet his eyes. Why? he wanted to ask them, but their faces were blank, focused on their tasks. In anguish he searched their faces for any sign of compassion, of warmth, of concern. But he was nothing to them. A deep, angry humiliation coursed through him: to think his colony had once thought they were their friends, that they would help them, and now to be treated like this.

He could hear bats breathing hoarsely beyond the walls on either side of him.

"Hey!" he called out to the bat ahead of him. "What's your name?"

No answer.

"What have they done to you?"

There was only a whimper. Shade shivered. Maybe it was best he didn't know what awaited him.

He came to a stop, looking at the circular portals in the trough walls, waiting for the hands to push through, wondering what kind of horrible tools they would hold now. He didn't have long to wait. Simultaneously from both sides, four hands pushed into his compartment, and this time, he fought. Baring his teeth, he lunged at their fingers, trying to sink through their gloves and draw blood. He bit, and heard a satisfying holler of surprise and pain from the Human. One set of hands pulled back.

"I've had enough!" Shade bellowed.

But the hand returned, holding some kind of thin,

metal stick, and Shade could guess what it was. He jerked from side to side, trying to avoid it, but eventually it grazed his tail, and a familiar numbing jolt shot through every limb. He crumpled, wheezing.

Onto his back. A small piece of metal was pushed against the shaved patch on his stomach. He lifted his head to watch, but there were too many hands in the way now. He saw another needle, and some kind of stiff thread strung through it, and then, in horror, realized they were sewing this piece of metal onto his stomach. He caught a glimpse of the needle slicing through his skin, come out, and he felt only the dullest sensation, as if something blunt had poked against him. Again and again the needle passed through him, tying the metal circle to his belly. Something else sharp appeared and cut the thread. The hands pulled back.

He could see it properly now. From the middle of his stomach protruded a round, metal loop. With his claw he touched it timidly. It swung from side to side, so that it rested flush against his belly, and it was a part of him. They'd added a bit of metal to him. It looked so out of place against his skin. Already a dull pain was starting to encircle the spot. He remembered how much he'd envied Marina and Frieda for their bands, how he'd fiercely longed for his own—this thing that the Humans gave like a blessing. But this thing now attached to him felt so foreign against his skin and bone, unnatural. He could see strange Human hieroglyphs scratched into its surface. He hated it.

He was scarcely aware he was moving again, and when he stopped, more Human hands hovered over him, holding another piece of metal. This time it was a small disc, which was hooked with a short length of chain through the loop in his belly. He jerked to his feet and felt the disc pulling against him, surprisingly heavy.

"Is it over?" he called out hoarsely to the bat ahead of him. But all he heard in reply was a howl of pain. New terror coursed through him. What next, what was left?

The trough whirred again. Outside the shield, more Humans approached. He saw the hands reaching for the portals and stared, mesmerized, unable to look away. They came gripping a pair of pincers, like the jaws of some vicious metal animal. He recoiled, but hands swept in from the other side and held him firmly in place. He watched as the two-pronged instrument neared him, aimed straight at his head.

"No!" he screamed. "Don't! Please!"

He flattened his ears, tried to make himself small, tried to make himself disappear, eyes shut tight like a newborn. But it was no use. He felt the metal slide around his outer ear, and then came a horrible, piercing pain.

He thought his pounding heart would finally break free of his ribs. But already the worst was over, just a throbbing memory, and he sagged limply, watching the hand move away with the instrument. Thank you, he thought numbly. It was over at least; it hadn't killed him.

But they'd left something in his ear. He wagged his

head fiercely, trying to shake it loose. It was something embedded in the outer flap of his ear, something small and cold and hard. He twisted his neck to see it, but couldn't.

Suddenly the floor of the trough tilted, the wall before him dropped away, and he tumbled clumsily into darkness. His face hit the floor hard, and when he looked up, he saw other bats all around him, peering at him mournfully. They were all breathing rapidly, as if they'd just flown a great distance. He was in a large black container with no openings, except the one he'd just fallen through, at the side. He turned back to the bats and recognized a few faces from the forest, though he didn't know any of their names. Now he noticed the metal studs in all their ears, and he caught glimpses of metal discs clipped to their stomachs too. The same thing had happened to all of them. He sank down on his belly, his entire body bruised, as if he'd been knocked about by a gale. He felt infected by the atmosphere of defeat, too drained to even speak.

"Shade!"

All at once, another bat was all over him, practically strangling him with his forearms, nose pressing into his neck in joyful greeting. Shade recognized the smell, the bulk of muscle, and the glint of silver-tipped hair.

"Chinook!" he said with a surge of surprise and genuine delight. "Um, Chinook, could you loosen up a bit, you've got me kind of tight. . . ."

"Oh, sorry," he said, releasing his grip around Shade's

throat slightly. He looked over his shoulder. "Hey, everyone, this is Shade Silverwing! He's a big hero. He'll know what's going on!"

Shade gaped in amazement. Chinook calling him a hero? Was this a joke? But he could tell, just by the hopeful expression on Chinook's face, he was serious. Shade almost smiled, but then saw all the other bats turning toward him expectantly. He let out a big breath. He was sure he didn't have the answers they wanted.

"How did we get here?" asked a Hoary bat.

"They took a lot of you in your sleep," Shade said. "Hundreds of you. The Humans came right into the forest and pulled you from your roosts."

"My parents?" Chinook asked, and Shade could hear the edge of anxiety in his voice.

He nodded. "Them too. They must be in another cage," he added reassuringly.

"But how do you know this?" asked another bat. "None of us remembers anything. We just woke up and the Humans were . . . doing those things to us."

"I didn't get taken at the same time as you. We woke up in the forest, and you were all gone. So I came looking for you the next day. I found a way out—the stream." He was too weary to explain about the owls and Goth right now. "I got into this room and saw everything, what they were doing to you. They caught me when I came too close." He felt his throat tighten. "And maybe Marina too." All he could hope was that she'd stayed high, and maybe found her way back to the forest to tell the others.

"Marina came with you?" Chinook asked, and Shade thought he sounded pleased.

"Yes."

Chinook sidled closer, lowering his voice. "So she, you know, missed me?"

Shade looked at him, amazed he could be asking this right now.

"Because I'm pretty sure she likes me," Chinook said confidentially.

"What are these things they've tied to us?" said a Fringed bat, batting at the metal stud in her ear.

"I don't know," said Shade.

"And these heavy discs, what are they for?"

"I don't know," Shade said again, with mounting frustration.

"If Arcadia were here, she'd know! She was right about you: You're just a troublemaker. You don't know anything!"

"I know we should be getting out of here!" Shade retorted. "Have any of you tried that?"

"No."

Great, Shade thought, they're all useless lumps. Do I have to do everything, all the time?

"Why *should* we try to get out?" asked a banded Longear. "How do we know this isn't part of the Promise?"

"Well, you stay, then," Shade snapped. "I'm getting out of here. Who's with me?"

There was a depressing silence for a second, and then—

"Me." It was Chinook.

Shade felt a wave of relief and gratitude. "Come on, then." He hurried for the small opening in the side, and poked his head through. It was an almost vertical shaft, and high overhead he could see the glass, sealing them in.

A Brightwing suddenly came tumbling down toward him, and he pulled out of the way just as she skidded inside, dazed. Not Marina. He felt a mixture of disappointment and relief. If she was free, she might be able to get help. What kind of help, he couldn't even imagine right now.

Without warning, the whole container jerked suddenly. The side opening was quickly sealed off by a sliding panel, and the sudden total darkness unlocked the bats' panic.

"What's happening now?" one wailed.

"I can't take anymore!" another cried.

Their voices piled atop one another, growing in anguish and intensity. Shade tried to block them out. With his echo vision, he looked at the sliding panel and heard a precise metallic click come from a tiny hole about halfway up.

"Chinook, give me a boost, will you?"

He leaped up onto Chinook's back and raised himself on his legs. He could just reach the tiny hole with his thumb, and hooked his claw into it. With all his weight he tried to pull the panel back open, but it wouldn't move. It was somehow locked in place around that hole.

The container now swung wildly in an arc, and Shade lurched off Chinook's back and hit the floor. He could hear heavy Human footsteps. They were being carried somewhere. A door hissing open. And all at once it was much colder. The footsteps crunched.

Snow.

"Outside," he heard Chinook whisper.

Shade's heart nearly broke with yearning. On the other side of this container was the world, and if only he could get out, he could spread his wings and lift, and the Humans would never catch him. He hammered his wings against the wall, and then the pain brought him back to his senses. There was no point wasting his energy this way.

All at once the footfalls became harder, and louder, the sound echoing. They were inside something now, though it was only slightly warmer. With a slam, the cage was put down.

Loud, slow Human voices were all around them like a moaning wind. The cage jostled roughly, throwing him against Chinook.

There were other bats here; he could hear their voices welling up outside his container in a confused, ghostly moan. He remembered the echo chamber back at Tree Haven, so long ago, where Frieda had taken him to hear the old stories, centuries of sound whispering through the air. Is that all that would be left of them? Would they soon just be the dead makers of lost sound?

He felt Chinook nudging closer against him, and then

jolted at a tremendous slamming sound, metal on metal. Silence hung heavy for a few seconds. Seconds later, a deep, powerful vibration welled up around them, through the floor of the container, into the bones of his feet and spine and chest. To Shade it felt like they were inside the belly of a vast mechanical beast.

There was a rush of air, and his ears popped. He swallowed and looked at Chinook, both of them too frightened to speak. The vibration deepened, so that it seemed to be coming from the marrow of his very bones. The whole container hummed.

They were moving, not just the cage, but whatever it was around them. Shade got the sense of something with immense strength, moving slowly at first, and then with increasing speed. The cage tilted, and instinctively, Shade shot out his wings for balance.

All the other bats had fallen into a terrified silence, some mumbling under their breath, maybe prayers to Nocturna. But Shade's mind was blank, and he was ashamed of himself. Should be thinking, should be doing something. But all he could do was stupidly wait for what would follow.

Then suddenly the vibrations calmed, and Shade felt a strangely familiar weightlessness.

"We're flying," he said.

PART TWO

Part Two

Airborne

Marina clung to the outside of the flying machine as it angled into the night sky. She knew her claws couldn't hold out much longer against the wind. It tore at her body, screaming in her ears. An inch away, there was a small indentation in the metal hull, and maybe if she could reach it, it might shield her. If she moved, she might lose her grip—but if she didn't move, she'd surely be blown off.

She tensed and lifted her left claw. Instantly the wind ripped her loose, pelting her backward through the sky. She heard one of the machine's fins shriek past her head, almost cutting her in half. Tumbling, she saw the flying machine, already so far away from her, climbing higher.

"No!" she cried, spreading her wings and chasing after it. No bigger than a bird now, its lights twinkled on its belly, carrying Shade away. An anguished gasp escaped her mouth, as if her last breath were leaving her lungs. She looked at the flying machine until it disappeared, and recognized a wracking loss she hadn't known since her own mother and father had chased her into exile.

Gone, gone, he was gone.

Wings stiff, she let gravity pull her back down to the earth in a slow spiral. She'd seen everything: Shade being struck by the Human's metal stick, and trapped in one of the troughs. From the ceiling, she'd seen his body pass beneath the glass, shunted by busy hands. She'd caught glimpses of metal being fastened to his body. She'd heard him cry out. Then he'd dropped into the large container. A Human had sealed it, picked it up, and carried it toward a door. She'd followed, slicing through the closing door into the winter twilight.

There were lots of Humans with containers, carrying them through the snow to a long road at the end of which rested the huge flying machine. She'd hung back, afraid, as they'd loaded the containers inside the belly of the machine.

Coward, she now told herself miserably. He befriended you when no one else would; gave you a new home with the Silverwings. Should've gone inside the flying machine. Then at least you'd be traveling with him instead of watching him disappear.

South, that was the direction it was traveling, due south.

Beneath her was the Human building, glittering coldly in the dusk. No magical bat song swirled around it now, nothing beckoned her. It was just a big pile of stone and metal, like all their other buildings.

Free, she thought bitterly, I'm free now. But she'd

never felt less free. Tell Ariel, tell Frieda, that was the only thought she could latch on to. She had to get back inside. They all had to leave now, she was sure of that. Frieda would know what to do. They could go south, catch up with the plane, find Shade. Yes, that's right. Find Shade.

She recognized the stretch of roofline they'd flown over when they'd first arrived, and after several minutes, caught sight of one of the entrance portals. She dove toward it, then pulled back, afraid. If she went through, she'd never get out. She had to be able to get out.

She glared at the building, hating it.

She wanted to smash it.

So smash it.

She skimmed the ground and found the biggest stone she could carry. Clutching it in her rear claws, she flew high, took aim, and let it drop. She tracked it as it plummeted and hit a pane of glass square in the center. Nothing. Not so much as a splinter. Again she picked up a stone, labored into the air, and dropped it on the same spot. It bounced off harmlessly.

That left only one choice.

She'd have to use the portal.

It only opened one way, she remembered Shade explaining. No way was she going to be trapped inside that forest again. She glided low, and finally her eyes picked out what she was searching for. A stick, thick and not too tall. She grabbed it and flew to the portal. Just inside, she tried to remember what had happened last time, how quick the drop was at the tunnel's end. She started down, pausing at the edge. She took a deep breath, wings spread, and dropped over.

Sparks shot from her claws as she dug into the sides. Her flared wings pushed against the shaft, slowing her down a little. Slower . . . slower . . . she urged herself. With her echo vision now she could see the end of the shaft rushing toward her, the metal flap that only swung one way. If she didn't slow down enough she'd simply fly through, and that would be the end of it.

She jammed her wings even harder against the shaft walls, burying her claws in the metal, and—

The flap swung up as she neared it, and she wedged herself into the opening. Gasping with the effort, she quickly jammed the stick against the flap. It came down hard and caught, grinding. The stick skittered a bit, then held.

Through the portal she saw the forest.

She was back in.

But this time she had a way out.

Standing on Chinook's back, Shade blasted sound into the tiny hole in the metal panel. The returning echoes filled his head with a complicated weave of metal. Quickly he tried to make sense of it all. Some kind of lock. And the Humans must have some kind of tool to push inside and open it. Maybe he could make his own tool—with sound. Open the lock that way.

He didn't know what was on the other side of the

panel, but he wasn't about to wait around here any longer. The other bats were crouched on the floor, some silent and staring, others muttering forlornly among themselves.

"Can you open it?" Chinook asked from below.

"I hope so."

"You can do it," said Chinook, nodding confidently. "I've seen you knock those stones around. You can do it."

"Thanks," he said, touched by Chinook's loyalty.

He sang a needle of sound into the opening and watched in his head as it ricocheted off the metal pieces, making one or two move gently. But he saw the pieces he would need to move: three of them, all at the same time. He took a deep breath, took aim, and sent out a three-pronged bolt of sound. Metal tumbled, and there was a small *pop* that jolted the panel.

"I've done it," he whispered to himself, then more loudly, "I've done it. It's open!"

The other bats looked up at him.

"But we don't know what's on the other side," said the banded Long-ear. "Maybe we're better off here."

"Maybe this is what's supposed to happen," another bat said hopefully. "Arcadia always said that whatever the Humans do is part of the plan."

"Does this feel like something good?" Shade said bitterly. "When they cut into us back there? Tied these things to our bodies? Don't you remember how much it hurt?"

The horrible wail of that room still echoed in his head.

"But maybe we're supposed to endure the suffering. Maybe it's a test?" said the Long-ear.

"Maybe," said Shade, and for a moment, he wanted to lie down on the floor too, just rest and wait. Had this happened to his father too? How he wished he could speak to him now.

He looked at the bats and sighed. "The panel's unlocked," he said simply. "Anyone who wants to can leave. Come on, Chinook, we're getting out of here."

He saw a tremor of hesitation in Chinook's body, but then he followed Shade's lead, and together, they dug in their claws and dragged their weight along the panel, pushing. It slid back slowly but smoothly, and on the other side was—

Another black wall, blocking their opening.

Chinook slumped.

Shade peered at it in dismay, and then realized it was another panel, identical to the first, complete with a tiny hole for the lock.

"It's another cage," he said.

Faintly he could hear more bat noises around them, weary murmurings, the occasional cry for help.

"I can open this one too, maybe," said Shade.

"What's the use?" moaned a Graywing behind him.

"It'll just be another cage," said a second bat, "and how are we supposed to get out of that?"

"We'll never get free," whined a third.

"It's better than sitting here and waiting," said Shade

angrily. Once again he hopped up onto Chinook's back and peered into the hole with sound. Stupid bats. He didn't care what they said; he'd keep trying to get free until he died.

It was obvious they were inside some kind of Human flying machine. And if he could get out of all these cages, maybe there was a way out of the flying machine. Into the air. Back into the world.

The lock was slightly different from the first, but he recognized the same principle of tumbling metal. He took a deep breath, aimed, and fired sound. By the solid *clink,* he knew he'd succeeded. With Chinook he started sliding back. Probably more useless bats inside, he thought with a grimace.

They'd barely moved the panel a few inches when a huge snout lunged through the gap, knocking Shade over onto his tail. He saw the fangs and knew instantly what had happened.

He'd just unlocked Goth's cage.

He leaped back to his feet and hurled himself against the panel with Chinook, pushing it back.

"What is that?" Chinook choked out.

"Meet Goth," Shade grunted, then over his shoulder shouted to the other bats, "help us!"

Goth's head pushed farther through the gap, and it was all Shade and Chinook could do to keep the panel from sliding open even farther. If Goth got inside, it would all be over. It would be unimaginable.

A few other bats managed to beat back their terror at

the sight of Goth's teeth, and added their weight behind Shade's and Chinook's, pushing. Still, Goth held his own, his snout lashing from side to side, trying to wedge himself through. Just don't let him get his shoulders in, Shade told himself. Once that happened, there'd be no holding him.

Goth's head pushed hard, and now his eyes were inside. Shade looked into one wild black eye, not an inch from his own face, and winced as the scalding breath washed over him. He almost gagged. He knew Goth was going to get inside unless he did something fast.

He released his hold on the panel, darted forward, and sank his teeth deep into Goth's cheek. Goth tore back his head with a roar of pain and rage, and the panel slammed against the spiked tip of his nose. Goth howled again and pulled back altogether.

The panel slammed shut.

"Keep holding," Shade panted, disgustedly spitting out the taste of Goth. "I've got to lock it again."

But already Goth was hurtling his weight against the panel, making it bulge inward with each blow.

"What was that?" one of the other bats stammered.

"A bat, from the jungle. His name's Goth."

"You know him?"

Shade just nodded. "He eats other bats. We need some fresh help."

Reluctantly, five new bats came forward and braced themselves against the panel as Goth pounded on the outside, trying to lever it open once again.

Shade had no idea if he could close the lock—opening it was one thing, but he wondered if he could even reach the right pieces with his echoes, to force them back into place.

He threw sound into the lock, but had it crushed by Goth's roaring on the other side. Eye to eye they peered at each other through the tiny hole in the thin metal panel.

"I'm going to eat you alive, Shade," he said through his hot, rank breath.

Shade didn't have time to make another try with the lock. A deep machine *whir* enveloped them, and suddenly their whole container was tilting slowly backward. Shade tried to cling onto the panel, but it was no use. He was skittering down the floor, falling against the other bats, all elbows and claws and wings flaring to keep balance.

The panel. There was no one left to hold it.

Even as the container tilted higher, dumping the bats into a jostling heap, he watched the panel in dread. It jerked, opening a whisker, then slid all the way in a rush.

Goth plunged toward them, fangs bared, and in that split second, Shade had time to notice that there was a stud embedded in his ear too. And from his belly swung a metal disc, like his own, only much, much larger.

Shade kicked with his feet and caught Goth under the chin, knocking his jaws away for a second, just a second. All was confusion, a seething mass of limbs and wings. Goth was on top of him, on top of all of them, saliva spraying from his mouth. Shade saw his fangs sink into fur, and cried out in pain before realizing it was someone else's.

Then the whole top of the container sprang open. There was a deafening roar of wind, and Shade was sucked up into the air, tumbling. He had no time to trim his wings, no time for anything. He caught only skewed glimpses of things. The vast insides of a flying machine. Huge doors parted like jaws. And beyond the doors, the night sky.

Around him were hundreds of other bats, hurtling toward the doors as they were sucked out of the flying machine. There was no fighting it, and Shade didn't want to. He was free from Goth, free from the Human container.

He hit open air.

Marina didn't waste a second. She had no idea how long her stick would hold the flap open. Cold air whistled through into the artificial warmth of the forest. She swooped down.

"Hurry!" she cried. "We have to leave! We have to leave here. Now!"

With the setting sun, everyone was already awake and hunting, and bats wheeled in surprise at her voice. But she didn't slow down to explain. She flew to the stretch of stream where the Silverwings liked to feed, and there she found Ariel and Frieda, looking anxiously toward her.

"Where've you been?" Ariel demanded immediately, and then, her voice suddenly husky with dread: "Where's Shade?"

"They took him," Marina gasped, roosting.

"Catch your breath," Frieda said firmly.

But Marina was shaking her head urgently. "I've blocked the portal. Please, don't ask me to explain now. We have to go."

"What's happened to Shade?" Ariel insisted.

"They took him away with the others."

There was a snap of wings, and Arcadia was dropping down toward them, her brow furrowed angrily. "What's this all about? You're causing a panic!"

When Marina's breathing had calmed somewhat, she quickly told how she and Shade had gone down the stream, through the owl's forest and into Goth's. She told them about the room where the Humans put metal on the bats, and how they were loaded into cages and taken to a flying machine.

And with every beat of her heart, she was thinking of that portal, the stick, how long would it hold the flap open?

"We've got to hurry," she said pleadingly. "The flying machine's going south, and—"

"Why do you think any of this is cause for worry?" said Arcadia sternly.

Her question seemed so absurd, Marina was dumbstruck.

"What is it that's so different from banding?" Arcadia insisted. "We've welcomed the bands for years; this is no different."

"No, I had a band. It was different. Or maybe it wasn't, maybe it's all the same, but it wasn't good what they were doing in there. I saw it."

Lodged in her nostrils was still the smell of the room, the fear and pain, like some poisonous smog.

By this time, a huge crowd had gathered around them, anxious bats listening to Marina's story. But Arcadia's voice was powerful, and confident.

"Do you presume to know more than the Humans—than Nocturna herself! We are puny creatures. We must trust in the signs and await! How do we know the owls aren't imprisoned here to keep the skies safe for our brothers and sisters on the outside? And this cannibal bat you speak of, perhaps he too is a prisoner for our benefit."

Marina looked imploringly at Ariel and Frieda, and they were looking back at her, as if trying to find the truth in her face and eyes.

"We're leaving," said Frieda, "and any who want to come, come now!" She spread her wings and climbed through the branches, her voice welling out of her, crashing through the leaves of the forest. "All those who wish to leave this place, fly with us. We have reason to think the Humans are harming us. Come now if you will!"

Gratefully, Marina soared after her with Ariel. Arcadia followed them.

"Do not go with these bats!" she bellowed. "They are leading you astray. They are not chosen, but are here to bring fear and suspicion and tempt you away from Paradise. Stay here!"

And as Frieda cried her news across the treetops, only a very few bats came forward to fly with them, mostly the other Silverwings who'd originally set out with them from Hibernaculum.

"You see," cried Arcadia smugly. "We put our faith in a greater power than yours."

"I wish you well, then," said Frieda.

The sound of heavy footfalls overhead made Marina quicken her wingstrokes. Two Humans were making their way carefully along the metal latticework of the glass roof—toward the portal.

"Quick!" she said. "They must know I've jammed it."

With relief she saw that the stick still held, though shuddering with the strain. Acrid smoke curled out from the wall, and the whine of machinery was more labored.

"Hurry!" she called, waiting at the threshold and ushering the bats through.

The Humans, she could hear, were very close, and there was the sound of metal on metal, things being lifted. Beside her, a panel slid open suddenly, and a Human hand pushed in and felt around. It touched the stick, closed its fingers around it, and started to pull.

Marina sank her teeth into the soft flesh, not without some satisfaction.

There was a yelp, and the hand drew back.

She watched as Frieda squeezed through, then Ariel, and now it was her turn, and the Human hand burst back through, this time clutching a wickedly pointed dart. Marina skipped clear, but the Human was waving it around wildly, blocking her way into the portal. She heard Ariel calling to her from the top of the shaft.

Marina held back, waiting, watching the dart stab blindly around. She saw her stick begin to slip, saw the flap drop. She lunged, the flap snapping down on her tail. She pulled, wincing as some of her skin was ripped off. But she was through. She opened her wings, claws skittering on metal as she clambered up the steep shaft. Perched above her was Ariel, waiting anxiously. Marina heaved herself over the top, darted down the tunnel after Ariel, and burst out into the star-filled sky.

The savage impact of cold air punched all the breath out of him. Tumbling, tumbling, head over tail, Shade saw clouds, though he didn't know whether he was falling away from them, or toward them. He was falling so quickly, he was afraid to unfurl his wings in case the wind tore them off. He could barely breathe, the wind shrieking air away from his nose. He was suffocating. In the sky, and no air to breathe.

How could he be falling *toward* the clouds? His stomach lurched and he retched. His vision puckered and flared. Stars overhead, that was right, wasn't it? Yes. Stars overhead. Good. Clouds below? Not good. You didn't fall toward clouds.

He was thinking like a newborn, a few days old, trying to puzzle things out. Slowly it occurred to him that he might be *higher* than the clouds.

And then the world made sense again.

He'd never been so high. No wonder he was cold, no wonder he could barely breathe. Was there even air up so high? He was still tumbling, but gradually he edged out just a bit of wing to stabilize himself.

There were stars overhead, and a hunk of moon, and he could see other bats speckled through the night sky, falling like him. He was plunging straight down now, and he realized that the metal disc chained to his body was making his fall dangerously fast. In the container, where he'd mostly been on all fours, he hadn't realized how heavy it was. Now it was like ballast. Below him was a white sea of cloud.

Gradually he unfurled more wing. The wind caught under them, and his spine took the hit as his arms were snapped up like whips. He slowed so quickly, he felt as if he were being sucked back up into the sky.

Still, the clouds were racing toward him, and he couldn't stop himself from closing his eyes and holding his breath when he smacked into them. There was a definite impact as he broke the surface, then turbulence, and he was buffeted as he plummeted, punching through the bottom of one cloud bank only, seconds later, to go plunging into another.

It drenched him. His fur was coated with frost, and he was shaking violently. Inside the clouds he could see nothing. Where was Chinook? Where was Goth?

It was suddenly getting warmer.

Within seconds his wings were thawed, and then bone-dry.

Whumph, through another blanket of cloud, *whumph* again, and then the heat really took hold of him, the same, soaking heat he'd felt in Goth's artificial jungle.

Alarmed, he peered back up into the sky. Through the gaps in the clouds he saw stars, and tried to mark out familiar constellations. The stars didn't join up, they were all in the wrong places. His stomach felt queasy again.

The metal stud in his ear began to sing.

He jerked in surprise. It was drawing a crude sound map in his head—a simple arrangement of lines and dots. A city, maybe. A night city. And then the shape of a single building began to glow brighter than the rest. A big block of a building, not very interesting to look at, with several narrow buildings radiating from it like spokes.

Wagging his head, he tried to dislodge the image, but it persisted, flaring in his mind's eye over and over again.

Whumph!

He cleared a final layer of cloud, and a dense constellation of lights flared before him. He was still very high, and the city spread to all horizons, bigger even than the last city he'd seen up north. As he swung closer, he saw that the buildings didn't look so high, nor were their auras as bright.

The city below him, and the one blazing in his head, seemed to mesh one atop the other. And he saw the blocky building, off toward one of the horizons.

Go there.

The command shunted its way rudely into his head, and he caught himself angling his wings, setting course. He stopped. Why should I?

But it was like hearing a voice telling you something

over and over again; after a while, you just did it. Go to the building. But why, why? Go there. He couldn't clear it from his head; it would drive him mad if he didn't go there.

The Humans obviously wanted him to go there for some reason, and that was reason enough to disobey.

But what if his father was there?

Go there.

He was tired, and the weight of the metal disc was wearing him down. He had to roost somewhere, why not on this building?

You're an idiot, he told himself.

But, still, he tilted his wings and began a slow descent toward the building. Around him now, he could see the other bats, all converging on the same place. Their studs must be singing an identical image in their heads. Go there.

Despite the heat, he shuddered, breaking out in a sudden sweat. It was just like the way the Humans had lured them to their artificial forest, with that melodious bat song. And he'd been pulled in faster than anyone— hadn't even thought about what he was doing. And look what happened. This was just another trap.

He wouldn't do it. He wouldn't go.

But what if it really was some part of the Promise, some kind of test, what if his father was there, waiting for him, hoping he would pass it?

"Don't go!"

He heard the voice, and it took a moment before he realized it was him shouting.

"Don't go there!" he wailed into the wind, again and again.

But none of the other bats listened. They seemed locked on to their sonic targets, heedless of all else. A Brightwing passed by quite close, and Shade yelled at him to stop, actually struck his wing to get his attention, but the other bat looked at him as he might an unappetizing insect, and sailed past, eyes glazed.

"Don't listen to it!"

They were grazing low over the city, almost at the building now. Shade held back, circling, fighting against the weight of the metal disc. The first bats neared the roof of the building. Shade watched as they braked, rings flaring, and came in to land.

They touched down.

Flames blossomed from their discs, delicate licks of fire that in less than a second became an eruption of smoke and sound. More bats were landing now, all across the vast roof, and as their discs knocked hard on stone, they too exploded, gouging craters from the building.

"Stop!" Shade's screams raked hotly at his lungs. "Don't land. Stay away!"

It was futile. In the confusion, Shade watched more and more bats land like dazed things, adding to the geysers of flame and flying stone and metal. It was as if they were hypnotized by the song in their ears, unable to wrench themselves free of its pull. Horrible Human sirens rent the air.

Shade tried to fly higher, to get clear of the spiraling

debris. Black smoke stung his eyes, tarred his fur. His wings were lead, threatening to buckle.

So this was the secret of the bands. This was what the Humans did to them. His eyes blazed with the reflected flames. He had nothing inside of him. He was going to die. The thought came with no panic, just a numbing certainty. He could not stay aloft forever.

Soon he would have to land.

JUNGLE

A large Silverwing dove past Shade, careening headlong for the seething flames.

"Chinook!" he shouted. "Don't!"

Chinook glanced back at Shade, confusion furrowed in his face, and faltered for only a moment before continuing on his course. With the last of his strength, Shade caught up to him just as they were entering the plumes of smoke. He sank his teeth deep into Chinook's tail.

"Hey!" Chinook flipped around sharply, eyes narrowed. "What're you doing?"

"Stopping you!"

"But I've got to—"

"You'll explode! Look down there! We land, and we explode. We're carrying fire."

For the first time, Chinook seemed to notice the flames, the thunder of explosions. A section of the building's wall sheared away and avalanched to the ground. Shade looked around the sky; he could see no other bats.

They had all flung themselves onto the building, to their deaths.

"Come on, let's get away from here."

"Yeah," said Chinook, dazed. "We'll land somewhere else."

"No," said Shade in frustration. "We can't. If that metal disc hits anything hard, it explodes."

"We have to land sometime," said the other bat.

But how? What could they land on that wouldn't trigger the explosive? Something soft, so soft. Water? A bed of leaves, would that be soft enough? He didn't want to even risk it. Guiltily, he wished Marina were here. She'd have ideas too, or at least tell him which one of his was the least stupid. There wasn't much time. Weighted down by the metal disc, he had to struggle just to keep from losing height.

"We've got to get them off," he said.

"How?"

"Bite them off." He was thinking furiously. "Okay, Chinook, I'm going to come underneath you and bite it off, all right. You'll have to carry my weight for a bit."

Chinook looked down at the ground doubtfully. "I'll fall too fast."

"Find a thermal and try to circle over it," Shade said. Shouldn't be too hard to find one, he thought, it was so hot here. He felt his wings billow warmly and locked on. "Here, right here. Feel it? Just don't lose it; it'll help keep us up. I'm going to fly underneath and grab hold now. Ready?"

He didn't even know if this would work. Would landing on Chinook trigger his own explosive? Couldn't. It had been banging against the container floor, and against his own body as he fell from the plane. It must need something harder, like stone, metal, a good crack. Or maybe he was just being hopeful.

He swung out from Chinook and then came in fast from an angle, as if about to roost. He could see Chinook brace himself.

"Furl your wings!" he shouted.

Chinook pulled his wings tight, and in that split second, Shade braked and, with all claws, grabbed hold, trying to avoid knocking against the metal disc dangling from Chinook's stomach. He flattened himself against Chinook's right flank, and ducked as his wings snapped out over him. Nobody blew up. They slowed, Chinook rocking crazily as he tried to balance himself. Through Chinook's fur, Shade could feel his chest muscles straining.

"How'd you get so heavy, Shade?" he grunted. "You used to be nice and small."

"But you're big and strong, Chinook," said Shade encouragingly. "Shouldn't be a problem for you."

"No problem."

They were falling quite rapidly, and he knew he didn't have much time. At least the stud in his ear had finally stopped singing. He shifted down toward Chinook's stomach, craning his neck toward the chain that held the disc. He tested it with his teeth, grinding with his incisors. It showed no signs of fraying. He'd never get through it in time. He looked at the metal loop sewn into Chinook's belly. "I'm going to have to rip out the whole thing."

"What?"

"The stitches; I'll rip them out."

"You sure?"

He didn't waste time on reassurances. He sank his teeth into Chinook's skin, trying to hook out the careful loops of Human thread. He felt one give, then another. He could taste the saltiness of Chinook's blood, and feel the pain singing through his tense muscles. I'm sorry, he thought, sorry. But it was the only way. Three stitches he'd worked out. His muzzle was spattered with blood. Almost done. The last loop of thread ripped out with the weight of metal, and Shade watched as the disc plunged away from them.

"It's gone!" he shouted, and he tumbled off Chinook, spreading his own wings. Below them, a fountain of flame shot up with a crumpling roar from a Human road. Shade was startled at how much closer they were to the earth.

"Me now," he said. "Rip mine out."

He was worried that Chinook would mess it up, worried he wouldn't be able to hold the bigger bat's weight. Worried he'd run out of airspace.

"Move your wings, I'm coming over!" Chinook yelled at him.

Shade felt claws close around his fur, and nearly

capsized with the burden. He unfurled his wings, and beat as hard as he could, straining to keep them both aloft. Slowly but surely, they were sloping in toward the peaks of the city. He quickly plotted their course to a stretch of trees, mist pooling around the branches. From this height it looked soft and coolly inviting, and he longed to bury his tired body in it and sleep.

Chinook's teeth cut into him, and he winced. He clenched down, imagining that metal disc getting looser, falling away. A hot wind knocked him from above, slamming them earthward. He beat faster, trying to compensate.

"Chinook?"

"Just a few more."

"Chinook, get off, we're going to hit!"

The trees were soaring to meet them.

"I've just got a couple—"

"Get off!"

Chinook rolled clear. Shade glanced down at his belly and saw the metal disc dangling by just one loose stitch.

Drop, he thought fervently, drop!

He was skimming over the treetops, close enough to see the water droplets glistening in the cupped leaves. It was beautiful, and he was going to die very soon. The disc knocked a few leaves, and his face clamped in dread, but nothing happened, not yet. Suddenly the trees gave way to a clearing, and down below was a long ribbon of swampy water. Desperately Shade wheeled and dropped toward it, fanning his wings and pounding the air with all his might.

He was almost hovering when he set down on the steaming surface, eyes shut tight, waiting for the end.

Nothing.

Chinook landed warily on the bank. "Weird. You didn't blow up," he said, with more surprise than relief.

"It's still there," panted Shade. "Can you swim under and chew off the last bit?"

"Just come ashore."

"I'm not risking it. Come on, Chinook." Already he could feel the weight of the metal disc pulling him deeper into the water, and he didn't want to splash too hard with his wings, in case the movement triggered an explosion.

"I don't like water," Chinook said.

"Neither do I," said Shade, losing his patience, "so get over here and chew this thing off me."

Chinook wrinkled his nose distastefully at the oily water. It was filmed with rotting leaves and grasses, and produced a rich smell of decay. The big bat sighed and folded his wings tight and dipped gingerly into the water, keeping his head clear.

As Shade watched Chinook approach, he thought dolefully, Why aren't you Marina? And then felt guilty.

"Thanks, Chinook."

"You want me to go under?"

"That's the general idea, yes."

Chinook took a breath and ducked beneath the surface. Shade felt him nudge against his belly, but almost right away he was spluttering up beside him.

"Something brushed me down there!"

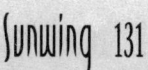

"You sure?"

But Shade instinctively drew up his legs. Chinook's eyes were darting all across the water's surface. It was so murky, it was impossible to see underneath.

"Maybe it was just some bark or something," Shade said.

Then something grazed his tail. He felt it, the whole quick, scaly length of it, before he whipped his tail away, half-tipping himself over in panic.

"That's not bark!"

Chinook was already thrashing his way toward land.

"The disc!" Shade hissed. How did he know it wouldn't explode when he clambered up out of the water? But off to one side he saw a long furrow bulge the water, and a head with bulbous eyes broke the surface, followed by a slick, scaled back, several feet long. It was some kind of fish, unlike any he'd ever seen. This one had teeth. Thick triangular teeth in its open jaws.

Then it was gone, somewhere beneath him, invisible. Waiting.

He couldn't bear it. Disc or no disc, he was getting out of here. He started rowing after Chinook toward shore. He was halfway there when he was pulled under in one smooth, quick tug. Flailing, he saw nothing in the swampy water, but he could tell by the stabbing pain in his stomach that the fish was dragging him down by his disc.

It had it in its mouth.

Shade tried to pull back, but his sodden wings were useless as the powerful fish plunged deeper. He made a last violent backward jerk and felt the final stitch in his stomach rip clear. He was free. With difficulty he folded his wings tight and kicked furiously. Unbearably slowly, he rose. The fish could overtake him in a second if it wanted.

At last he broke the surface, wheezing, and saw Chinook, crouched on the shore, a look of relief flowing across his face. But before Shade could even form a word, there was a muffled but powerful bursting noise deep beneath him. The water boiled, swatting him up into the air on a colossal geyser. Blasted almost to the height of the trees, he whipped his wings out, and spiraled back down to Chinook.

"It ate the disc," he panted.

For a few moments they said nothing, watching the water slowly calm. Then Shade's eyes turned upward to the towering trees, the foreign stars, and his ears pricked to the calls, far and near, of strange animals. Weird shrieks and hoots and crowing sounds, some disconcertingly close.

The forest was unlike what he was used to. The trees grew tall and bare—without branches or foliage for fifty feet or more—and then spread to form luxuriant canopies. Beneath them, flowers coiled the trunks, and other plants seemed to have found purchase on vines and bark. Some of the leaves seemed vaguely familiar to him from the north. But much fleshier, with a waxy sheen.

He felt queasy. He'd seen all this before, back in the Human building. And the strange stars, the smothering heat, it all fit. He said the word softly, as if afraid of giving it too much strength.

"Jungle."

The Humans had dropped them in Goth's homeland.

After the warmth of the forest, the winter night was piercingly cold, and Marina felt all her resolve, all her energy, seeping out of her. She looked back at the Human building, shuddering. What if Arcadia was right? What if the Humans really were readying them for some glorious future, and she'd gotten it horribly wrong. . . . She clamped down on the thought: No, she'd seen what they were doing to the bats, the way they handled them like worthless things. It was not right.

When they reached a small stand of pines, Frieda called a halt, and they roosted close together, Marina huddling against Ariel for warmth.

"We must all decide what to do," Frieda said, "and quickly."

Marina looked at their small group. Apart from Frieda, Ariel, and herself, there were only six others, and they all looked as cold and scared as her.

As if reading their minds, Frieda said, "Anyone who wants to return, to go back to the forest, is free to do so. I exert no hold on you. You must do what you think is right."

A male called Windsling shifted awkwardly. "Why don't we go back to Hibernaculum?"

The question hung temptingly in the air for a

moment. Marina felt its warm lull. To return to the security of that cave behind the waterfall, to fold her wings, to sleep and forget everything until spring . . .

"Shade," she said. "I saw which way the flying machine was headed. South-southeast. We can't leave him."

She looked at Ariel as she spoke, and saw her eyes reflecting back her own sorrow.

"That plane could be millions of wingbeats away by now," Frieda said gently. "It could have changed course."

"I should've gone aboard," Marina said bitterly. "I would've, if I were . . . braver."

"Then you wouldn't have been able to warn us," Ariel reminded her softly.

The kind words unlocked Marina's tears, and Ariel enclosed her in her wing. "I know," she said soothingly, "I know. I've had lots of experience with males flying off somewhere without telling me. I'm even getting used to it."

Marina laughed gratefully, then coughed, wiping away the last of her tears with her forearm.

"I say Hibernaculum should be our destination," said Windsling. "I'm sorry, Ariel, for your son, and all the others, but Frieda's right. This flying machine could go anywhere, and faster than us. How could we hope to find it? And if we did, how do we know we could help?"

"You're right, we don't," said Ariel. "But I've lost my mate, and now my son, for the second time. The first time I gave him up for dead. But never again. You go back to Hibernaculum, but I'm going after that flying machine."

"Me too," said Marina. She'd lost her family once before, and she'd do everything she could to stop it from happening again. Her brain darted with guilty thoughts. Why hadn't she gone inside the flying machine? They traveled quickly. A million wingbeats in a night . . . and who knew how far it would fly. But at least now, she would not be traveling alone.

"Your journey may be too long for me," said Frieda, "but I'll make it until my wings stop beating."

Two others agreed to go with them, but Windsling and the rest chose to go back to Hibernaculum.

"Good, then," said Frieda, with no sign of ill will. "You will carry the news of what has happened to our colony. Make sure no others come to this place, and spread the word to any others you may meet. This place is cursed for us. Good fortune, and let us go on our ways."

As Marina rose into the air with Ariel and Frieda, she saw a thick smudge of movement across the eastern sky. Owls, was her immediate thought. But moments later came the telltale squeak of bat wings in the cold. It was a large group, perhaps a hundred, and they were heading for the Human building.

"Hurry," said Frieda, "we should warn them."

When they were near, Marina saw Frieda's face wrinkle with a smile. "That, unless my eyes fail me, is Achilles Graywing."

Marina stared. Achilles Graywing was a name known

to virtually every bat in the northern world—a great warrior who had fought in the last rebellion against the owls, fifteen years ago. Even though the bats had been beaten, Achilles's bravery and shrewdness in battle became legendary, and there were few newborns who hadn't fought imaginary battles in his name.

"Frieda Silverwing!" called out the majestic warrior. He looked old, older even than Frieda, if that were possible, but his wingstrokes were still sure and strong.

"Achilles," said Frieda, "it is a pleasure to see you again. And a great relief."

They circled one another in tight aerial greeting.

"The relief is all mine, Frieda. We have bad news to relay. Hibernaculum has fallen."

It was as if Frieda had been struck in the chest; for a moment it looked to Marina as if she'd stopped breathing altogether, her eyes dull. Then she said, "The owls."

Achilles nodded. "They've broken all hibernation laws; they've been attacking any roost they can find, taking all inside prisoner, or rooting them out into the winter. These"—he nodded at the bats around him—"are some of the survivors I've gathered together. We were on our way to rouse your colony. But we were too late. We saw it under siege by the owls, too many for us to fight. Your colony is imprisoned, Frieda Silverwing, and I am sorry."

Frieda's shock was short-lived. Marina had never seen the Silverwing elder angry in the short time she'd known her; now, Frieda's eyes burned, and her voice was hoarse with fury. "Never has there been such an outrage. To attack a colony's Hibernaculum. These are ancient laws . . . not in a million years have they been broken."

Achilles nodded wearily, stretching out a wing to touch hers. "I know, my friend. They are intent on crushing us, and their strategy is wise."

Marina glanced at Windsling and the other bats who had hoped to return to Hibernaculum, and their faces were limp with disappointment. Their safe haven, a cage. Worse, a dying ground. She shuddered. By waking up a hibernating bat, you were forcing her to fight for life. First she had to warm up, thaw herself and, with what little energy she had left, hunt voraciously. But in winter, there was little to eat. Sleep wasn't merely a choice; it was a life-or-death necessity for wintering bats. And if the owls didn't even let them leave to hunt, few would last till spring.

"We will go back and free them," said Frieda.

Achilles shook his head. "There is nothing we can do. The detachment there is too strong for us. We must go south."

"It is my colony!" Frieda shouted.

"I know, and if you go to them, they will lose their elder, and you will not have helped them. We must go south. There are other groups like ours, plotting course for Bridge City."

Marina had heard of the place, the greatest of the bat havens. It was, of course, a Human city, but beneath its great bridges lived a massive colony of bats, millions upon millions, undisturbed for decades. So long as the Humans hadn't imprisoned them too, Marina thought bitterly.

"It's our last hope," Achilles said. "We will gather there and collect our forces. If there is to be a great battle, it will be there. Come with us."

"We were about to embark on an equally perilous quest," Frieda said, and now it was her turn to tell Achilles their story. With Marina's help, she told the Graywing general about the Human building and all they'd found there, and about how the Humans were taking the bats away in their flying machines, somewhere to the south.

"We're on a common path, then," said Achilles. "Travel with us. The skies are too perilous to fly in small groups. Owl squadrons are everywhere. We lost fifteen in a skirmish just two nights ago."

"Let us go south then," said Frieda, "together."

And find Shade, Marina added silently.

Goth flew over the jungle, its glorious warmth rising up to him, wrapping him in its wings. The stars, bless Zotz, blazed in their familiar constellations: the jaguar, the two-headed serpent, the eyes of the Underworld, searing down at him. Zotz had looked over him, and had brought him back home by way of the witless Humans.

The metal disc hung below him heavily.

He'd seen what it could do. When he'd been swept into the open air, he'd followed the small bats as they'd plunged toward the city. Curious, he'd hung back as they'd hurtled themselves at a single building.

When he'd seen the explosions, he'd understood what it was he carried. His hatred of the Humans intensified, but took on a new respect. They were using him as an instrument of destruction. He hadn't known they could be so clever.

The stud in his own ear was still singing, as it had been from the moment he'd dropped from the Human's flying machine. A building, it sang to him. A small, low-lying building on the outskirts of the city. Go there, the picture urged him insistently.

How typical of the Humans, Goth thought, to think him so weak-willed, so stupid. That was their real failing: The Humans were idiots. Of course, it seemed to work on the northern bats—they'd hurtled themselves with glee to their deaths. Always so eager to please the Humans. He had to smile.

Still, as he'd watched the upward torrents of flame and smoke caused by those little metal discs, he'd had a startling thought: Imagine what mine would do.

He would use it for his own purposes, for the glory of Zotz.

Now, he steered away from the building that still flared faintly in his head. The metal disc was heavy, but his wings were stronger—stronger than they'd ever been, thanks to Zotz. He set his course for the deep of the jungle.

He was home.

THE STONE

In the distance the undergrowth rustled, and Shade's claws felt the vibrations of heavy footfalls through the earth.

"We should get off the ground," he told Chinook, "get higher."

"Okay, good idea," said Chinook, nodding quickly.

They lifted from the stream's bank and flew in tight, cautious spirals up toward the jungle's canopy. Shade didn't want to get too deeply into the foliage—who knew what roosted there?—so he kept his distance, searching the tall trunks of the understory for a roost. He settled on a network of frail branches, which he thought were probably too weak to support anything bigger than him and Chinook.

He locked his rear claws, hanging upside down, and for the first time, was aware of the pain in his stomach. Ripping off the metal had left a raw gash in his flesh, still bleeding slowly. He caught a glimpse of Chinook's wound, similarly ugly. "You all right?" he asked.

"It's not too bad," said Chinook. "How's yours?"

Shade shrugged. He was impressed with Chinook. Somehow he'd expected him to fall apart, but he was doing pretty well. Nothing on Marina, Shade thought with a pang, but after all, Chinook didn't have nearly as much practice almost getting killed all the time.

Below them came a great thrashing of fronds and leaves, and Shade caught sight of a huge beast. It had a narrow, shaggy back that was easily four feet in length, and a thick, broad tail almost as long. Most unusual, though, was its snout, which looked like some kind of thick snake attached to its face. The beast plunged its snout into the earth and made a loud sucking noise. As it dragged back, Shade saw a long, whippy, ant-covered tongue dart out and slap around the edges of the snout, then disappear back inside. Good, Shade thought distantly. It ate ants, and it didn't seem interested in climbing trees. After a moment it ambled out of sight, walking on the knuckles of its feet.

He'd never seen a more unusual creature, but nothing surprised him anymore. He felt dazed. So much had happened, and so quickly, everything was like a memory that belonged to someone else: the owls, Goth, the Humans chaining him with the metal disc, the cage, the flying machine, then the explosions. A fish that nearly ate him. It was all something distant, on the horizon of his mind, but like an approaching thundercloud he couldn't avoid.

"Thanks, Shade," said Chinook dully. "For stopping me."

"Sorry I had to bite you."

"If you hadn't, I would've—" He flattened his ears and winced, as if trying to block a painful sound. Quietly he said, "Did you see them, my mother and father?"

Shade felt his breath go jerking out of him. He'd completely forgotten Plato and Isis had been taken too, and if they were loaded onto that flying machine . . . He swallowed hard, scrambling for words.

Chinook's voice was urgent: "I was looking for them, but there was all that echo noise in my head, and I couldn't . . . I'm pretty sure I saw them once, and I called out, but they were so far away, they . . . did *you* see them?"

Shade shook his head, sick. "We don't even know they were in that flying machine, Chinook. They might still be back at the Human building. . . ."

"You don't have to lie. I'm not that stupid." There was no anger in his voice, just a horrible hollowness.

"I'm not lying," Shade said desperately. "We don't know! Even if they got dumped with us, they might've survived." But in his mind's eye he saw the hundreds of bats streaming down into the inferno, vacant expressions on their faces. He couldn't believe any of them had pulled away in time.

Marina.

His heart gave a horrible lurch. Was she in one of those containers too? Stop it, he screamed inwardly. You don't even know she was on the flying machine. But what if she'd been blasted out into the sky with him and

Chinook, and he just hadn't seen her? She wouldn't have followed the sound picture, he told himself; she was too smart for that.

"If we survived, they could too," he forced himself to say. "We'll go back and see in a bit, all right? We'll rest up, and then we'll go check it out. There'll be others. There've got to be."

Chinook didn't seem to be listening. He was slowly turning his head as if seeing his alien surroundings for the first time.

"We're going to live, Chinook. But we need a plan, all right?" He knew if he let go, his fear would gallop off with him. He needed to talk so he could drown out the whimpering of his own terror. How he wished Marina was here. Ideas, he needed ideas. "Let's make a plan, Chinook."

The other bat was still staring, stupefied, into the jungle.

"Chinook!" Shade said. "Are you listening?"

"I want my father," Chinook said quietly.

All Shade's impatience evaporated instantly.

"I know," he said. "Me too."

Chinook turned back to him, and Shade saw in his miserable face that same desperate, bottomless longing he himself had felt for so long. I want my father too. He had to look away, his body rigid as he fought the wrenching sob caught in his throat. He wasn't afraid of crying in front of Chinook; he was afraid of not being able to stop.

He forced a shaky breath through his mouth.

"We're going to see if there're any survivors, then we've

got to get out of here. We've got to warn the others."

"All right," said Chinook, sniffing back his tears. "Good. We should be able to make it back before dawn, right? We weren't inside that flying machine too long."

"No, but it goes much faster than us," Shade said.

"Oh, right, right," said Chinook. "So how far is it?"

Shade inhaled. "Well, we were inside the flying machine for, say, three hours, maybe more?" He didn't expect an answer from Chinook; but he found it comforting to talk aloud. It made him feel more organized, like he was thinking clearly, solving a problem. "So how fast does one of those fly?" He really had no idea. "When we got dumped into the sky, we were going pretty fast, what do you think, maybe a hundred wingbeats a second?" Chinook's face was blank. "So what's that work out to . . . in three hours that's, what is it . . . over a million wingbeats." He swallowed, feeling queasy. "That's a long way."

"Why'd they do this to us?" Chinook whispered.

"They're just using us," said Shade darkly.

"To burn their own buildings?"

"When we met Zephyr back in the city, Marina and me, he said the Humans were fighting a war of their own. Against each other." It had surprised him at the time, and he'd quickly forgotten it. Now it came horribly back to him. "The Humans up north must be fighting the ones down here. And they're using us to carry fire."

"They were supposed to be our friends." There was incredulity and dismay in Chinook's voice. "What about the Promise?"

Shade was ashamed to admit, even to himself, that until he'd seen all those bats dying in flames, part of him still wanted to trust the Humans. Hoping, hoping that Arcadia was right, and it was all part of some plan. And no matter how horrible, how painful it was, it would all work out in the end. And maybe he'd even find his father too. All lies.

"There's no Promise," Shade said bitterly. "Goth was right all along about the Humans. They're evil. They trap bats to study them. They knew how to put pictures into our heads, just like our song maps. And now they've gone and dumped us in the jungle."

Something *clicked* behind him, and he turned hurriedly, but there was nothing there. Must've been a water droplet hitting a leaf.

"We've got to get out of here, Chinook," he said. "I'm pretty sure this is where the cannibal bats come from."

"Like Goth?"

He nodded, wondering if he should've told him. But what was the point of hiding things? He was too tired to lie, and he was going to need Chinook's help if they wanted to survive.

"It'll be dawn soon," Chinook said miserably, looking up through the trees. "You figure there're owls here too?"

Shade shook his head. "I don't know."

"The stars are different here," said Chinook. Shade was surprised he'd noticed: He'd never thought Chinook was very observant. Then again, Chinook had surprised him quite a bit lately. "How are we going to know where north is?"

"We'll use the setting sun," Shade said. "That tells us east, and we guess at north. We fly high enough, and keep the glow on the horizon as long as we can, and reset our course every twilight." It wasn't perfect, but it was the best he could come up with right now.

Click.

That same sound. He turned, and this time a leaf was bobbing slightly, as if recently touched. Shade frowned. That twig wasn't there before. It was closer.

Couldn't be, he told himself impatiently. He stared hard. It was a fat twig, with a knobbly tip.

It twitched.

All at once the twig unfolded itself, and a hideously long neck rose up from a winged body, topped with a spear-shaped head. Jagged spines bristled from pincered claws. It was a bug, but the biggest bug he'd ever seen, almost a foot long—and that made it twice as long as Shade. Its camouflage was so excellent, he'd thought its body and arms and legs were just jutting twigs. It had big, blank, globular eyes. Two antennae sprouted from its head. Its mouth was beaked.

Before Shade could drop from his roost, the bug sprang onto him, its four gangly legs sinking into him as it reared up, claws open, trying to crush his head. He smacked the bug's face away with his wing, but felt one pincered claw close around his left forearm, making it impossible to fly. He saw the bug's other claw flex and come swinging in for his neck—

And then in a blur of silver-tipped fur, Chinook was

upon the bug, sinking his teeth through the base of its gangly neck. Shade heard the *crunch,* and watched as the two halves of the insect fell from the branch, its legs and spiny claws still thrashing.

"That," Shade said, shaking violently, "was one big bug. That was really close, Chinook. You"—he looked at the bigger bat in true amazement—"you saved my life."

But Chinook was hanging motionless, eyes unblinking.

"Chinook, you all right?"

"That thing nearly ate us!" Chinook shouted. It was as if all his fear was only now flooding over him.

"Chinook, not so loud," Shade said anxiously. "We don't want—"

"The bugs here *eat* bats. What kind of place is this, Shade? You've got to get us out of here."

"Chinook—"

"This is your fault! We could be back in the forest, but you kept complaining and saying it was no good, and . . . and . . . you made the Humans angry at us, and now look what's happened. There're cannibal bats, and giant fish and bugs bigger than us that can bite off our heads!"

Panic-stricken, he was making no sense, and he was going to wake the entire jungle. Shade struck him across the face with his wing, not too hard, but hard enough to shut him up for a second. Sudden anger smoldered in the bigger bat's eyes, and Shade wondered if he'd done the right thing. He carried on, anyway.

"Chinook, you've got to take control of yourself, all right?" he whispered urgently. "You're a big bat, a powerful bat. Look what you just did! I froze, Chinook. But you didn't. You killed that bug."

Chinook just stared at him, panting.

"You killed that bug, Chinook."

"Yeah," he muttered.

"You didn't think about it. You just did it. Instincts, Chinook, you've got the best instincts. You always have. You're the best hunter and flyer in the whole colony!"

"We're going to get eaten!"

"No way, Chinook. You know what? I'm glad you're here."

"You are?"

"Oh, yeah," said Shade, and was surprised at how fervently he meant it. "You saved my life. Now I need you to be calm; I need you to help me out here. We're going to get out of here alive."

"Not if you're this noisy."

Shade jerked around and saw a bat beating the air overhead, inches from them. With a cold shock of relief, Shade saw he wasn't a cannibal but a northerner, bigger than any he'd seen before. His fur was thick and dark, and he had low-scooped ears and the most ferocious set of incisors Shade had seen since Goth. Most unusual of all, he had a tail, not like Shade's little stub, but a proper tail like a rat's tail, pointed and whippy.

"Didn't hear me, did you?" said the strange bat. "I could've been anything. Owl, tree snake, cannibal. And

you'd be dead. You're not in the northern forests now."
He peered at them intently. "You ripped off the discs,
good. You're not idiots, then."

"Who are you?" Shade asked.

"Caliban, from the northwest forests. I survived too.
And there're others. Now be silent, and come with me."

As Goth flew deeper into the jungle, he could see
huge craters and furrows carved from the earth by fire.
The Humans obviously did not just attack the city,
though from what he'd seen, the damage was immense:
buildings crushed and blackened, streets buckled. And
now, as he flew farther over the jungle canopy, it struck
him how quiet it was, as if the multitude of creatures
who made their homes here had been bludgeoned into
silence, or simply fled.

Still, it was impossible not to rejoice at being back in
the jungle, the smells, the heat. Home at last. Zotz had
brought him home.

The metal hanging from his stomach was heavy, but
he knew he could reach the pyramid. The only question
was how to remove the disc safely. He was not too worried. He knew the royal pyramid was home to some of the
finest stone artisans in the kingdom. Their teeth were
their tools, and they had honed and shaped them so they
could cut stone and design intricate doorways—like the
doors of the prison cells that held the sacrificial victims.
He trusted them to remove the disc from his body.

And there.

Rising from the jungle was the pyramid, home to the royal family, the Vampyrum Spectrum. It was almost completely overgrown, its stepped terraces cloaked under a blanket of creepers and ferns and palms that had somehow found root in the cracked stone.

The Humans had built the pyramid hundreds of years ago, in honor of Cama Zotz, the bat god of the Underworld. Now they seemed to have forgotten him. They let the jungle swallow the pyramid up. Even so, small groups of Men and Women sometimes hacked their way through the jungle to leave offerings on the bottom steps of the grand staircase. Cut into the east face, the stairs led to the royal chamber that crowned the pyramid. His home.

There was another entrance, midway up the terraces, and Goth could see bats streaming back toward it as the dawn's light filtered through the jungle. His brothers and sisters. Goth took a deep breath.

"I have returned!" he bellowed. "It is I. Prince Goth. I have returned!"

His voice echoed off the trees and stone like a roar of thunder, silencing the bird and insect song from the jungle.

"I am here!" he shouted again, and the Vampyrum swirled around him to look. Soon he was encircled. After so many months, it was a pleasure to be among his own kind: large, powerful bats. And yet, they weren't as big as they should have been. Many had a lean, hungry look to them, their ribs showing through the fur of their chests. Still, he basked in their excitement as they greeted him.

"Prince Goth!"

"Where have you been?"

"We thought you'd been killed!"

"Everyone! Prince Goth has returned!"

"Hail, *King* Goth!"

He snapped his head around to find the speaker of the last words. "Who said king?"

"I'm sorry, My Lord," said the bat, taken aback by the ferocity of Goth's expression. "But your father has died. You now are king."

The words of Cama Zotz slithered through his head. *Do my bidding, then, and you will be king.*

"When?" he demanded. "When did this happen?"

"Only four nights ago, during one of the firestorms. He was out hunting."

"This is the cause of your firestorms," he roared, lifting his wings high above his shoulders and revealing the metal disc sewn to his belly. "This is the Human fire that's ravaged our jungle. They have used the northern bats as their carriers. They thought they could use me to destroy other Humans, and myself. But we will use this against them, you have my promise. They have insulted us, and Cama Zotz, and they must be punished. I will avenge my father's death!"

"Hail to King Goth!" the bat cried, and his words were taken up by the others, building to a chant that thundered deliciously in Goth's ears.

"Now," he said, ready to give orders, "send for the carvers. I want this metal shorn from me and stored carefully!"

"Your Highness, I've been waiting for you."

Goth looked and saw Voxzaco, flapping his crippled wings toward him. He was the chief priest, and his father's closest adviser. Goth found him as repellent now as he had when he was a child. His spine was arched, and it made him a poor flyer. His fur had almost all fallen away with age, leaving mangy patches of strawlike gray among raw-looking flesh. His breath stank from the noxious berries and leaves he ate to fuel his visions; and even Goth had trouble meeting his gaze sometimes, his eyes so huge in his gaunt head that they seemed to swallow you up. He had always looked like this, as long as Goth could recall.

"Waiting for me?" said Goth in confusion. "You knew I would return?"

"Yes," said Voxzaco. "It is on the Stone."

Then the old priest's eyes saw the disc beneath Goth's belly, and a small cry escaped his throat. He could barely stay aloft for the trembling that wracked his body.

"What is it?" Goth asked in alarm.

"Yes," muttered Voxzaco, eyes still locked on the Human disc. "Yes, I see now. It fits perfectly." He wrenched his eyes away and looked at Goth. "Come, let me show you."

Inside the royal chamber, Goth hovered over the deep bed of soft leaves which the carvers had prepared for him. Then, wings churning, he carefully lowered the metal disc onto it.

"Free me of it," he ordered, and the carvers set to work instantly, their specially sharpened teeth raking at the chain that connected the disc to Goth's body. While Goth hovered in agony, the carvers sawed through the metal links within seconds, and Goth soared upward in relief, and roosted. The metal ring was still in his stomach, and he did not welcome the idea of it being torn from his flesh, even by one of the royal surgeons.

"Now," he said, turning to Voxzaco, who had been anxiously watching over the whole procedure, "show me the Stone."

The royal chamber was rectangular, made of huge granite blocks, and all around the upper walls were jewel-encrusted carvings: twin jaguars, their eyes gleaming onyx; a two-headed serpent, winged in silver; and in every corner of the room, a pair of eyes, watching.

In the east wall, a large portal gave onto the outer staircase, all but sealed off by vines and ferns and crumbled masonry. In the flat, high roof was a circular opening, and it was always kept clear by Voxzaco, for it gave a powerful view of the stars and moon.

Directly beneath this opening was the Stone. It too was circular, thick, and twice the diameter of Goth's wings. It lay flat on the floor of the chamber, its surface intricately carved with strange glyphs of Humans, birds and beasts, and bats—and Cama Zotz himself, his slitted eyes gazing out from various locations. It was Humans who had made the Stone, and the pictures were blackened and smoothed with age. They ran around the outer rim of the stone and then spiraled gradually in toward the hole at its very center.

Goth had spent much of his life in the royal chamber, but had never examined the Stone in much detail. That was the work of Voxzaco, to crouch over these tiny little pictures and scratch away at the mold and dust of centuries. It was said he could predict the seasons with the Stone, the length of the nights, the phases of the moon. And it was his duty to perform the sacrifices upon the Stone: ripping out the hearts and offering them to Cama Zotz. The hieroglyphs had become permanently stained with blood.

"Come," said Voxzaco, scuttling onto the Stone and leading Goth closer to its center. "Look. This is the here and now. It is all on the Stone. Your capture by the Humans, the firestorms . . ."

Goth used echoes to peer impatiently at the Stone, but all he saw were a series of jagged lines. Was that supposed to be a bat there? Or flames?

"And here, the hardships of the kingdom," Voxzaco continued. "The hunger we have faced."

Goth remembered the leanness of the bats he'd seen. "Why hunger?"

"Many birds and beasts have fled the firestorms. They've gone into hiding, or gone farther south, even north. Hunting has been very difficult. But there have been the small bats." The old priest jabbed a scaly claw at another picture.

Goth ducked his head closer to the Stone, wrinkling his

nostrils at Voxzaco's stinking breath. There was a plant in the jungle that smelled always of rotting meat. That was how the old priest smelled. There, in the stone, he made out the shape of numerous small batwings. He thought of Shade. It made him uneasy, for some reason, the idea that these small northern bats could be on the Stone.

"They are easy prey," said Voxzaco. "We have several dozen in the dungeon, and have been offering them to Zotz before eating them, and praying for more abundant times."

"Good," said Goth, wondering if Shade had survived. He remembered his dream of wrenching out the small bat's heart. If Shade was still alive here in the jungle, Goth would eat him himself. In his mind, the Humans and the northern bats were linked forever—both had defied him and brought hardship on him.

"We will strike down the Humans, and the small bats," said Goth. "That has been my plan since I was first caught. We must raise an army and go north. We will annihilate the bats, and the Humans we will attack with their own weapon."

"Yes," said Voxzaco with a knowing smile. "That too is on the Stone. But there is something we must do first."

"Show me, then!" demanded Goth. He didn't like that superior way Voxzaco had with him. He could rip his heart out; he was king. He didn't need some rotting carcass to tell him the future. Voxzaco was rumored to talk with Zotz himself. But so can I, thought Goth, and without berries and potions to help me.

Still, there was a tremor in his gut. He wanted to know more.

"What do you see here?" the priest asked him.

"A circle," he said. "The sun."

"Look closer."

"Part of it's missing."

"And over here . . ." Voxzaco drew his sonic gaze to the next picture, where an even larger sliver of the sun was missing.

"What does it mean?"

"There will be a total eclipse of the sun," Voxzaco said, voice crackling with excitement. "Total night in the midst of the day." He guided Goth through the pictures as they spiraled, quickly now, toward the very center of the Stone, the sun getting skinnier and skinnier until it had disappeared and was replaced by a slitted eye, Zotz's eye. And then there were no more pictures, for they had dropped into the hole that was the stone's center: a circle of darkness.

"Do you realize the importance of this?" Voxzaco asked him.

Goth glared back haughtily, silent.

"You know nothing of the gods, then."

"I know about Zotz," Goth growled.

"Perhaps, but do you know of Nocturna?"

Goth bristled in anger. "The little bat, Shade, he spoke of Nocturna. She exists?"

"As much as Zotz does. They are twins. Nocturna presides over the upper world. She ushers in the dusk, but also brings on the dawn. She is a thing of the night, but she draws her power from the sun. She is selfish. She keeps her twin brother, Zotz, in the Underworld, because she knows if he were above, his power would thwart hers."

"No one is more powerful than Zotz," Goth insisted. He was enraged at the idea of a rival to Zotz, angrier still that he hadn't known about it. To think that those runty northern bats had Nocturna as their god.

"At one time Zotz and Nocturna were equally matched," Voxzaco told him, "but over the centuries Zotz lost many of his followers in the upper world. The Humans here, who built this temple, who carved this Stone, they once knew and worshiped him. But they turned away, to worship the sun, perhaps. Still, there are more souls in the Underworld than above, I can tell you, and they want passage to this upper world. Nocturna uses the sun to keep Zotz below. But the eclipse will give us our chance. We can bring our god back, bring him to the upper world to reign over all creation."

Goth could only stare in amazement. Not for the first time, he wondered if Voxzaco was deranged. Too many potions, too many visions. But you too have had visions, he reminded himself, thinking of the cave.

"How?" he asked.

Voxzaco was scuttling across the Stone. "We had a chance once before, and failed. Three hundred years ago, look. That was the last total eclipse, but the priest then, he wasn't prepared, he knew nothing. This is our chance here. We will be the ones to succeed."

"But how?" Goth demanded again, jaws grinding.

"I wasn't sure until I saw you, King Goth. But then I knew." Wings spread, he leaped off the Stone and landed beside the metal disc. Before Goth could stop him, he'd picked up the chain in his own claws and heaved the disc up into the air, carrying it back over the Stone.

"No!" Goth cried. "It will explode if it hits!"

Voxzaco didn't listen. Lurching down unsteadily, he inserted the metal disc into the Stone's very center.

It fit perfectly. As if it had been made only to fill the hole.

"You see," wheezed the priest. "Now is the time. This completes the Stone. It is the *end* of the Stone, the end of time as we have known it. Now, we must make a double sacrifice, and ask Zotz to show us how to destroy the sun."

Goth watched as the two northern bats were brought up from the bone room, their wings gripped tightly by a guard on either side. He scanned their faces, hoping maybe to see Shade, but was disappointed. Normally, it was birds they sacrificed here, owls, and for special rituals, their own kind, a Vampyrum who was chosen for the great honor.

"Put that one on the Stone," Voxzaco instructed the guards.

Goth watched as the first terrified bat was hefted up, his wings pulled tight, and pinned by two guards. The old priest drew closer, eyes closed.

"No!" said Goth suddenly. "I will make this sacrifice."

Shock convulsed Voxzaco's face. "Only a priest can perform the rites, King Goth. You will anger Zotz if—"

"I have spoken with Zotz. He will speak with me again."

The priest smirked. "You think so, do you? You think you are closer to him than me, after devoting my *life* to serving him and tending the Stone. I, his high priest?"

"He has chosen me as his servant," Goth growled. "He has sent me visions. He has made me king, healed my wings, and *I* will make the sacrifice."

Without waiting for the priest's reply, he lunged for the northern bat and plunged his jaws deep into its chest, tearing out the shuddering heart.

"Zotz!" he cried. "I offer this to you. Tell me, your servant, what we must do to kill the sun!"

Rearing onto his hind legs, he flared his wings and whirled so they billowed with air.

"Zotz!" he cried again. "Here is your servant! Tell me what I must do!"

That instant there was a tremendous roar, and then a huge sucking sound, which left the chamber in absolute silence. Then, from all corners, came a maelstrom of wind so loud, it was like a moan, a chorus of dark angels, all singing different notes.

Goth flinched, and could see Voxzaco hide his head under his wing. The guards holding the remaining northern bat fell back in horror, and the small bat broke free and hurled himself into a crevice in the floor. It was unimportant. What was important was the presence he felt in the chamber, carried on this tide of sound.

Suddenly the presence wasn't around him, it was *inside* him. He felt his jaws being pried open by an unstoppable force, and air surged through his throat.

"Ask!" he bellowed at Voxzaco, and he knew it wasn't his own voice, but Zotz's, speaking through him.

Voxzaco was still cowering under his wing, but he looked up at Goth, trembling violently.

"Ask!" Goth shrieked again.

"What must we do, Lord Zotz, to kill the sun?" Voxzaco asked.

"Give me more *life!*" Goth felt himself roar. "The lives of one hundred, their hearts! All in the darkness of the eclipse!"

"And what will happen then, Lord Zotz?"

Goth felt his lungs swell to suck in more air. Then he was speaking again. "I will come. Now I come only as sound, a whisper of my full power. But kill the sun and the Underworld will be the whole world, and you, Goth, will lead my armies across its face. You will scour the Humans from this planet, those Humans who have tried to obliterate you. You will reign supreme over all things, all birds and beasts, and all the bats too. Your empire shall grow to the north, to take over the kingdoms of the Silverwings and Brightwings and all others. The owl kingdoms too shall be yours. Alive and dead. And we shall cross oceans to make new lands our own. That is to be your reward for serving me so well."

Another huge breath of air was forced into his lungs.

"You will help the Humans finish the work they have started, wiping each other off the face of the earth. And the metal disc they gave you shall be our first assault. There is a place called Bridge City, where you can drop the disc. It is home to millions of bats, and to as many humans . . . it is their greatest city, and you will destroy it."

Goth felt himself wrenched off his feet and slammed to the Stone. It was as if a huge beast had had him in the vise of its jaws, and finally let go. He choked in more air. His ribs sang with pain.

"I'm sorry, Your Highness," whimpered a guard, "one of the little bats escaped."

"Find it, then," Goth snapped, but his thoughts were elsewhere. He turned to Voxzaco. "This eclipse, how long does it last?"

"No more than seven minutes," the priest replied.

Seven minutes to sacrifice one hundred offerings.

"And according to the Stone, it will come in only three nights," Voxzaco added.

Goth whirled on the guards. "We will send out our soldiers immediately. Capture owls and birds, and as many northern bats as we can find. Take them all from their roosts and bring them back here. We have three nights to find one hundred offerings—fall short of that number, and you yourselves will lie on the Stone. Do you understand?"

"Yes, King Goth."

"Then make all preparations. Hurry."

STATUE HAVEN

With every wingstroke, pain seeped through the gash in his stomach, and Shade had to struggle to keep up with Chinook and Caliban. They flew in urgent silence over the city, and for the first time, he noticed how battered it was: streets buckled, buildings collapsed in rubble, huge spaces where there was nothing at all but a scorched crater. Their flight path took them over sullen stone buildings with tiled roofs, many in ruin. Off to the west, he could still see the flicker of flames from the big building the bats had destroyed, and the wail of Human sirens filtered through the pungent air. He wondered if the Humans down here used bats to carry their weapons too. The eastern sky was starting to pale: Dawn was coming.

Flying behind Caliban, he could see the ugly scar in his belly. Must have ripped his disc off too. He was a big bat, larger even than Chinook, but his ribs pressed through the skin of his flanks, and his face had a gaunt, somewhat savage look to it. Shade wondered how long he'd been down here, and what he'd had to do to survive.

"What's your colony?" he asked.

"Mastiffs," Caliban said bluntly, without looking

back, "from the western forests."

He didn't seem very eager to talk. Chinook had said nothing since they'd set out; he just flew, his stunned eyes fixed on the horizon. Shade didn't even know where they were being led. He tried to comfort himself with what Caliban had said earlier: There were others searching around the burning building for more survivors.

Maybe Chinook's parents.

Maybe your father.

He clamped down on his thoughts, angry with himself for even hoping. He'd hoped for so long and had been disappointed so often—what was the point?

From behind him came a sudden intense flash of light, and for a split second it was as if the night had become day.

"Don't look back," Caliban snapped.

Shade looked. A huge plume of light and smoke was billowing up from the far horizon. Even after slamming his eyes shut in pain and horror, the image of that monstrous thunderhead still burned before him. Moments later, the earth and air rumbled as the sound from the explosion reached them.

"That's one of the owls," said Caliban.

"What d'you mean?" Shade asked.

"They put little ones on us. But the owls carry much bigger ones."

Shade remembered seeing the Humans enter the owls' artificial forest with their metal sticks, and cage the drugged birds. He thought of the young owl with the lightning in his plumage, and felt sick. The sheer size of that blazing cloud—nothing could have survived the sweep of it.

"The Humans pick night flyers," Caliban was saying quietly back over his wing. "Bats, owls, both of us have echo vision. That's important. That's what they use to guide us. I saw a dead owl once; it had a siren in its ear too—you know that metal stud—just like us. The Humans pick their targets, and send us in to do the work for them. They don't get hurt. The owls can carry more metal. Far bigger explosions, like that one behind us. Lucky for us, the targets are usually way out of the city. So far, anyway."

Shade thought of the large disc on Goth's belly. Would his make an explosion like that too? But Shade knew Goth would survive. He always did. He was somewhere out there in the jungle, carrying his disc, a flying catastrophe.

"We're close now," said Caliban, jerking his chin. "Up there."

It was the last place on earth Shade would have flown for safe haven right now. High on a cliff overlooking the city towered a giant metal statue: a Human Male, arms outstretched beseechingly—except that his right arm had been blasted off above the elbow, by fire, judging from the melted, twisted look of the stump.

"Statue Haven," said Caliban, leading them in high toward the peak. Shade could now see the metal

Human's face. There was something achingly kind about the expression, and it made him angry. What right did Humans have to look this way, after what they'd done to all of them? It was a lie. The Humans were evil, like Goth had said all along. He didn't want to go any closer but Caliban was diving down to the amputated right arm, and Shade followed with Chinook.

Amid the fused and twisted metal of the stump was a small opening, and Shade trimmed his wings for landing. As he approached, he could make out, just inside the entrance, two bats standing guard. With surprise he noticed they clutched wickedly sharpened sticks.

Caliban shouted out to the guards, and the sticks were quickly pulled back inside. Never had Shade known bats to fashion weapons, and it made him shudder—what terrible things they must be protecting themselves against. The bug that had nearly eaten him was frightening enough. He imagined an army of them, leaping up the statue and flooding inside. The bats needed those weapons.

He landed behind Caliban and shuffled farther inside to make room for Chinook. Shade eyed the guards, a Brightwing and a Graywing, both worn down by hunger but with ferocious determination in their weary faces.

"We're glad to have you," one of them said to Shade as they passed.

The passage sloped upward inside the statue's arm, working back, Shade reckoned, toward its shoulder.

There, at the summit, the passage ended, opening out into a yawning vertical cavern: the hollow inside of the statue. It reminded him, just a little, of Tree Haven, his and Chinook's lost home back in the northern forests, and he felt his throat swell dangerously with homesickness as he heard the echoing flutter of wings, the squeak of voices.

"How many are here?" Shade asked Caliban. He couldn't bring himself to ask about his father directly—he was too afraid of seeing Caliban shake his head, mumble an apology. It had happened too many times.

"Thirty-six, including you two," said Caliban with a weary sigh. It was obvious to Shade he was used to keeping track, day by day, as the numbers of this makeshift colony changed, sometimes for the better, sometimes the worse. "But let's hope they find more survivors back at the building."

It was a tragic assortment of bats he saw now as he fluttered down into the cavern. He swept the ledges with his echo vision, desperately searching for a banded Silverwing male. Many of the bats still had bits of metal chain dangling from their bellies. Some had wings cruelly clipped by injury; others had large patches of furless scar tissue caused by horrible burns. All had a lean, wild look to them, and none of them was his father.

At least now he knew for certain. His father, like so many others, had died in flames. He was surprised and guilty that he felt so little. He felt like a colossal empty cave without even echoes inside. What was wrong with him?

He looked up as two more bats swept through the entrance tunnel into Statue Haven, and heard Caliban call up to them: "Did you find any other survivors?"

"We searched all around the building for as long as we could. There was no one."

Shade looked at Chinook. All the life seemed drained from his eyes. Even his body seemed smaller, somehow. How was it he could feel only numbness for his own father's death, but seeing Chinook like this was almost too much to bear? He'd have done anything to get the old Chinook back: boasting, swaggering through the air, calling him Runt.

"I'm sorry, Chinook," he said, pushing his nose against the other bat's neck.

"I knew I saw them," said Chinook dully.

Anger boiled through Shade's head. You're such a fool, he raged at himself. Marina lost her parents, and now Chinook has too. You at least always had your mother. Others too: Frieda, Marina, and Chinook. You had a family, but it was never enough. Should've just stayed in Hibernaculum with them all, been grateful for having something. Because now what was there?

"You've lost family and friends," Caliban said matter-of-factly. "We all have. But we're going to survive."

"How long have you been here?" Shade asked.

"Varies. Some several weeks, some over two months, like me."

"You haven't tried to go back north?"

Caliban gave a harsh laugh. "A long journey. You've

seen what the jungle is like. The bug that nearly ate you was the least of it. There are owls, and snakes big enough to swallow you alive and give you a long look at their gullet before you're squeezed to death. There're eagles, falcons, vultures. And the cannibal bats. Thousands of them."

Even though he'd known, hearing Caliban say it still filled him with dread. Goth by himself had been terrifying enough. Thousands was beyond imagining.

"I know these bats," Shade said.

"How?" Caliban said.

"There was one the Humans had up north, named Goth. They took him to the same building as us, and chained him with a metal disc, a big one. He got dumped out with us tonight."

"Chances are he's dead, then. At least that's one less."

"He doesn't die," said Shade simply.

Caliban looked at him strangely. "Doesn't matter either way. There are enough of them to run the night skies. Even the owls stay out of their way." He shook his head. "The total reverse of what we're used to. Owls scared of bats. We've lost a few to them. Nothing on the number the cannibals have taken, though. They hunt in packs. Just a few weeks ago we were almost fifty here."

"We've got to get back north," said Chinook, and Shade turned to him in surprise; he'd been so quiet. "We've got to try to warn the others before it's too late. There's Frieda, and your mother. And Marina too, maybe."

"No argument," said Caliban. "And we would have embarked much earlier. But we've still got wounded.

We've had to wait for everyone to heal. No one gets left behind here. That's the rule. We all stay, or we all go."

Shade nodded, filled with admiration for this small group of determined bats.

"You two need some rest now if you're coming with us. There're some berries I came across that seem to quicken the healing. You'll want some on your wounds."

"Thank you," said Shade. He wanted sleep. Deep sleep that would take him through the weeks and months until he could wake up somewhere else, somewhere safe. With surprise he realized how relieved he felt. Someone else was in charge here, and Shade trusted Caliban on instinct. He didn't want to make plans anymore; he only wanted to follow orders. All his life he'd never done what he was told; he'd always doubted what others said—and look where it got him. He was finished with all that. Take a break from being a hero. Marina was right. He was tired of the very idea of thinking.

Caliban returned with a berry in his mouth and proceeded to chew it into a paste, and spread it onto Chinook's stomach.

"Every few weeks," the big mastiff said, "more bats get dropped over the city. And every time we go see if there're any survivors. There used to be more. Sometimes the discs wouldn't explode; sometimes the bats would veer away in time." He smiled angrily. "The Humans are obviously getting better at it. I'm amazed you two survived. Good thing I found you when I did, though. That place where you roosted was a bug nest. More would have come. I've seen them eat each other while mating. The female just bites the male's head right off. Still, they taste all right."

"You eat them?" Chinook asked in amazement.

"When we can. Plenty of meat on them. Which is good, because hunting's tricky here. We go out in twos and threes, and stick close to Statue Haven. Without this place, we wouldn't have lasted a night in the jungle."

Caliban mulched up another berry in his mouth and began applying it to Shade's wound now.

"We were getting ready to leave a few nights back, but then we lost our leader. If anyone could've led us back north safely, it was he. I'm just a pale replacement. He was one of the first to get dropped here. Saved me when I came. He'd been in the Human forest for months, and he'd seen some of the things they did to us. Tests."

"What kinds of tests?" Shade said.

"Making sure the bats were strong enough to carry the discs, figuring out how to make them explode. Getting the sirens to work, and stay in their ears. A lot of bats died in that building, burned to death, or their wings singed so they could never fly again. He survived it all. But the jungle beat him. He was a brave bat. Cassiel saved a lot of us."

"Cassiel Silverwing?" Shade could hear himself asking the question, as if he were hovering high in the air, watching himself speak.

"That's right."

"What happened to him?"

"The cannibals ate him." Caliban looked at him

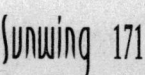

strangely, and his matter-of-factness faltered for a moment. "You knew him?"

"He was my father."

Marina flew south.

Every night, Achilles Graywing's convoy grew as it was joined by other refugees driven from their winter roosts by the owls. Marina felt comforted to be flying with so many bats, even though she knew a single elite platoon of owls could slash a bloody path through their ranks.

She and Ariel tried to talk to all the newcomers, asking them if they'd seen any Human flying machines, either on the ground or in the air, heading south. The answers were vague: The sky was full of Human machinery, going in all directions. Shade could be anywhere by now. Anywhere.

It was getting warmer. They'd left the snow behind, and last night her heart leaped when she saw grass again, and even a few flowers.

But despite the weather, Frieda was flagging. She lagged behind, her breath rattling. Marina and Ariel and the others had started taking turns carrying the Silverwing elder on their backs. Marina was amazed at how little she weighed, as if her ancient bones were starting to hollow out. During the day, she slept long and hard.

Marina looked across her wing at Ariel. Even at dawn she combed her hair, and made a fuss of her, asking if she was warm enough, well fed. At first it made Marina feel awkward—she'd spent so much time alone, she wasn't used to such attention. She was used to taking care of herself and doing things her own way. But she couldn't deny she liked it. And being so close to Shade's mother was strangely comforting, a way of being close to Shade.

"I should've gone with him," she said hopelessly, probably for the tenth time, she realized. "We're never going to find him this way."

Ariel shook her head. "You did the right thing, not going inside that flying machine. Shade made his own decision. You're not responsible for that. I could never understand why Cassiel did some of the things he did, either. Plain stupidity, I think."

Marina laughed, then looked off with a frown.

"I should've been . . . I wish I'd been nicer to him beforehand. I guess I was kind of ignoring him."

Ariel said nothing, but her silence wasn't questioning, just patient.

"I *was* ignoring him," said Marina quickly, with the relief of making a guilty confession, "but only because he was ignoring me. All his searching and moping around, that's all he did, it was like nothing else existed—and, okay, yes, it turned out he was right about the forest, but—"

"It's not easy taking second place to a great cause. Cassiel was the same, so wrapped up in the secret of the bands and the Promise, he didn't see much else."

"Exactly," said Marina, relieved. "He got to be so important and he wasn't making it any easier for me, trying to fit in with all of you. Living alone was one thing—you could sort of resign yourself to it, make your own rules, get set in your ways—but then Shade came along and I got this second chance, and I was afraid of losing it all over again."

Ariel nodded.

"Yeah, well, I tormented him," Marina admitted, without being able to conceal a smile. "Chinook paid me a lot of attention, and . . . it was nice."

"Of course it was."

"I don't know why Shade couldn't figure it out," she said irritably. "It just made him even angrier. For a smart bat, he can sure be stupid."

She remembered Shade's body moving along that terrible trough in the Human building, and her smile disappeared.

"He's good at surviving," she said firmly, but she was looking at Ariel, as if asking an urgent question. "He made it home to Hibernaculum." She frowned. "But I was there to help him. I doubt he could've done it without me. You know what he's like; he doesn't think, and he does these stupid things sometimes."

"I know," said Ariel gently. "Don't worry. We'll find him."

Dawn approached, and they found roosts high in a forest of cedars. As Marina folded her wings about her, eager for sleep, she saw Frieda alone on a distant branch, very still, peering intently into the brightening sky. What was she looking at? Ariel was already asleep beside her, and Marina didn't want to wake her. She lit silently from the branch and darted up to the tree's peak, settling behind Frieda at a respectful distance so as not to startle her.

"Do you see them?" Frieda asked, without turning around.

Marina followed the elder's gaze, and in the pale light saw a shimmering mass above a distant stand of flowering trees. What were they? They were too large for insects, and certainly too small for birds. But there were dozens of them, flitting from flower to flower.

"Hummingbirds," said Frieda.

"Those are birds?" She saw that the elder's face was grave. Surely she couldn't be worried that these birds were a threat. They were so tiny. "What's wrong?"

"The fact they're here at all," Frieda replied. "They winter in the far south. To see them here . . . something must be very, very wrong. Come with me, but be slow, let them see you coming."

Marina lit from the branch, following Frieda. "We're going to talk to birds?"

"They aren't like the rest. They're so small, they've never been at home with other species. They live apart. They eat insects like us, as well as flowers."

"Flowers?"

"They drink their nectar. And they too have a distrust of the owls. They've never fought with us, and we have no quarrel with them."

They flew well above the treetops, in plain view so the hummingbirds could see their approach.

"I am Frieda Silverwing," the elder called out. "I mean

no harm and ask only to speak with you."

For a moment, it seemed to Marina as if all the hummingbirds froze motionless in the air, their gossamer wings still, their tiny heads turned toward them. Then, faster than her echo vision, they disappeared.

"Where'd they go?"

"Please, we only want to talk," Frieda called out again as they circled the tree.

"Come no closer, Silverwings."

Marina looked around in surprise and saw a hummingbird above her head, darting so quickly, she kept losing track of it—side to side, up, down, it could even fly backward.

"Why do you risk breaking your dawn curfew to talk with us?"

The hummingbird's voice was slightly peevish, pitched high, and seemed to vibrate in time to the beat of its wings. How fast were its wingstrokes? Marina wondered in awe. Much faster than bats, maybe a hundred beats a second.

What a fabulous creature it was, she thought in admiration. Slightly smaller than a bat, it seemed to fly almost vertically in the air. Snow-white plumage covered its chest, and gave way to a brilliant patch of feathers around its throat. Its beak was thin as a pine needle, elegantly curved downward at the tip.

Now she could see others reemerging from the trees, dipping their beaks into the flowers. She knew why they had no reason to fear bats, or any other creature, for that matter. They were so alert, and moved so quickly, so effortlessly, they seemed to weigh nothing at all, more an element of the air than creatures of sinew and bone. They could fly forever. She felt a twinge of envy.

"Why are you here, so far from your wintering grounds?" Frieda asked.

"They have been destroyed," the hummingbird replied simply.

"By whom?"

"The Humans, with their interminable fighting. The northern Humans send their flying machines and spray down fire. Our trees have mostly been burned. We have been driven from the jungle, and not just us. Many birds and beasts have fled. You have heard nothing of this?" the bird asked pointedly, its head cocked. It took a few backward skips through the air.

"No," said Frieda.

"Because there have been rumors," the hummingbird said in its shrill voice.

"Please tell us," said Marina, her heart thumping heavily. Human flying machines traveling to the south, carrying fire. Carrying Shade.

"At first the Humans came with many flying machines, low in the sky, and the machines themselves seemed to spit out fire. But the southern Humans shot them down with their own missiles. Several months ago, the northern planes started flying higher, above the clouds, where they couldn't be attacked. But, still, their fire came down. And it is rumored they are using birds and bats to carry it."

"You've seen this?" Marina asked, her mouth parched.

"Not I. But others say they have. You know nothing of this, truly?"

Marina looked at Frieda, speechless.

"If this is true, we do not do it willingly," said Frieda. "The Humans have captured many bats, and owls, and tied metal discs to them. Then they take them away in their flying machines, to the south."

"The fire pours from these metal discs. That is what I have heard," said the hummingbird.

"What happens afterward, to the bats?" Marina asked.

"I cannot say. I think they must die, many of them, for the explosions are great. I do not see how they could survive."

"But you have seen some bats, alive, in the forest?"

"There have always been bats, but much bigger ones than you. The Vampyrum."

"Vampyrum," said Marina, knowing what the hummingbird must mean. "Three-foot wingspans. Meat-eaters."

"Yes."

Marina shut her eyes so tightly they hurt. Goth and Throbb had come from the south. The Humans were taking the bats to their homeland.

"They used to ignore us in the jungle, but now with their food supplies destroyed, they have turned on us. That is another reason we have fled. I am sorry to tell you this news," said the hummingbird. "It is monstrous of the Humans to use us in this way."

"Thank you, hummingbird."

"We know the owls have declared war on you. We will not be fighting alongside them."

"We are very grateful for that."

"Good speed," said the hummingbird, and in a flash, all the birds were gone.

"Marvelous creature," Frieda murmured to herself.

Marina turned wearily after the elder, and flapped her wings listlessly back toward the cedars.

"My colony was right," she said, near tears. "They were right to banish me after I was banded. All those stupid stories about banded bats disappearing or bursting into flames. They must've known somehow, heard rumors or something. They were right. The Humans are evil."

"At least now we know where the Humans take them," said Frieda. "The hummingbirds winter in the great southern isthmus. That is where we will find Shade."

If he's still alive.

Neither of them needed to say it.

"Tomorrow we reach Bridge City," said Frieda. "Let us try to take some comfort from that."

But she sounded as worn out and hopeless as Marina felt in her bones.

BRIDGE CITY

Shade hoped this would be the last night he spent in the jungle.

He hunted distractedly, paying more attention to the sky around him than to the insects he was trying to catch. With Chinook and Caliban—who had insisted on accompanying them—he stuck close to Statue Haven, warily snapping up any bugs that looked like they wouldn't snap back. Anything too big, with too many antennae, or weird markings, or strange odors, he stayed away from. He also avoided the trees because there were snakes, and owls, and more of those bugs that had nearly bitten his head off; he stayed away from the ground because there were giant cats, and who knew what else.

Tomorrow night they were leaving.

That was their plan. For the past three nights they'd discussed it in the twilight and dawn hours inside Statue Haven. Shade knew it was the only chance at survival for any of them. For some reason, after his arrival, the jungle had become even more deadly. Two nights ago they'd lost one bat, and last night, three more. It was the cannibals. Normally they hunted alone, but lately they were traveling in packs, and they were scouring the jungle in some kind of feeding frenzy. Crouched in the narrow entranceway of Statue Haven one night, Shade had seen them strafing treetops in the near distance, and with a shudder he recognized the familiar outlines of their broad, jagged wings. They'd killed his father.

This was only one of the thoughts that made up the constant, low roar in his head now. His father, here, alive, just nights ago. It was too cruel, and he wished he could stop thinking about it. But, still, it tugged at his heart like a hook. For the first time since plunging into that stream back in the Human forest, he had time to think about things, and they came crashing over him like a violent thunderstorm, leaving him spent with sorrow and rage. He could barely summon the energy to speak to Chinook or Caliban. He retreated deep inside himself.

Even his sleep was no escape. The bad dreams he'd had since returning to Hibernaculum had metamorphosed into something even more ominous. He dreamed of an eternal night, a night with no coming dawn, night without even the hope of the sun's warmth. He dreamed of violent winds gusting across the earth, carrying the most horrible sounds he'd ever heard. Yesterday, he'd woken trembling from a vision in which the sun had been suddenly blotted out by a dark eye, but there was no center to the eye, no light in it. It was like a hole that only led to more pure darkness.

Escaping the jungle was the only thought that gave him any strength. It was what his father had wanted to do, and he was right. He had to get back north, find the forest, warn the others. If only he could know if Marina had been caught like him, or somehow made it back to Ariel and Frieda. Even so, could they have escaped the building? Maybe even now they were loaded onto a flying machine, sirens in their ears, discs tied to their stomachs. He lived in dread of hearing the sound of explosions across the city rooftops, but mercifully, none came—yet.

He was desperate to leave, and, most maddening of all, it was he who held back their departure. Caliban told him there was no way he could set out until his wound had healed a bit more. Chinook too needed time to recover. And no one left until they could all leave.

Shade was healing, but slowly. A few days ago, he'd been alarmed to find his hair was falling out vigorously. Worried this might be the symptom of some horrible disease, he'd asked Caliban, and received a smile from the free-tailed bat. Shade had never seen him smile before; he didn't suppose there was a lot to smile about down here.

"It's called molting," Caliban had told him with a laugh. "It's natural with the heat. Just that it usually happens in summer." Shade nodded, wishing Marina were here. She could have told him that. He'd never molted before. Molting in the middle of winter, in the jungle. It was so hot here, he almost wished for a real northern winter.

Shade caught another beetle, and glanced over at Chinook, who'd been hunting alongside him. For the past three days and nights, they'd never been far apart, roosting side by side, hunting together. They didn't talk much, but Shade felt comforted just having him nearby. Part of it, he knew, was that Chinook was the only reminder of home he had right now. But what was home? he thought bitterly. And where? Tree Haven was gone forever. Ariel and Marina and Frieda were trapped in the Human building—or worse. You promised yourself you'd stop thinking about it, he told himself.

"Do you think Marina's okay?" Chinook whispered.

"I hope so."

"Because I feel like it's all my fault. I mean, it was me she came looking for, right? Back in the Human building? She took a big risk all for me."

"Well . . . partly, yes, but—"

"So loyal," said Chinook with a lovelorn shake of his head. And for the first time in nights, Shade felt irritated with him, and was almost glad.

"She also wanted to find out what was going on," Shade couldn't resist pointing out. "In general."

"But she missed me. I knew she would. Did she ever say anything to you, you know . . . about me?"

Shade ground his teeth. Handsome. She'd called him handsome, how could he ever forget that!

"Can't remember, to tell you the truth," he muttered.

"Hm," said Chinook. "Well, she talked about you all the time."

Shade waited expectantly, but the other bat didn't continue.

"And?" he said after another few seconds of agony.

"Oh, just about how puffed up you were."

Shade's ears shot up indignantly. "Puffed up? What's that mean, puffed up?" It sounded like something a vain pigeon did, fluffing up its feathers. It sounded ridiculous.

"She just thought you were too important for everyone. A big hero. I tried to stick up for you, but she seemed pretty angry."

"Uh-huh."

"I've got to find her," said Chinook. "Save her."

"She's pretty good at saving herself," muttered Shade.

"I was going to ask her to be my mate," Chinook confided. "I think she would've said yes, don't you? I mean, you and she have been friends for a while, so I thought I'd ask."

Shade swallowed wrong, and tried to choke back his cough, water streaming into his eyes. Marina, Chinook's mate? It was incredible! Didn't Chinook have any clue at all that he, Shade, the runt, might be interested in Marina too? Well, he'd been missing the old, thick-headed Chinook, and here he was back in full force.

"I don't know, Chinook," he said finally. "It's hard to predict what she'd say. She's kind of difficult."

"Really? I've never noticed that."

"Give it time."

"Hey, she's got a great laugh, doesn't she? It's so—"

"Tinkly?"

"Yeah, tinkly."

"Beautiful," nodded Shade.

Caliban flew alongside and signaled that they should be heading back to Statue Haven. An hour was all they risked for hunting now, and it was scarcely enough time to keep Shade's stomach from gnawing itself hungrily through the day. And how could they hope to keep their strength for the long journey north? All the bats here were so thin; at least he and Chinook were still relatively fat after gobbling the piped-in bugs in the Human forest. But hunger, he knew, would probably be the least of their problems. All that stood between them and the cannibal bats was Statue Haven—and without that, they would be horribly vulnerable in the night skies.

Shade banked and started back toward the giant metal Human. But in the trees that crested the cliff, he saw a blur of wings through the branches. He threw out sound, and a picture of an owl flared in his head. That was all he needed to know. By now he'd caught glimpses of a few southern owls: They had blazing circles of white plumage around their eyes, and a screech that was, if anything, more terrifying than that of their northern cousins.

He hunched his shoulders and started flying hard, hoping he hadn't been spotted.

"Wait!"

It was impossible not to look back, the voice was so desperate. He turned and saw the owl rising above the tree line: a young owl with lightning bolts across his chest. And from his stomach hung a large metal disc.

"Shade, fly!" he heard Caliban call out up ahead.

"I know him," Shade called back.

"Don't be a fool!"

The owl wasn't giving chase, just circling, and looking after Shade forlornly. He couldn't tear his eyes away from the disc. It was the same size as Goth's, and he knew what it could do if it exploded.

"Help me," said the owl.

"Shade!" Caliban said warningly, anger flashing in his eyes.

Shade faltered. He didn't want to disobey Caliban; he trusted and respected the mastiff bat. And he'd promised himself just two nights ago he would follow orders from now on, stay out of trouble. But he just couldn't desert the owl. "I'll catch up."

Without waiting for a reply, he banked sharply and flew toward the owl. "Listen," he called out. "That thing, the metal disc, it's—"

"I know. It doesn't work."

"What?"

"It didn't explode. I've already landed where I was supposed to, and nothing happened. Not like the others. I saw what happened to theirs."

Shade stared at the disc, still not trusting it. He started as Chinook suddenly pulled up beside him.

"Go back with Caliban!" he said impatiently.

"I'm staying with you."

"Go on!"

"No!"

Shade was surprised at the determination in his face. "Why not?"

"Feel safe," mumbled Chinook, then, almost angrily, "I feel safe when I'm with you, all right? It's the only time."

Shade's irritation melted away. It seemed almost impossible that Chinook could be saying these words, that Shade, the eternal runt, made him feel safe. He grinned gratefully.

"Likewise, Chinook. Believe me."

Behind them, he heard Caliban say, "I hope you know what you're doing, Silverwings. Whatever it is you plan to do, be quick about it. Dawn's not far off." And he was gone.

Shade turned back to the owl. "Why're you alone?" he asked.

"The others, the owls who live here, they won't get near me. They nearly killed me when they saw the disc. They're worried it will explode."

Shade didn't blame them. For all he knew, it might erupt in flames at any moment.

"They did it to me too," said Shade. "To all the bats. Look." He tilted steeply so the owl could see the still-healing wound on his belly. "That's why we were all there in that building. The Humans have been using all of us."

"I want to go home," said the owl miserably. "But I don't know where that is."

"There's a group of us who survived," Shade told him. "And we're leaving tomorrow night. Come with us."

He saw the frightened glance Chinook shot at him, and he knew he was taking a chance, maybe a fatal one. But he wasn't just being kind. There was a self-serving side to his invitation. A group of northern bats in these skies was easy prey; but with an owl as escort, they might avoid attacks by other owls—and even cannibal bats. Caliban would see the logic in his plan.

"You know the way north?" the owl asked.

"Yes." It occurred to Shade that owls didn't have as much experience reading stars as they did.

"But this disc weighs me down so much," said the owl. "I nearly got eaten by a snake last night. Barely had time to light before its jaws closed around me."

"You're sure it's dead?" asked Shade, nodding at the disc.

"I hit the building, hard, and nothing happened."

Shade took a deep breath. "Listen. I can get it off you. It'll hurt. I'll need to rip out the stitches in your stomach. I've done it before, though. All right?"

"Why're you helping me?"

"You saved my life."

"You saved mine first. Why?"

"You looked scared," said Shade simply.

"That monster, the giant bat in the Human building, was that the one you said killed the pigeons in the city?"

"Yes," said Shade with a sigh, as if finally a huge weight had been lifted from his wings. "That's what I've been trying to tell you all along. It wasn't we who started killing the birds, it was these jungle bats."

"I believe you now."

"Can you land in that tree?" Shade said. "It's easier if you keep still."

Watching the owl roost in a high branch, Shade's muscles tensed as the metal disc knocked repeatedly against the bark. It did seem to be dead, though he'd feel a lot better when it was off the owl, if he was coming with them.

With Chinook, Shade landed nearby, still grappling with the strangeness of being so close to an owl, his deadly enemy for millions of years. He couldn't say he liked its smell, but he supposed it might not care for his, either. The feathers made his nose itch.

"Here we go," he warned the owl. "It'll hurt, but I'm not doing it on purpose, all right?"

"Go on," said the owl.

"You just keep an eye out for anything that might want to eat us. You too, Chinook."

"I'm watching," said Chinook.

Shade began, sinking his teeth delicately into the bare patch the Humans had shaved on the owl's belly.

"What's your name?" he heard the owl ask, his voice strained.

Shade pulled back for a breath. "Shade. This is Chinook."

"My name's Orestes." After a moment he asked, "You don't know who I am, do you?"

Shade grunted no. There was owl blood on his nose; amazingly, it tasted almost identical to bat blood.

"I'm King Boreal's son."

Shade faltered. Not only was he gouging his teeth into an owl, he happened to be the prince of the most powerful bird king in the northern forests.

"Where's your father now?" he asked, pulling back to see how he was making out. "Was he in the building with you?"

"No, luckily. He sent me away while he . . ."

"What?"

"Organized his armies for war," said Orestes quietly.

Shade looked away. War with the bats. He felt a sudden impulse to leave. Let Orestes fend for himself; why should he help him, when his father was getting ready to wipe out every bat in the sky?

"Do you want a war too?" he asked Orestes coldly.

"I don't know. Do you?"

"No, but I don't want us to be banished to the night forever." He sighed. It all seemed so far away, somehow, like someone else's life. Right now he was in the jungle, and that was all he knew. Staying alive, making it out alive. And for that, he needed this owl.

"Can I trust you?" he asked Orestes. "When I take this off, you'll escort us back north, and you'll protect us from any owls we might meet?"

"Yes."

He looked into the owls' huge eyes, and knew there was no way of knowing whether he was telling the truth.

But he chose to believe he was. What more could he do? He went back to work, slashing at the stitches until there was only one left.

"When I cut this one, catch the chain with your claws," said Shade. "I don't think we want it hitting the ground. Just in case."

Orestes nodded. Shade sliced through the thread quickly, and the owl, with amazing agility, hooked the chain with his talons.

"Put it down slowly, on the ground."

He waited up top, while Orestes flew down through the tree with the disc.

"You trust him?" Chinook whispered.

"We have to."

"He might just go back and gang up with the other owls now. Tell them where we're hiding."

"Maybe," said Shade, needled by Chinook's possibility.

Orestes returned to the branch, free at last from the Human explosive. "Thank you."

"Let's go. I'll show you where we're staying." He measured the owl with sound. "You should be able to just squeeze inside Statue Haven."

"You'll have some convincing to do beforehand," said Orestes.

Shade grinned.

A set of claws sliced down from the sky and sank into Orestes' feathered back. Shade's eyes snapped up to see a huge cannibal bat dragging Orestes up off the branch. A shadow fell over him, and he could only drop away

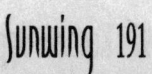

instinctively as a second set of claws whistled past him. Instead, they plunged into Chinook's shoulders and heaved him up into the sky.

"Shade!" he heard Chinook cry out in confusion and pain.

Peering through leaves, Shade watched as the two cannibal bats flew off, Chinook and Orestes gripped in their claws.

He watched them disappear, his heart pounding. You did nothing, nothing. There was nothing to do.

I feel safe when I'm with you, Chinook had told him.

He was shaking, and for the first time since the Humans had captured him, he was crying uncontrollably. He was stupid and weak and he'd lost everything, everything. He lurched back toward Statue Haven, blinded by his tears.

A wide river cut the city in two, and spanning the water was a soaring metal bridge. Even from this great distance, Marina could see the flicker of movement around its underside, and then, huge, long, shimmering tendrils twisted into the sky in all directions, turning, arcing over the city like dark rainbows.

Bats. Millions of them.

They had arrived at Bridge City.

Marina felt a wave of pride: She never thought she'd actually visit this place, this legendary city where the bats filled the skies, and seemed more like the rulers of the place than the Humans who had built it. Relief too flooded through her. They were nearing the greatest of all bat strongholds, home to the western free-tailed colonies, the biggest of all northern bats. If there was any place left on the earth that was still safe for them, this was it. Still, the sight of the Human city set off a queasy swirl in her stomach. The idea of living so close to them seemed disgusting to her now. And how could the bats be safe from the Humans' hideous plans?

As they flew closer, she saw how the bridge could be home to so vast a number of bats. Its length was immense, a latticework of metal beams, supported at intervals by thick, stone piers that plunged deep to the river's bottom. The top of the bridge served, Marina could see, as some sort of Human roadway, lit now by their noisy machines, going to and fro. But the bridge's underside, with its multitude of ledges and niches, provided roosts along its entire span, from one side of the river to another.

As they approached they were met by gleeful squadrons of bats encircling them, and Marina felt something close to exultation. To be in the midst of such a throng! How would they be defeated? Anything was possible now.

Beating the owls.

Rescuing Shade.

The next few hours passed in a whirl as she and Ariel and the other newcomers were led to different parts of the bridge and shown where they could rest. She learned that the population of the bridge had swollen hugely over the last two months, and it was now home to bats of all species, from the west coast to the east. The roosts were crowded, and everyone seemed to be in high spirits, telling the stories of their own adventures, their narrow escapes from the owls, sneak attacks, and desperate flights for freedom.

"You should sleep," Ariel told her. "We've been flying hard for a million wingbeats."

"When can we continue south?"

"We'll ask Frieda," Ariel said, then frowned. "I'm worried about her."

The Silverwing elder was not with them; she'd been summoned with Achilles Graywing to report to Halo Freetail, the chief elder of the bridge. Marina was worried about Frieda's health too. More and more, over the nights, she'd had to rely on others to fly for her, and her breath rattled almost constantly. Even her bright eyes seemed slightly bleary, wandering off to the far horizons.

"This last journey was too much for her," said Ariel.

Marina shook her head, alarmed. "She'll be all right. She just needs rest." She didn't want to hear about anyone dying. But Ariel said nothing.

Amazingly, Marina slumbered, despite the constant thrum of activity around her, despite the impatience coursing through her veins. Pure exhaustion won out. When she woke, Frieda was beside her, and Marina broke into a glad smile.

"The elders are holding a war council in an hour," said Frieda, suppressing a cough, "and I would like you both to accompany me. You may need to be my voice."

The war council was held in the highest of the bridge's soaring towers. It was here that Halo Freetail and the other elders made their roost, and the location gave a sweeping view of the Human city, and the open skies above the flatlands.

Marina felt horribly out of place among the elders—and such a large collection she'd never seen. There were hundreds from all the different colonies, and their faces were all wrinkled and lined and awfully sober as they spoke. Like all the Freetails, Halo was an imposing figure, considerably larger than a Silverwing or a Brightwing, with a huge chest, and the distinctively long tail membrane which enabled her to be incredibly agile in flight.

"We have now been joined by Achilles Graywing," she said, "and Frieda Silverwing, and for that we are extremely glad. Welcome to you both."

There was a chorus of greeting from the other elders.

"Our scouts have told us that the owls are massing from the north and are within several nights' journey of Bridge City. Much as it saddens me, we must now talk of war." Her chest fell as she sighed. "I know that some of you put great faith in the teachings of Nocturna's Promise, and had high hopes that the Humans would somehow come to our aid when it came time to fight. But I understand from Frieda Silverwing that these hopes have been disappointed."

Marina listened as Frieda slowly, but with force still

left in her aching voice, began the story of the Human building, and the forests it contained. When the Silverwing elder turned to her and asked her to continue, Marina's heart beat so quickly, she thought she would faint. All the elders gazed at her, and she tried to quickly tell what she and Shade had seen in the Human building—the way the Humans had treated the bats, how they were carrying them south in their flying machines—and then what the hummingbirds had told her several nights ago, about the Humans using the bats to carry fire.

A defeated silence stretched out when she stopped talking, and she looked at her claws, wishing someone would speak.

"I won't pretend that we Freetails ever put much faith in the Promise," said Halo finally. "We've thrived in the night, and never had much appetite for the light of day—as I know some have."

At this she seemed to look directly at Frieda and Achilles Graywing.

"We never thought it worth fighting the owls for the sun, and I know many of you resented us for it. As for the Humans, we've lived side by side with them for a hundred years, with no reason to distrust, or trust them. They've not disturbed our roosts here, and few of us have been given the bands. But this news of yours, Frieda, does gravely disturb me. If they are using us to carry weapons, we must consider them our enemies, and be more vigilant here on the Bridge. But all our energies now, I think, must be turned toward the owls."

There was a general rustle of wings in agreement to this.

"We could tolerate the banishment from the day, but these other atrocities we cannot tolerate. The seizure of Hibernaculums, the surprise attacks during the night. Their actions tell us they are intent on war, and we have no choice but to fight."

Marina looked at Frieda and saw how tired she looked, not just in her face, but in her whole frail body. She looked away, frightened.

"The owls are powerful, but we have here an army the size of which has never been seen before, and we may now have to fight for our very survival."

"It will be terrible," said Frieda, and there was such sorrow in her voice that no one spoke for a few moments.

"You surprise me, Frieda," said Halo, trying to chuckle, as if to wash away the sense of doom that Frieda had created. "You were one of the loudest voices in the rebellion of fifteen years ago. You've lost your appetite for battle?"

"I suppose I have, yes," said Frieda, "because I realized this is not a battle we can win, not alone. . . ."

"But there is no help," came a bitter voice, another elder. "You yourself have said the Humans are not our friends. So what are our alternatives?"

"We must at least try to talk to the owls. We may find they are our allies."

"Allies against whom?" asked Halo.

"It seems to me that the most powerful creatures on

this earth are the Humans, and they have used both of us for evil ends."

"Perhaps, but the Humans are not systematically forcing us from our homes," said Halo impatiently. "As for speaking to the owls, I sent a delegation to them some weeks ago, and they had to flee for their lives before they could even get an audience with King Boreal. We will speak to the owls, yes, if we can, but we must prepare to fight, and fight alone."

A Freetail swept up from below, breathless from his rapid ascent to the tower. "Halo Freetail," he said, "a rat envoy has tunneled up beneath one of the piers. They bring offerings of peace, and say that King Romulus is eager to meet with you."

Hearing the name, Marina felt a surge of surprise and joy. Was it the same Romulus she and Shade had met last fall? Back then, he was far from being a king. Imprisoned in a muddy dungeon by his brother, Prince Remus, he'd managed to save them from being drowned as spies. If Romulus was now indeed king, that could only be good news.

But a tremor of alarm and anger spread through the assembly.

"How dare they tunnel beneath our pier!" said one elder.

"They must be in collusion with the owls," said another.

"Will you talk to them?" Achilles Graywing asked Halo. "It may be a trap."

"A preemptive strike to weaken us before the owls come!" cried yet another anxious elder.

"No," Marina blurted out, and had to shout louder to be heard, "no, I don't think so. I know him."

"*You* know King Romulus?" Halo's bushy eyebrows shot up dubiously.

"I think so." Quickly she told Halo Freetail and the others about how she and Shade had met Prince Romulus. "He saved our lives; he showed us the way back to the surface from the sewers. And I think he's a friend to all bats."

"Come with us, then," said Halo. To his messenger he said, "Summon five of my best guards to accompany me, and alert the garrisons. If this is a trap, we'll not be taken by surprise."

As Marina spiraled off the tower, down and down, their group was joined by five formidable Freetail soldiers. They swept beneath the underside of the bridge, and skimmed the water toward the south pier, a huge mountain of stone slammed into the earth.

There, at its foot, was a deceptively casual heap of sticks and straw, but as they neared, a rat appeared, crouched watchfully. Marina realized the sticks must cover the hole they'd tunneled out from. The rat's whiskers twitched as the bats found roosts overhead on the stone, a safe enough distance from the ground. Marina felt a tremor of dislike and suspicion. Apart from Romulus, Marina's memories of rats were not pleasant.

"Halo Freetail," said the rat, "thank you for coming. King Romulus is here to speak with you."

With no further fanfare, a solitary large white rat

appeared from the shelter of the sticks and looked up at the assembled bats. And as he raised himself on his legs and spread his arms in greeting, Marina saw, with relief, that this was indeed the same Romulus she remembered.

For it was as if he were half a bat himself. A fine membrane of skin stretched between his upper arms and chest, making it look like he had some kind of malformed wing. And on his legs too, you could see these strange flaps of skin between limb and belly, hopeful wings again.

"Halo Freetail, my thanks for giving me an audience, and to all the other elders, my sincerest greetings."

"What brings you to us in Bridge City?"

"We're aware of the owls' rage against you," said Romulus, "and there seems little reason for it. We will add our voice to yours during any talks."

"King Romulus, this offer is most kind, and we will gladly accept, though the owls, so far, do not seem inclined to diplomacy."

Romulus nodded. "If they will not listen to us, we will fight with you."

A moment of stunned silence burst apart with happy exclamations, and Marina broke into a smile.

"This is a powerful pledge of friendship," said Halo. "Are you certain you wish to bring this upon your fellow rats?"

"We've fought each other too long, the rats and bats," said Romulus. "It's time to lay claim to our common past"—and with this he spread his arms again to show his strange half-wings—"for at one time I believe we creatures were fashioned from the same materials."

"Have you any idea why the owls have embarked on this course?" Halo asked.

"The owls, I know, are claiming that you started this war by killing pigeons in the city, and then other birds through the northern forests, but I know that you are not responsible for this. I have seen the jungle bats who created the carnage—and I know they are no friends of yours, or any bird or beast, for that matter. But I fear the owls are simply using them as an excuse for war—if not this, it would be something else. Their quarrel goes back to the Great Battle of the Birds and the Beasts. But as I said, if it comes to war, we will fight for you beneath and above the earth, on the land, and in the trees."

A huge cheer went up from the elders, one of delight and huge relief, and Marina could no longer restrain herself.

"King Romulus," she said, "do you remember me?"

She saw the rat look up at her, and she dropped from her roost and fluttered down to him. She could hear the whispers of surprise from the other elders, and knew she was breaking some kind of rule about distance between different creatures. But she had been closer to rats than this. She settled respectfully at a distance on the ground, and saw Romulus smile.

"Here is a face I remember well," he said. "You escaped, then!"

"Thanks to you."

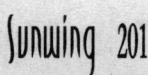

"But where is your friend, the Silverwing?"

"Well, that's a big story."

"Tell it, please."

So Marina shyly told him about what had happened to her and Shade once they'd escaped from the sewers. The rat's face was pained when she finished with Shade being chained with Human metal and taken away by one of their flying machines.

"We have seen this building, I think," said Romulus, "though we have not dared to enter it. And I fear it is not the only one of its kind."

Marina looked up at Frieda and Ariel in horror. "There're more of them?"

"It would make sense," said Frieda, "if the Humans need a great many of us to carry their war to the south."

"We've heard rumors from our cousins down there," Romulus admitted, "though I never knew what to think of them before now. It is appalling. I will send messengers at once, to see if we can tunnel inside these buildings and undermine them. The Humans have never been very good at keeping us out if we want to get in." He grinned. "The machinery they take so much pride in is, after all, only bits of metal and plastic for us to take apart."

"We're going south to find Shade," said Marina.

Romulus looked at her with what seemed like admiration. "You are brave to attempt a rescue. . . ." He trailed off, thinking. "I cannot go with you, but I can perhaps speed your journey."

Marina looked at him hopefully, but wondered how rats could travel faster than winged creatures.

"Certainly nothing is faster than flight," said Romulus, as if hearing her thoughts, "but you may find that the skies, as you go south, may not be as hospitable as these. And more importantly, you cannot travel through all the hours of the day and night. But my barge can, on the underground waterways."

Marina remembered the maze of tunnels she and Shade had been ferried through on their way to the court of Prince Remus. "They go that far south?" she asked, amazed.

"Oh yes, our system is extensive, and I believe there is a branch . . . it's been so long since it's been used . . . but it would take you down, yes, I believe it would."

"You've been a good friend to us," said Marina. "Thank you."

"The boat is at your disposal, when you're ready."

"You're coming with us, aren't you?" Marina asked Frieda. She couldn't explain it, but the bat elder, though frail, made her feel immeasurably safer, as if she generated some kind of protective aura around them.

Frieda smiled sadly and spread her old wings. "Every bat is born with only so many wingbeats. I have too few left. And I am needed here now, I think."

Marina looked away guiltily. She felt pulled in two different directions: to stay here at Bridge City and fight if need be, or go looking for Shade. She knew what her heart wanted her to do. Was it selfish? Would the others think she was a coward, just trying to avoid war? She didn't care; she was going after him.

"You must go," Frieda told her, as if reassuring her. She looked at Ariel. "It's right that both of you go."

Marina looked at Frieda and was suddenly overwhelmed by the feeling she would never see her again.

"All right," she said, glancing down at her claws. She felt the gossamer touch of Frieda's wing on her head.

"Make a safe journey, and bring him back, and Cassiel too."

Marina forced a smile, said good-bye, and flew off after Ariel, holding on to herself tightly. She hated leaving almost as much as being left behind.

Down by the bridge's great south pier, a rat messenger was waiting for them. "King Romulus is expecting you," he said. "Follow me, please."

These rats were certainly a lot more polite than the ones she and Shade had known. She supposed Romulus had whipped them all into shape when he became king. She didn't like tunnels; they made her feel breathless, and cramped her wings uselessly against her sides. But the passage wasn't long, and soon she could hear the sound of water.

Romulus was waiting for them on a large, flat stone that jutted out into a swift underground stream. And tied up alongside the rock was his barge, a long and narrow craft exquisitely fashioned out of wood. Just by looking at it, Marina knew it must have been made by

Humans. Not even rat artisans could have chiseled something so elaborately detailed. She wondered what purpose it might serve for Humans, though. Much of her life she'd spent on an island, watching Humans come and go in their ships. This wouldn't even fit a Human child.

"It was found, decades ago, on a Human junk heap," Romulus explained, "and it's surprisingly watertight. It's served me well. It will take you safely south."

"Thank you," said Marina.

"I can't spare many," the rat continued, "but these few are among my most trusted and able servants." He introduced her to Ulysses, who would guide the ship south, and who knew the waterways of the world better than many fish. Two hulking soldier rats were to come with them too, as well as Harbinger, one of Romulus's chief ambassadors.

"You're going well beyond the limits of my kingdom . . . and I cannot guarantee how you will be received by my southern cousins. Our relations have been . . . difficult lately. But with Harbinger you will get the best treatment possible. Take care of them," Romulus said, turning to his rat crew, "and treat them as if it were me you were carrying."

"Yes, Your Highness," came the reply.

"Don't worry," whispered Romulus in Marina's ear. "You'll be safe with them. I've made changes since my brother's reign."

"What happened to Remus?" she asked.

Romulus smiled faintly. "You imagine I finally over-threw him? No, he overthrew himself. He fled his own kingdom, certain that a plot was afoot to poison him. He left the kingdom in such a shambles that it was not diffi-cult for me to come in and restore order. Good speed, now."

With Ariel beside her, Marina stepped onto the boat. The rats cast off the line that had tethered it to the stone, and the boat leaped into the current.

Marina's heart leaped too. On their way. It was a jour-ney, and she couldn't help feeling a sense of jubilation at its beginning. To go south. To find Shade.

PART THREE

Part Three

ISHMAEL

Inside Statue Haven, Shade hung numbly from his roost, sleepless, watching the first light of day seep up through the long tunnel of the statue's arm.

He almost hadn't wanted to return, so filled with shame and dread at having to tell Caliban what had happened. The mastiff had listened grimly and said only, "Your friend paid for your recklessness with his life."

Shade didn't have the energy to explain why he'd talked to the owl, what he'd hoped might come of it. It was impossible for him not to think back to Tree Haven, when he was just a newborn, and how he'd dared Chinook to break the laws of dawn and come see the sun with him. He'd done it to shut Chinook up, show him how brave he was—with disastrous consequences. He'd seen a sliver of the rising sun, but the owls had nearly caught him, and later in punishment, burned Tree Haven to the ground.

I told him not to come, he told himself. But he felt safe with me. It was agony, seeing Chinook's face again in his mind, saying those words. All the jealous, unkind thoughts he'd had about Chinook, and yet the other bat had trusted him. Chosen him over Caliban and the safety of Statue Haven.

His thoughts were interrupted by a clamor of excited voices from the entrance. He saw Caliban, instantly waking and lighting from his roost, and he assumed the worst. An attack. Bugs, owls, or, worst of all, the cannibal bats. But he couldn't stop himself from following Caliban as he raced down the tunnel toward the entrance; it was better to know the trouble right away rather than worry guessing.

"Is it Ishmael?" he heard one guard saying.

"I don't . . . who else could it be?"

They were peering at a Silverwing, collapsed at the mouth of the entrance, his flanks heaving for air, head hidden by one of his wings. He was little more than a skeleton, his skin and fur stretched painfully over protruding bones. Caliban sat down beside him, bending closer to the other bat's face.

"Ishmael?" he whispered.

"Yes," came the ragged voice. "It's me."

Shade had not heard Ishmael's name spoken of, so he knew this must be one of the many bats who had disappeared before his arrival. Caliban looked at the guards in amazement, and then said to Shade, "Help me bring him inside."

It was almost an hour before Ishmael had rallied enough to speak. They brought him a leaf drenched with dew so he could quench his parched throat.

"We thought you were dead," said Caliban. "Ramiel said he saw two jungle bats carry you off."

"They did," Ishmael croaked. "They took me to their pyramid." Brokenly, he described a huge stone structure buried deep in the jungle, rising in stages to a peak almost as high as the tallest trees. "Thousands of them roost there," he said, and Shade felt a chill run beneath his fur.

Ishmael coughed, and took another sip from the leaf. "There are others," he said, his voice an echoing whisper inside the giant statue. "More of us."

"What do you mean?" Caliban asked sharply.

"The others who went missing, who got caught, lots of them are still there. Imprisoned in a stone mound deep inside the pyramid. Must be Humans buried there, because there are big bones, and bits of cut stone and metal."

"Why did they imprison you?" asked Caliban.

The same question was in Shade's head. Why didn't the jungle bats just eat them right away? Like Goth and Throbb: They hunted, and ate immediately. With a sick heart he knew that something terrible was coming.

"They use us, first," said Ishmael, his eyes blazing.

Shade was suddenly aware he was shivering, his skin cold and moist. Stop, he almost shouted at Ishmael, no more. But he had to listen as the skeletal bat began his story.

"They came, almost every day, and took one of us. Just one."

Shade could see it, the cannibal guards thrusting themselves inside, and all the other bats cowering toward the back, trying to hide behind the ones in front, trying to think themselves invisible. Take him, take her, take anyone but me! Did the sheer terror allow any room for bravery?

"They never came back," Ishmael said. "We assumed they were eaten. But it was much worse than that. Three days ago, they came and took two of us. Hermes. And me. They dragged us past other stone mounds, and I could hear other creatures inside. Owls, I'm sure I heard owls, and rats too. They took us up to a chamber. It must've been near the top of the pyramid, because there was a portal in the ceiling, a round hole. I remember it, because I looked out and I could see stars, and I sent part of myself out that portal to escape, so I wouldn't have to think anymore. It didn't matter. I saw what happened."

Shade listened, as if gripped in the hold of a terrible dream, unable to thrash free.

"I remember there were two cannibals there, waiting for us. An old male, maybe some kind of elder, and another, much younger one, huge, with a black band on his forearm."

And Shade knew who it was, even before Ishmael named him. Of course he had survived; Shade was beginning to think he was immortal. "Goth," he whispered.

"Yes, King Goth, that's what the old bat called him." Ishmael laughed unsteadily. "The king of all those monsters."

Shade wanted to ask about the metal disc: Was Goth still wearing it? Was his dead like Orestes', or had he too ripped it from his flesh? But Ishmael was already continuing.

"There was a stone, and the guards slammed Hermes on it. And King Goth said, *I offer this to you, Zotz,* and he tore out Hermes' heart. I saw it still beating, as he ate it."

The silence in the room was suffocating. Shade closed his eyes, tried to flush the image from his mind. Zotz. He remembered Goth telling him about this god: The strong feed on the weak, and in eating them take their strength into themselves. Zotz was the only god, Goth had said.

"The guards were moving me toward the stone, but something happened. Goth had Hermes' heart in his mouth, and suddenly the chamber filled with noise. It was like nothing I'd ever heard; it . . ." Ishmael had to stop to catch his breath, his thin flanks heaving.

"Drink," Caliban said softly.

Ishmael drank. "There was something in that chamber, some kind of presence that raced around like a tornado. It seemed to go right into King Goth's throat, and he began to talk in a voice not his own. The guards were terrified too, and they fell back and I pulled free. Before they could grab me, I found a gash in the stone floor and threw myself into it. There were other crevices, leading deeper, and I was thin enough by then to squeeze myself through like a bug. All I could hear was the noise above me, and I crawled until my claws were bloody." He held them up for the others to see. Shade's stomach clenched. There was virtually no talon left.

"I found a network of air shafts, too narrow for the cannibals, and waited, I don't know how long, for my chance to fly. It took me three days to get back here. The cannibals were everywhere. I could hardly fly. I never expected to make it."

And then, his story told, Ishmael crumpled, and the noise that came from his broken body was unlike any weeping Shade had ever heard, blunt and ugly, as if it were chiseled from his own bones.

As Shade watched, four or five others flew closer to Ishmael and enclosed him in their wings, until he was completely hidden from view, his sobs muffled by their bodies. After a few minutes, the group broke apart, and Ishmael seemed calmer.

"The others still in the dungeon," said Caliban gently, "who are they?"

Shade could feel everyone tense in horrible anticipation as Ishmael raggedly began to recite names. He could barely listen, because he knew what he was hoping to hear. The list seemed agonizingly long, up to twenty-one now, these other names nothing but cruel sounds to him.

" . . . Lydia, Socrates, Monsoon . . . and Cassiel. He was there too."

Shade remembered to breathe. He was aware of Caliban's eyes on him, and couldn't figure out the expression in his eyes: pity, maybe, mixed with something hard and determined.

"We leave tomorrow night," Caliban said tersely. "We can't risk staying any longer."

It took a few moments for Shade to understand what he'd just heard. "What d'you mean? We've got to free them! Chinook's there too, now!"

Ishmael turned his haunted eyes on him. "No. You can't."

"I'm going to get them!"

"We leave tomorrow," said Caliban fiercely. "That is the plan, and we won't break from it. This is our chance for life; the others have already lost theirs."

"I'll go alone, then," said Shade, turning to Ishmael. "Just tell me the way."

"It was three nights ago," Ishmael said. "Cassiel might already be dead."

"He's my father!" he said pleadingly.

"And I left my brother," Ishmael hissed, his eyes dancing with anger. "I didn't even try to go back to get him out. I just left. I saved myself and left him to die. Do you know what that's like? But there's nothing I could've done. There's nothing anyone can do. Are you listening to me? There're thousands of them."

"You escaped."

"It was . . . they made a mistake; I had a chance to fly." Ishmael shook his head. "It won't happen again."

"We take to the skies tomorrow, at sunset," said Caliban. "It's the only way. And may Nocturna look over us."

Shade laughed, and it came out like a bark of pain. "Nocturna? You won't get any help from her. If she even exists."

Caliban and the others looked as if they'd been struck across the face.

"How can you say this?" Caliban asked, shocked.

"Where is she, then?" Shade demanded, feeling his anger swell inside him. "How do you know it hasn't all been a big mistake, a lie, and we've been idiots and clung on to it? Just like we were fools to believe in the secret of the bands, and the Humans helping us. Look what they've done to us! Where was she when we needed her?"

"You've survived," Caliban reminded him, sweeping his wing around the statue, "we all have. But we've got to leave this place now. Look around you, Silverwing. Haven't these bats suffered enough? You want them to go into the jungle with you, in the hopes you can save one or two others? No. You know what these cannibals can do. There's no real hope of winning."

"I don't expect help," said Shade defiantly.

"We won't wait for you," said Caliban. "I'm sorry, but if you go, you go alone."

As the sun burst free of the horizon, Shade flew higher still, straight up from Statue Haven, in tight spirals. He wanted to go as high as he could, not just for safety, but so he could see into the distance.

And maybe even *hear* into the distance.

It was madness to fly in the light of day, and he knew it. There were eagles, vultures, and maybe even Human flying machines. But he wanted to be alone, to try to clear his mind and decide what he must do. It had been a long time since he'd flown in the sun's full glare. He didn't count those days in the Human forest, under that dulled sun.

He could feel his black fur burning unpleasantly with its heat. But as he rose higher and higher, the air cooled. Higher still. When finally he looked down, he saw all the city spread below him, reassuringly distant. The statue, and high hills, and then, the darkness of the jungle as far as he could see.

To the east was water, a long coastline extending north in a slow curve. That would be their way home. Whatever was left of it. What should he do? How he wished for Frieda or Ariel, and especially Marina, who could help him make the decision.

It had been so simple before. To flee north with the others was the only thing to do. But now the cannibals had Chinook. And his father was still alive—at least he was three nights ago. The hook that had drawn him millions of wingbeats had just snared his heart afresh. How could he leave now? Without at least trying to rescue him?

It wasn't so simple—there was a pull in another direction. If he went north with the others, he might be able to find the Human building, and warn them before more were taken south to their deaths. He might be able to save the lives of thousands—and Ariel and Frieda and Marina with them. He pointed his nose into the wind, feeling its cool caress on his hot face. Above him, banks of clouds scudded to the northeast, and his heart went with them—how easy it was for them to make the journey, their passage so safe, their arrival certain. And he wanted to fly right now. Fly north, fly home. Leave this hideous jungle behind.

But maybe Marina had already warned the others, and there was no need of his journey. For all he knew, maybe they'd escaped. But there was no way of knowing, unless . . .

He tilted to the north again. Sound was supposed to be his gift. Frieda said he was good at listening, that he would hear things others wouldn't. And Zephyr, the albino bat, the Keeper of the Spire, had once told him that you could hear even the stars if your hearing was good enough. More than that, you could hear into the past and future, to sounds long ago, and ones that had yet to be made.

He doubted he could hear the whispers of the past or future, or hear the distant stars, but could he send his voice over the millions of wingbeats to the north and hear a reply?

It was ridiculous, of course. He'd never heard of such a thing. But Zephyr's ears were so good, maybe he could hear a cry for help. The albino bat had helped him once before; maybe he could help him now.

He aimed his voice at the northern horizon and cried out. He didn't try to make his voice as loud as possible, but imagined projecting it on the air, as if the sound had wings and might carry itself. He imagined the city, and the cathedral and the spire where Zephyr made his home, and he imagined Zephyr's white fur and whiter eyes, and his ears flaring to catch his voice.

He made his message as short as he could. He told Zephyr how he came to be in the south, and how he was separated from the rest of his colony. Had he heard anything about Ariel or Frieda or Marina? Were they safe? Should he fly back to them, or should he stay and try to save his father?

When the last words left his mouth, he felt foolish, a newborn crying for comfort. He was alone, high in the sky, in a foreign land, and he would have to help himself. That was the hard truth.

Still, part of him hoped. He opened his ears wide, heard only the whisper of the wind. He wondered if Caliban was right about Nocturna. Was she looking over them, was that why they had survived so long? But what about those who hadn't? Was there a reason for that? None he could understand. It was just luck, maybe. All his childish dreams about bringing his colony the sun, fulfilling the Promise. He'd been so hopeful then, so certain of a good ending, and his place in it all.

How long did it take sound to travel? And how long before it died, evaporating on the wind, his voice dispersed like little bits of dew on tree leaves.

"Shhhhhhhhh," said the wind in his ears. "Shhhhhhhhhh." Like his mother trying to get him to sleep back at Tree Haven.

He was so tired. He should go back. There was no point staying up here, hoping for someone to solve his problems. And the longer he stayed up here, the better chance of getting eaten. His voice wasn't strong enough, or perhaps his ears weren't sensitive enough to hear a reply. There was nothing but the great emptiness of the sky.

"Shhhhhhhhh," was all the wind could say to him, and then:

"Shhhhhaaaaaade."

His name? Or just a trick of the wind? He flared his ears as wide as they would go.

"Shhhhhaaaaade. Lissssten careffffffulllllllyyyy."

Was that Zephyr's voice? It was so hazy, he couldn't tell. But he locked on to the sound, rocking in the wind to find the best position.

"I ssssennd you greeeeetingsss from the sssspire."

Zephyr! It *was* Zephyr. He was so surprised and overjoyed, he laughed out loud, and then immediately shut his mouth in case he missed something.

"Aaaaaariel . . . Mariiiiiinaaaa . . . traaaaavvvvvelliiii-ing to youuuuu."

He frowned, concentrating so hard, his head ached. Traveling to you? And why no mention of Frieda?

"I don't understand," he shouted, then realized this was not a conversation, only a message, traveling millions of wingbeats to his own ears. He would only hear it once. But what did it mean? Were they already on a flying machine, with metal tied to their stomachs? Or were they looking for him? But how would they know where to look?

"Zzzzzotzzzzz willlll reignnnnn . . . unlessss . . . ssssstaaaay . . . and sssssavvvvve the sssssunnnnn . . ."

He was worried he was losing words now, only getting fragments. Save the sun?

" . . . and your faaaaaattthhher . . . ssssstilllll alllllive."

Eyes shut, he listened for more, but the message had ended. Still alive. Still. It didn't have a very reassuring ring to it. Did that mean his father was close to death, barely clinging to life, and if Shade didn't hurry up and do something, he'd be too late?

He felt irritated. He wasn't a whole lot wiser after all this. He still didn't know if Marina and the others were safe. And saving the sun?

He shook his head with a snort. "The sun's fine," he muttered to himself. "It's doing fabulous up here, shining away. I don't think anything's going to happen to the sun. It's me I'm worried about. Me and a million other bats."

Save the sun.

Why should I? Anger suddenly blazed through him. What kind of thing was that to ask someone? How? When? Why couldn't Nocturna save the sun if it was so important? Let her do some of the hard work for a change, instead of passing it off on runty little bats!

Tired of being used, he thought as he quickened his descent. By Goth, by the Humans. He'd had enough. He would try to save his father, save Marina, his mother, Frieda. That was all that mattered to him now. No more big ideas, no more promises.

Just to survive.

But from the message, it sounded like saving the sun

and saving his father were somehow connected; how, he couldn't imagine. Now, images from his recent dreams were beginning to surface in his mind. An eye opening behind the sun, a permanent night.

He glanced over at the sun, well above the horizon now, skirting across it quickly with his eyes and then shutting them tight to stop the pain. The sun's shape flared against his eyelids. He frowned.

There was a piece missing.

Not a lot—you'd barely notice unless you were look-ing hard—but on one side, a tiny sliver had been scraped off its curve, in the same way that the moon gradually withered over the month.

The moon always came back.

Would the sun?

"This is the end of the northern waterways," said Ulysses from the rudder. "What follows belongs to the kingdoms of the south."

For the past several hours, Marina had noticed that the tunnels through which the barge floated seemed less well maintained. Their walls were now only mud, soft, oozing. Once, the water had seeped away altogether, and she and Ariel had to get off the deck and work with the rats to drag the boat over a long stretch of muck. Often there was next to no light to guide them, and Marina would use her echo vision to help Ulysses steer through the increasingly mazelike tunnels.

This was their second night on the barge, racing

beneath the earth on the rats' waterways. They had only stopped twice on their journey south. Ulysses would tie the barge to the side, and tunnel to the surface and check the stars to make sure he was still on course. Then they would spend a few hours hunting. Marina circled cautiously with Ariel in these strange new landscapes, the air growing ever warmer. On their last trip upground, there was nothing but sand stretching as far as she could see, and tall, spindly cactuses; but the sky was alive with insects.

On the barge, there was little for Marina or Ariel to do besides sleep; her body seemed to remember its lost winter hibernation, and she passed many hours dozing on the gently rocking boat. At first, she'd kept some part of her mind awake, still suspicious of the rats, but they seemed kind and, most of all, bent on fulfilling the wishes of their gracious king. Harbinger, the ambassador, she particularly liked. He had a shrewd, animated face, his whiskers twitching for emphasis as he spoke.

"Have you been to the south before?" Ariel had asked him shortly after they set out.

"No. In my lifetime there has been little communication between us and our southern cousins. They have always resented the rule of the northern kings, and prefer to remain apart. General Cortez, unless I'm mistaken, is the current ruler, a very independent-minded rat."

Harbinger must have seen the worried glance Marina gave Ariel.

"I don't think there's any cause for alarm, though. They may not assist us, but I doubt they will protest your presence when it is made clear you are under our protection."

When she wasn't sleeping, Marina passed time speaking quietly with Ariel, about what might await them, what they should do to find Shade—and sometimes they talked about other things too, better times back in the northern forests, favorite roosts and hunting grounds.

She must have slept again, because a sudden grating jolt woke her. She cast out sound and saw that the river had simply ended. For several hours the water had been flat and stagnant, requiring the rats to pole the barge forward with long sticks. And now the boat had bellied onto the shallows of a broad, muddy bank within a cave. Marina was suddenly aware of how hot it was, even beneath the earth. It made her fur itch.

"The waterways go no farther," said Ulysses. "We've arrived."

Harbinger, flanked by the two soldiers, hopped off the boat and waded ashore. Marina followed with Ariel.

"We must make ourselves known to General Cortez," Harbinger said, "and then—"

"Stop!" came a gruff voice from a tunnel opening low in the cave wall.

In seconds, a dozen rats had emerged and were facing them at the top of the muddy bank. They were scruffy-looking creatures, powerful in the shoulders, with blunt snouts and pale muzzles.

"Bats!" hissed the lead guard to Harbinger. "You've brought bats with you?"

"They are under our protection," said the emissary coolly. "We travel under orders from King Romulus and—"

"King Romulus," snorted the guard. "What do we have to do with this northern king? He is no king of ours."

"—and we ask an audience with General Cortez." Even as the southern rats shuffled closer threateningly, Harbinger did not flinch, nor did his voice falter. Marina was impressed. She herself was ready to fly.

"We are a small, diplomatic envoy," Harbinger said. "These two soldiers here are my solitary escorts."

"We know that," said the guard. "We've been watching your boat for the last six hours. We know you're alone."

"Then you know we pose no threat. I'd ask you to take us to the general."

The southern guard sneered again, and turned his back on them. "Follow," he said curtly, and led the way.

General Cortez looked nothing like Marina had expected. Judging from the southern guards, she'd imagined a slovenly, fat rat lounging in a heap of garbage. But the general, in his dry, rock citadel just above the earth's surface, was slim, and almost elegant. His whiskers grew so close together as to almost form a mustache beneath his nose, and on his chin, his dark hairs formed a trim, triangular beard. Most arresting of all were his eyes: Unlike all the other rats' eyes Marina had seen, his were incredibly light and translucent. The effect of his gaze was penetrating, like that of two diamonds, which could cut through anything.

Marina could see light through the chinks in the stone-and-stick citadel, and was grateful to finally be aboveground, even if the heat had thickened uncomfortably. She wished she could make herself molt.

"General Cortez," said Harbinger, "I am an emissary from King Romulus. He has asked me to deliver these two bats to you, in the hopes you may help them look for others of their kind, brought here by Humans."

"We do not feel generous toward bats," said Cortez, looking from Marina to Ariel with disdain. "Your cannibal cousins have been ripping the jungle apart, and hunting far more than even they could possibly need. They are violating all laws of sustenance. We have lost countless newborns to them in the last five nights alone. Including my youngest son." Cortez looked back at Harbinger. "I am surprised your king is so eager to befriend these putrid creatures."

"General, I am very sorry to hear of your son, but my bat friends have had no part in it, and no knowledge of what the cannibal bats are doing in your kingdom."

"And do they also have no knowledge of the fire their kind has been pouring down on our jungle and city?"

"We know a bit about that," said Marina. "But we've been forced to do it for the Humans."

"Have you, now?" Cortez said coolly, and he sounded far from convinced.

"Not us," said Marina. "We escaped. But there're

others—thousands, maybe—who've been sent here in Human flying machines. They have metal discs chained to them, and they explode when they land."

"My son was among them," Ariel told General Cortez. "And I want to find him. If he's still alive."

"Her son," said Harbinger, "is a personal friend of King Romulus. And it is very important to him that Shade Silverwing be brought home."

"There are not many survivors, I think," said Cortez, and his voice had lost some of its iciness.

"But there *are* survivors?" Marina said hopefully.

Cortez turned to one of his guards. "Rodriguez, I have heard you speak of a place where these northern bats are gathered."

"They've taken up inside the statue on the cliffs. We have been monitoring them from the base."

"Take us there, please!" implored Marina.

Cortez said nothing.

"King Romulus would be indebted to you, General. And should you need some favor from him in return, now or in the future, he would surely oblige."

"Very well," said the rat general curtly. "But only on the condition you take them out of my kingdom. The fewer bats of any sort I have here, the more content I will be. Agreed? Good. Rodriguez, lead them to their friends."

ETERNAL NIGHT

"A voice on the wind," said Caliban with a snort. "The wind plays tricks, you should know that. It'll tell you everything you ever wanted to hear, or maybe what scares you most. You'd be a fool to give it much attention."

After returning to Statue Haven, Shade had found Caliban hanging awake from his roost, and told him about Zephyr's message—or what he *thought* was Zephyr's message. Part of him was relieved by Caliban's disdain. Maybe it really was nothing more than his own desperation at high altitude. But he was too scared by what he'd seen to give up just yet.

"Look, there's something wrong with the sun," he pressed on.

"Flying off alone in full daylight," muttered Caliban angrily. "Don't you learn, Silverwing? Do you know how dangerous that was? Not just for you; for everyone. You could've been spotted, and led something right back to all of us."

"You're right. I'm sorry." Shade nodded, contrite for a

moment before adding doggedly, "But what about the sun? Ignore my dreams if you want to, ignore the voice. But just go take a look at it yourself."

"I don't need to take a look at the sun," Caliban hissed, hackles rising, lips pulled back over his jagged incisors. For the first time, Shade was afraid of him. He saw how determined he was to leave the jungle; he'd survived two months here, and that was a kind of miracle that could only be temporary. "We're leaving, first dark. Like I said, you can stay if you want. But I don't want you trying to change anyone else's mind. Understand: You poison our escape, and I'll silence you myself."

Shade swallowed, feeling utterly alone. Maybe Caliban was right. He'd become dangerous, to himself, to others. Look what had happened to Chinook. And if it weren't for him, maybe none of the Silverwings would've even gone to the Human building in the first place. He'd led them right to it, their dark Promise.

Caliban's powerful neck relaxed, and he looked away. "The sun is no concern of ours," he said more quietly.

"No, the Silverwing's right."

Shade turned to the voice, and was surprised to see Ishmael's eyes wide open. The emaciated bat was breathing rapidly, and had obviously heard everything.

"You need rest, Ishmael," said Caliban, with a trace of irritation. He shot Shade a warning glance.

"I'd forgotten until now," Ishmael whispered, "but Goth said something after he murdered Hermes. He said, *What must we do . . . to kill the sun?*"

"What else did you hear, Ishmael?" Shade asked.

"I was moving, and there was so much noise and wind. Something about the darkness of the eclipse, and more sacrifices."

"What's an eclipse?" Caliban asked.

"The sun going out," said Shade numbly, remembering his dreams, and the image of the sun being eaten away. He shuddered despite the heat. "When?" he asked Ishmael.

The other bat shook his head. "But there was something else about a city, Bridge City, and destroying it with fire."

"The disc," said Shade with a start. "He still has a disc from the Humans. Did you see it on him?"

"I can't . . ." Ishmael's forehead creased, eyes closed with the effort of remembering. Shade felt guilty, forcing him back to such hideous images. "I . . . no, I can't remember." His breath whistled through his throat, and he hung limply, exhausted.

Shade looked carefully at Caliban, trying to gauge his reaction to all this.

"Zephyr said Zotz will reign unless we save the sun."

"Any ideas, little bat?" Caliban said grimly. "I've never had much interest in prophecies and riddles."

"I'm not too crazy about them myself anymore," said Shade with a bitter laugh. "I don't like this any more than you, believe me."

Caliban turned away. "I'm not the leader your father was," he said to Shade. "Maybe he would've known what to make of all this. I don't. All I want is to save as many as I can, bring us back north. Home."

The word tugged at Shade's heart. How he longed for it, wherever and whatever it was now.

"But it doesn't matter where we go if Zotz kills the sun," he said. "If this is the god they worship, then he must be strong. Stronger than Nocturna, I suppose, or why hasn't she stopped him herself?"

From deep below them, at the very base of Statue Haven, came the faint but distinct whisper of earth and rock shifting. Caliban heard it too, and lit.

"Come with me," he told Shade.

Shade followed him lower through the statue's torso, and then down its left leg, which veered off at a slight angle. When they'd reached the knee, Caliban pulled back, circling. Shade peered down into the darkness at the foot of the statue.

"Rat," he heard Caliban mutter in disgust.

With his echo vision, Shade could see the rodent's head poke up from a narrow opening inside the foot. It wrinkled its nose high in the air, sniffing, its sharp front teeth bared. Then its head pulled back suddenly. Shade looked after it, anxious; were there more coming? Still, he didn't see how the rats could scale the sheer, smooth surfaces of the statue's interior. Even if they could, the bats would simply fly clear.

A second rat struggled up through the hole and began to shake the earth carefully from its fur. There was something in this brisk, almost elegant motion that was remarkably familiar to him. He noticed that this rat's fur had a startling brightness to it, much thicker and softer-looking than any rat he'd ever seen. Then he saw wings flare, rustle briefly, refold.

Shade gaped. How could this be? A *bat* in the company of a rat? Maybe he was mistaken. He looked more closely, bombarding the creature with sound, and when he saw the eyes, he knew. Instantly he was hurtling downward, hearing Caliban's exclamation of warning behind him, telling him to come back, but it sounded a million wingbeats away.

"Marina?" Shade called out. "Marina!"

They were a tangle of wings as they tumbled over one another, nuzzling their faces into the other's neck and cheek, sniffing ecstatically. He pulled back and looked at her, just to make sure it really was her. It absolutely was.

"You came for me!" he said in amazement.

"Of course I did," said Marina with a laugh, her eyes glistening. "We both did." She nodded off to one side.

We? Shade turned. His mother waited beside him. She took his face gently between her folded wings. Forehead creased, she just gazed at him intently, as if mapping his every feature. Then she caught sight of the ugly scar on his stomach, and tears spilled from her eyes. She looked so tired, he was overtaken by a wave of regret and gratitude.

"Thank you," he said hoarsely. "How did you find me, how did you know where . . . ?" He looked from his mother to Marina, suddenly at a complete loss for words.

For the first time in so many nights, he was suffused with an unexpected sense of safety, and he felt all the tightly wound things inside him start to uncoil; he couldn't stop his body from trembling. He felt Marina fold her wings around him along with his mother, and he let himself surrender, just for a moment, to the feeling that everything was going to be all right now.

He made them tell their story first, and Marina launched into a hurried account of how they'd escaped the Human building and met up with Achilles Graywing, then the journey to Bridge City, and their meeting with King Romulus. When he heard about Frieda's flagging health, he felt no sudden shock of dismay: It seemed just another sorrowful weight to add to all the rest. "Will she live?" he heard himself ask.

Ariel shook her head, as if to say, I don't know.

"But we can go now," Marina said to him. "The boat's waiting."

Shade could say nothing for a moment, so strong was his urge to simply nod and hurry away with them. He exhaled, and pulled back. Where to begin?

"There are others here," he said.

"Sure," said Marina impatiently. "They'll come too." She glanced over at Caliban, who had by this time settled warily on the ground, at a suspicious distance from Harbinger and the two guards who had accompanied them.

"How many others survived?" Ariel asked the mastiff bat.

"Twenty-six," he said, eyes not straying from the rodents.

"Just twenty-six?" Ariel murmured, her face sorrowful. "But they took hundreds. . . ."

"Most got killed in the explosions," Caliban said simply.

"Caliban found me in the jungle," Shade explained. "He brought me back here to Statue Haven. Me and Chinook," he added painfully.

"Chinook too?" said his mother, and Shade saw in her face genuine surprise and joy that another Silverwing—a newborn she'd seen born and grow—had survived as well.

"He's not here," he said with difficulty. "It was my fault. The jungle bats caught him last night while we were hunting." He cast a quick, guilty glance at Marina, wanting to see her reaction: Had she really come for him, or was it really Chinook she'd most hoped to find? "But he still might be alive," he told her.

"How?" Marina asked, ears pricking.

"They've taken a lot of us as prisoners," said Caliban, "back to their pyramid."

"Cassiel?" Ariel said, looking at Shade; he knew she expected to hear the worst, but there was still a tremor of hope in her voice.

"He's alive, Mom. The cannibals caught him five nights ago, before I even got here. But he's alive."

"How can you be sure?" she asked.

"That's what Zephyr said."

"Zephyr's here?" said Marina in amazement.

"No, but I talked to him," Shade said breathlessly, "and he told me Cassiel was still alive, and also that the sun was in danger, and if it dies, Zotz rules the skies forever."

He knew he must sound half-crazed; he could see the way everyone was looking at him. He started at the beginning, from the moment he was caught by the Humans and chained with the metal disc. Even now he felt removed from it. They were things that had already happened, and he'd spent so many days and nights just surviving minute by minute. Only the now seemed real to him.

"Goth survived?" said Marina in dull horror when he told them about Ishmael's escape from the cannibals' pyramid.

"*And* he's king now."

Marina just snorted in disgust. "Of course he is. Couldn't have happened to a nicer bat."

And then Shade told them how he'd shouted a message across the world to Zephyr in the spire, and heard his muffled reply: *Save the sun or Zotz will reign.*

"My plan was to fly north tonight," said Caliban. "And I still say we keep to it. I'm sorry for Cassiel; I'm sorry for Chinook and the others. But there's nothing we can do. And this matter of the sun, this isn't for us to deal with. We need the guidance of our elders, and maybe we can come back with a bigger force."

"It'll be too late by then," said Shade with a conviction that surprised him. What was it, the urgency of his dreams, or the missing piece of the sun he'd already seen? But he was certain they only had a matter of nights, maybe even hours, before the sun would be swallowed up altogether. "We can't go."

"What're you saying, Shade?" Marina demanded, and he could already detect that familiar edge of exasperation in her voice. "That *you've* got to save the sun? I mean, this is big, Shade, right? Even for you, this is huge! Were you planning on doing this all by yourself?"

"You think *I* like this!" Shade snapped.

"Yeah, I do. Trust you to come up with the biggest problem ever—"

"I didn't *come up* with it—"

"—save the sun! You know, we came a long way to get you. It wasn't easy. Don't you want to just go home?"

"What about the others, what about *Chinook*—"

"This is not helping, you two," said Ariel sharply, and Shade looked down in shame, face burning beneath his fur. Bickering in front of everyone like newborns.

Ariel turned to Caliban. "Even if we made it back north, there's no help there. The owls are ready to wage war. Every free bat's needed to fight. There're a million of us at Bridge City, and the owls are on their way."

"Bridge City?" Shade shot a worried glance at Caliban. "Ishmael said that was where Goth would drop his disc after the eclipse." He pictured the size of the owl's explosion he'd seen from a distance: One of those in the right place could wipe out a million bats.

Shade squeezed his eyes so tightly shut that light flared behind his eyelids. How could they stop all this? It was too much.

"Why won't Nocturna help us!" he demanded in fury. "I've seen what Zotz can do. Save Goth from lightning, heal his wings, eat the sun bit by bit! Why doesn't Nocturna ever show herself!"

"You've survived," said Ariel. "You didn't die in the explosions."

"No, but a thousand others did."

"We found you."

He grunted, unconvinced. Was that Nocturna's doing, or just luck?

"And she'll help us rescue Cassiel and Chinook and all the others," Ariel said.

Shade was startled by the certainty in her voice. All his life, she'd never talked much about Nocturna, or the Promise. How could she have so much confidence in her now?

"I'm not leaving," Ariel said.

"You don't know what you're saying," Caliban said angrily. "There are thousands of these cannibal bats at the pyramid. You'll never even get inside."

Shade shook his head, fearing that Caliban was right. Marina was wrong if she thought he wanted to be a hero. He wanted to go home right now, just like her. "And what about saving the sun?" he said heavily. "What does that mean?"

"The sacrifices."

Shade looked up to see Ishmael, limping down through the air toward them.

"I remember now," Ishmael croaked. "King Goth said

they need to make a hundred sacrifices during the eclipse. That's why they're taking so many prisoners in the jungle. Bats, owls, rats. They need a hundred offerings for Zotz. And that gives him the power to kill the sun."

Shade nodded slowly, understanding. "So, what if we take them away? Stop the sacrifices, and Zotz can't kill the sun. Does that make sense?"

"Then saving the bats and saving the sun is the same thing," Ariel said.

Caliban was shaking his head. "I admire you all, your determination. But this thing you're talking about, it just isn't possible. We don't have the force."

"By yourselves, no, I would agree," said the rat, Harbinger, speaking for the first time. "But we may be able to enlist some help. If there are indeed rats held prisoner by the cannibals, perhaps General Cortez would provide some assistance?"

Ariel nodded. "He lost his own son, he said. If he thought he might get him back . . ."

"Yes," said Harbinger, "I will propose it to him at once."

"Thank you," said Ariel as the rat emissary and his guards slipped down into the tunnel.

Shade turned to Marina. "You don't have to come, you know. I'd understand."

She just laughed. "And have you get all the glory for saving the sun? Nice try, Shade. Besides, you'd only mess it up on your own. You need me more than you think."

"I know," said Shade with a grateful smile.

With a hesitant claw, Ishmael scratched a picture in the sandy floor of Statue Haven. Shade watched as Goth's pyramid took shape: the stepped sides; the narrow, flat-roofed summit.

"It might've been as much as two hundred feet high," Ishmael said. "Hard to tell, it was so covered by the jungle, and I was only half-conscious when they brought me in."

"Yes, we know of this place," said General Cortez, eyes fixed on the drawing. "The Humans built it centuries ago, and the Vampyrum made it their home after they abandoned it. I know of no rat who has been inside and returned."

Shade studied General Cortez's face, trying to guess what he was thinking. His expression was unreadable. They were lucky he was here at all, Shade knew. Harbinger had returned to his stronghold and managed to convince Cortez to meet with them. The general's dislike of bats was obvious. His nostrils wrinkled frequently at the sight of them, and he rarely made eye contact when speaking. But he'd come, and Shade was determined to convince him to help.

"The entrance," Cortez said, prompting Ishmael.

Ishmael's claw hovered over the drawing. "I think they brought me in here." He made a mark, and then brushed it away. "No. Here, lower down. It was a big entrance, big enough for Humans. I didn't notice any others."

"Guards?"

Ishmael nodded. "Lots. All around the entrance, hanging from the top and sides."

Cortez grunted. "And where did they take you?"

Ishmael shut his eyes, thinking. "The passage sloped down, steeply, yes. That's where most of them seemed to roost; I'd never seen so many bats in one place. Then we passed another passage, stairs spiraling upward, but we kept going down until it opened out into a big chamber."

Clumsily he sketched out a long, narrow space quite near the base of the pyramid. "There were bones," said Ishmael tightly.

Shade felt his heart battering his ribs.

"Bones?" said Cortez.

"On the floor. From all sorts of birds and beasts. The chamber was lined with stone mounds; big, rectangular mounds. That's where they kept us. There was a door—"

"Where?" said Cortez.

"In the side of the stone mound. They all had doors. They were round, stone. There was a stick they used to roll one open. It ran in grooves, top and bottom. It took two of them to do it. They pushed me inside with the others."

"But you say there were other creatures there."

"Owls I certainly heard, I could smell them—"

"And rats?"

"Yes, in one of those other stone mounds."

"Be certain of this," growled Cortez.

"As certain as I can be."

Shade watched tensely, knowing that Cortez was only interested in helping if there was some chance his son was still alive, and could be rescued.

Cortez studied the drawing, silent. "This chamber, there was only the one way in and out?" He pointed at the sloping passage Ishmael had drawn.

"That I saw," the bat replied.

Shade admired his stamina, and his patience. Cortez's curt manner made him bristle with dislike. Couldn't he imagine what Ishmael had been through? To be hauled off in the claws of one of those giant bats, knowing that you were about to die—it was amazing you could see or hear anything at all. Shade just hoped Ishmael's recollections were accurate.

"And when they took you out," Cortez began again, "where did they take you?"

"Back the way I came, but then up."

"The stairs you mentioned?"

Ishmael nodded, sketching a zigzag from the central tunnel up to the pyramid's summit.

"How do you know?"

"I saw the stars through a round portal in the ceiling. This is where they do the killing."

"Back in the prison chamber," said Cortez, "were there guards, I mean outside these mounds where you were kept?"

"I don't know. I heard nothing. Why would they keep guard? There was no escape. The mound was sealed with stone roofs so heavy, it'd take a dozen Humans to lift one. Thick stone—top, bottom, and sides. We dug our claws down to nothing, just to scratch at it."

"They're fearless, these creatures," said Cortez. "The vulture is about the only bird they would shirk attacking."

Shade remembered the huge, ungainly bird Caliban had pointed out to him from a distance one night. It wasn't a fast flyer, but if it got its claws or its hooked beak into you, only death could follow.

"No," said Caliban, looking up from the map for the first time. "An attack is out of the question. Even with a huge force, the losses to us would be terrible."

Shade was unable to contain his disappointment. "What if we went to the owls too?" he said.

"The owls?" Cortez replied, turning his pale, piercing eyes on him.

"They must've lost plenty of their own kind, just like us. Maybe if we talked to them, they'd agree to help us attack."

"The owls are no friends of ours, or yours," said Cortez with icy contempt. "It would be a fatal mistake to think otherwise."

"Can't we even try to—"

"I say it again: There is nothing to be gained," Cortez said sternly. "We have heard rumblings of the war the owls intend to wage against you in the north. There will be no alliance."

Shade shut his mouth angrily; there was no point arguing. He looked hopelessly from his mother to Marina. If they had no help from the rats, could they even attempt a rescue?

"An attack is suicide," Cortez said, "but there may be another way." He turned to the chief guard, who had accompanied him. "Can we tunnel? Here?"

Surprised, Shade watched Cortez make a mark on the map.

"Very likely, sir." The rat darted his nose down at the base of the fortress. "The fortress walls and foundation are bound to have cracked and settled enough for us to find passage. Assuming, of course, this chamber really does lie so close to the outer wall. Yes, I think we can tunnel in from underneath."

Shade's whole body was tensed with anticipation. He forced himself to breathe.

Cortez considered the map a moment before he spoke. "Here is what I am willing to do. There is no point leading a frontal attack on the fortress. But if we can tunnel into the chamber, and it is unguarded, as we hope, perhaps we can release the prisoners and take them out through the tunnel."

"Thank you," Shade said.

Cortez lifted his nose in the air to silence him. "But if we encounter heavy opposition there, we may have to retreat. It will be my decision. Understood? We go to free my friends, and yours. That is all. Our force must be small. The more we take in, the greater our chances of being seen or heard."

"I'm going," said Shade.

"Me," said Ariel.

"And me," said Marina.

"I'm coming too." It was Ishmael, his eyes blazing.

"You're in no condition," said Caliban.

"I left my brother there," said the other bat. "I'm coming. You need me, anyway. I'm the only one who's been inside."

"Thank you, Ishmael," Shade said. He looked at Caliban, gouging a claw into the sand, eyes averted.

"Cassiel would've come back for us," the mastiff said quietly. "I'll go back for him."

"We'll leave at noon," said Cortez. "They will be roosting, and our chances at surprise are greatest then. No one's ever attempted to enter their pyramid. They will certainly not be expecting us. Even so, once we enter, and their cries ring out, we won't have much time before all their might comes crashing down against us. We must be quick."

Goth circled above the pyramid with Voxzaco as the sun broke from the horizon. He laughed with delight when he saw it, wizened to half its size.

"It will be eclipsed at the height of day," said Voxzaco. "You have enough offerings I trust?"

"One hundred and ten," Goth said. A few hours ago he had gone himself to the bone room to count them, just to make sure. How the northern bats had cowered when he'd thrust his head inside! But he was disappointed not to see Shade among them. For a moment he was sure he'd spotted him, but when he'd gone closer, pinning the bat to the ground so he could examine him, he'd seen that he was an older Silverwing, banded by Humans. Not Shade, but with a startling likeness. He frowned. In his dream, he'd ripped Shade's heart from his chest and eaten it while the runty bat watched. Maybe it wasn't important now.

What was important was that they offer Zotz one hundred hearts before the eclipse passed, or the sun would live on. But he knew he would succeed.

"Let us prepare for Zotz's coming," he told Voxzaco, and flew back to the temple to sharpen his claws for the sacrifices.

THE BONE ROOM

After three hours beneath the earth, Cortez called a halt. Shade, grateful for the rest, sank down on the tunnel floor. Crawling was not particularly easy for any bat, but the rats' underground system was the safest way to travel unseen into the depths of the jungle. The tunnels themselves were low and narrow, wide enough for a single rat, or maybe two bats tight abreast. Shade hated the airlessness, the discomfort and frustration of keeping his wings tightly folded when he wanted so badly to spread them and soar. His claws and forearms ached from the strain of walking on them.

Their group was small. Beside him was Marina, and behind his mother, Caliban, and Ishmael. Harbinger had insisted on coming too. In the vanguard, and bringing up the rear, were General Cortez's guards, and his best tunnelers.

"This is as near as we come," whispered the chief tunneler up ahead. He lifted his front claw toward the ceiling. "Up there is the pyramid."

It was as if Shade could suddenly feel its massive weight on his own back, crushing him. All that stone towering up into the jungle, and within, thousands of Vampyrum and their prisoners: Chinook. His father. And Goth.

"Begin," said Cortez.

A small team of tunnelers squeezed past Shade and Marina and immediately went to work on the wall and roof. Shade was amazed at their speed and efficiency as they shunted the dirt from the new tunnel from rat to rat, stowing it further on in the primary tunnel so as not to block their retreat.

As quick as they were, Shade felt every beat of his anxious heart as lost time. The sun, as they'd set out from Statue Haven, had looked even more wizened, a huge crescent bitten from its side, as if by some huge set of jaws.

The tunnelers were already disappearing up their new hole, dirt flying down behind them.

"Be ready," Cortez hissed to them all.

Shade met Marina's eyes, and they stared at each other. He reached over and stroked her with his folded wing. And suddenly he was afraid in a way he'd never been before: He wished she weren't here, not her, not his mother. It was one thing for him to act alone, to try to save his father, save the sun, but now everyone he cared about was right here, and they could be destroyed along with him.

Panic galloped through him. What if this thing were all wrong, a big mistake? He'd been wrong before. Look at the Human building! Maybe now he was just leading them all into harm's way, like Chinook. Was it really Zephyr's voice he'd heard up high? Was he sure? All this about the sun, what sense did any of it make, really?

He opened his mouth to speak, and felt how dry it was. Could she see the panic in his eyes?

"We're together," she said softly. "That's good."

"Yeah."

"We move," Cortez said.

Immediately, Shade was on his feet, grateful to think no more. He followed Cortez into the tunnel. It was even narrower than the one they'd left behind, winding tightly among huge blocks of stone, jarred apart over the centuries to allow them passage. He caught himself panting for breath.

The passage was angling steeply now, and as Shade clawed his way upward, a tremor of sound passed through the earth beneath his talons. Dust misted the air, and he paused, trying to suppress a cough. There again, a second tremor, and then almost a breeze moving from behind, rustling the fur of his eartips.

"You hear that?" he whispered over his shoulder to Marina.

"No," she said, then more worriedly, "what?"

"No talking," came the general's angry voice from up ahead.

Still, Shade felt it, these vibrations of the air and earth around him. They were so faint, he could easily have missed them, little sonic eddies caressing his fur, slithering past him along the muddy walls and sketching quick pictures in his mind's eye. A long snake with feathers. A two-headed jaguar . . .

His heart galloped. These he'd seen before, in his dreams.

And suddenly before him he saw two eyes opening, twin black slashes in the darkness. Shade grunted in shock, shooting out sound. But there was nothing there. Seeing things now. Stop it.

But the tunnel trembled again, and this time everyone felt it.

"It's the weight of the stone," he heard one of the tunnelers hiss. "I don't like it. The soil's soft here."

But Shade knew it wasn't just the weight above them; there was something in the tunnel *with* them, something that could seep through rock and earth and air.

"How long will it hold?" Cortez asked.

"Long enough for us to do our work," said the chief tunneler, "but let's be quick about it."

From up ahead Shade heard a dull *clunk* of stone on stone. "We're through . . . ," the chief tunneler was saying above him, "but . . . I don't understand . . ." There was a short, sickening silence. "Some kind of burial ground . . ."

Following after General Cortez, Shade squeezed between two huge stones and was suddenly out of the tunnel.

Bones.

The tunnel had brought them out into a sea of bones. Shuddering with disgust, Shade fought his way up through the loose jumble after the others. A rat thigh-bone knocked against his wing, and a bat's skull thumped him in the back. There were feathers everywhere, severed batwings, patches of mummified fur.

He reached the surface, slipping and lurching as it shifted beneath him, then turned his attention to helping Marina and the others up. Within a minute they were all assembled in a tight group, perched precariously atop the floor of bones.

"Is this the place?" Cortez asked Ishmael.

Shade turned to look at Ishmael and saw he was trembling so hard, his legs almost buckled. He gave a quick, violent nod, mute with horror.

The entire floor of the long chamber was buried under bones, a testament to centuries of feeding. The stink of putrification was intense. The bones at the surface still had a slick sheen to them, some muscle and sinew still clinging. Shade felt a spasm of fear. His father's bones, somewhere here, buried in all this?

He tore his gaze away from the bones and swept the narrow chamber with sound. They seemed to be at its far end. Running down both walls were the rectangular stone mounds Ishmael had described, maybe a dozen in each row, the closest no more than ten feet away. Their outsides were ornate, studded with jewels and carved with figures that, with a shudder, Shade recognized all too well: a feathered serpent, a black jaguar. He let his gaze move higher, and almost cried out in shock.

The walls were made of skulls.

They were human skulls this time, stacked one atop the other up to the very ceiling. With his echo vision, Shade saw their eye sockets flare black, their jaws wide as if to shout: Intruder! We see you! We hear you!

Cortez was giving orders.

"This tunnel," he said, nodding to the shaft they'd just ascended, "is our life. If we lose it, we lose our retreat. I want it well guarded." He nodded at two of his guards. "Mark this spot, keep it clear, and be ready when we return."

"Yes, General."

"I want two airborne guards to fly to the end of the chamber and keep watch. You, and you." He nodded at Ariel and Caliban.

Shade looked at his mother in alarm. The idea of being separated from her . . .

"No arguments," said Cortez. "I need two bats who can do what I ask. Ishmael's too weak, and the young ones"—his eyes swept from Marina to Shade—"I don't trust. Too willful." He looked back at Ariel and Caliban. You're our advance alarm. You see or hear anything approaching the chamber, you let us know."

"It's all right," Ariel whispered to Shade, "I'll be back. Please, do what he tells you."

"Okay," said Shade, watching her rise in the air and fly off on silent wings toward the chamber's far end.

Cortez was talking to Ishmael now.

"Do you remember which mounds the bats and rats were in?"

The bat shook his head. "I'm sorry."

"Very well." Cortez looked at Shade and Marina. "Take flight with Ishmael and stay above us as we move. Be my eyes, the three of you. Probe the darkest corners. You see anything move, I want to know. We'll check each mound in turn. Advance."

Shade was grateful to open his wings and lift clear of the bones. He stayed close to Marina and Ishmael as they circled above the rats. Cortez and his guards seemed to have less trouble on the bones than he did; quick and agile, they leaped from spot to spot, heading for the first stone mound.

Shade skimmed over it, ears pricked. A mournful warble passed through the stone lid. He veered back to Cortez.

"Owls in that one," he said.

"I can smell them," said one of the guards, face crumpling in disgust.

"Move on," said Cortez without hesitation.

Shade considered saying something, but Cortez fixed him with a hard look. He pictured Orestes being dragged through the sky by the jungle bat. It seemed too cruel to let him die when they could save him just like the others.

"Move on, Silverwing," said Cortez. "We have little time."

Up ahead, one of the rat guards called out excitedly, "I can hear them!"

Crossing the chamber and dropping lower, Shade could now hear it too, the muffled squeak of rat language emanating from within the stone mound. On the far side of the mound, Shade found the blocked portal Ishmael had described.

"Over here," he called out, settling beside it with Marina. The rats reached them within moments. The door was a crudely chiseled round stone, hugely thick. It was slotted into grooved ledges above and below, and there was a narrow hole in the very center through which funneled the sound of rats.

Standing on his hind legs, General Cortez pressed his face against the hole and said, "We've come to free you. Be silent."

"There should be a stick," Ishmael was saying, "to open it."

Shade scoured the bone-strewn floor, looking for a stick narrow enough to fit into the hole.

"Is that it?" asked Marina. Shade turned and followed her gaze high up the wall to the racks of Human skulls. Balanced atop a row of skeletal teeth was a long, stout stick.

"We'll get it," said Marina, and she was flying, Shade right behind her. He didn't like being so close to the skulls, and felt that same uneasy premonition he had earlier—that there was a presence in this room, watching over them. He and Marina grabbed opposite ends of the stick in their claws and awkwardly flew it down to the stone mound.

Cortez and his rats took hold of it and slotted it into the round stone.

"Roll it," the general grunted, and four rats lined up on their rear legs, pushing with all their might. The stone remained fixed for several long seconds, and then with a low rumble began to turn. It quickened as it gained momentum, and within seconds the opening was clear.

Wasting no time, rats surged out, their eyes wild with disbelief. There were dozens of them, mostly young or old, easy victims for the jungle bats, though there were a few strong soldiers clearly weakened by their ordeal. General Cortez stood tall, eyes flicking from one rat to the next, searching. Then Shade saw his whole face lift, and he dropped to all fours and surged through the crowd.

"My son," said Cortez, pushing his face against the young male's.

Shade stared, transfixed, and desperately wanted this moment for himself.

When the last of the rats had left the mound, Cortez wasted no time. He turned to two of his guards. "Escort them back to the tunnel now." Then to Shade and Marina, he said, "Now let us find your friends so we can leave this blighted place."

Up in the air again, Shade cut wide arcs across the chamber's width, ears flared and swiveling for bat song.

"That one, I think," Ishmael said beside him, tilting his chin.

Shade swung down toward the mound, but even as he grazed its roof, he couldn't hear even the faintest of squeaks.

"Yes," said Ishmael, "I'm sure this is it."

"Find the door," said Marina.

The door was around the far side, but the stone

was already rolled fully back, revealing the opening.

"Can't be it," said Shade, landing.

"No," whispered Ishmael in horror, "this is it. I remember the markings above the door."

With mounting panic, Shade stuck his head through the opening. He called out sound and saw that the chamber was indeed empty. But his nose told him more. He could smell the warmth of the bats, and the gouged and bloodied stone walls still echoed with their cries.

Frantically, Shade backed out of the mound, knocking into Marina in his haste. "They were just here!"

Ishmael was still aloft, unable to bring himself any closer to his former prison. "They must've already taken them up," he said. The rest hung in the air, unsaid. Up to the temple, up for sacrifice.

"What is it?" General Cortez asked, catching up to them and frowning at the already open door.

"Too late," Shade wheezed. "We're too late. We've got to go after them!"

"No," said Cortez, "that's impossible."

"You got your son back!" Shade said. "Let me get my father back."

For a moment the general looked as if he might falter, but his face hardened almost instantly. "Remember what I said before. We will not launch an attack. You've done all you can. It's too late for them now. I'm sorry, but we make our retreat now! Go and tell Caliban and your mother. We're leaving."

A low, subterranean rumble shook the chamber, making

all the bones on the floor clatter together horrifically. Dirt rained down from the ceiling, and then a slow sigh passed through the air, rustling Shade's fur.

"What was that?" said Marina, lifting warily from the ground.

"Earthquake," said Cortez. "Hurry, we're retreating."

But Shade knew this was no simple earthquake. The presence he'd felt with them all along was making itself known. He looked up into the darkness of the high chamber and thought he saw a pair of eyes open and then close, disappearing into blackness.

Two guard rats, fur matted with dirt, faces streaked with blood, limped toward them, gasping.

"General, the tunnel!"

"Collapsed," croaked the other rat. "I don't know what happened. There was a noise, like rolling water, and then the roof was caving in and there was nothing we could do. We lost the tunnel mouth completely. Three were buried alive when it went."

"Did any get through?" Cortez asked quickly.

"Maybe half; they might be safe on the other side, but everyone else is still inside the chamber."

"My son?" said Cortez.

"He's alive, but he didn't make it through. He's with us here. The tunnelers are already at work, trying to reopen the passage."

Shade swallowed. Their retreat was cut off. They were trapped inside. Ishmael's flanks heaved wildly for air; it was too much for him, the idea of dying here.

"We've got to get out," he said, his voice becoming dangerously shrill. "We've got to!"

"It's all right," Marina said soothingly, trying to quiet him. "They'll tunnel through, don't worry."

"I'll go get Mom and Caliban," said Shade to Marina. "Go back to the tunnel mouth."

She looked at him closely. "You're coming back, aren't you?"

"Yeah."

"Shade?"

"I'm coming back."

"Because if you're going somewhere, it's not without me."

"It's okay," he said, and he lit, flying low through the chamber toward its far end, where a pale wash of light cut the darkness slightly. He didn't dare call out, but only used his echo vision, sweeping the walls and ceilings for his mother.

And there she was, flying toward him at breakneck speed, Caliban at her side.

"They're coming!" Caliban said. "We've got to leave now."

His heart pumped with panic. He wheeled tightly and raced with them back through the chamber.

"Have they found him?" his mother panted, and he knew she meant Cassiel.

"No," he said bluntly. "We're too late. They're already gone."

She said nothing, just kept on flying. By now everyone

was assembled at the chamber's far end, where they'd entered. The freed rats cowered anxiously as Cortez's remaining tunnelers tried to dig a way out.

"The jungle bats are coming!" Caliban said.

"How many?" Cortez asked.

"Lots," Ariel said. "They're coming from above, from the spiral steps. I shot up sound and all I could see were wings and teeth."

"They're coming back for more victims," said Ishmael.

Cortez looked down into the shaft of bones. "How much longer?"

"Ten minutes."

"They'll be here in one," said Caliban.

Shade looked at the general. "We've got to release the owls."

"They stay where they are!" said Cortez, baring his teeth at him. "I won't be slaughtered by owls!"

"With them fighting, we'll at least have a chance! I know one of them, let me talk to him!"

Shade looked at the far end of the chamber, jabbing sound as far as he could into the distance, waiting for the first silvery flarings of giant cannibal wings. "We don't have much time," he said.

"He's right, General." It was Caliban. "We need allies now. The rats are too weak to fight, most of them."

Cortez twitched his whiskers in annoyance. "Quickly, then, but only if they agree to our truce." He flicked his head at two guards. "Come with us."

Shade led the way over to the stone mound that held the owls. Marina found the stick perched atop a row of skulls and helped Shade drive it into the hole.

With the rats on their hind legs pushing, and Shade, Marina, and Ariel driving against it using their wings, the stone door began to move quickly.

"Stop!" called Cortez when it was open just a crack. "Speak to your friend, Silverwing."

"Orestes!" he called into the mound.

He waited for the surprised hoots to subside, hoping desperately that Orestes was still alive. He had no idea how he would talk to the other owls, convince them to a truce.

"Who is that?" came Orestes' voice, and then Shade saw half his face pressed against the opening. "Shade Silverwing?"

"We're letting you out, but you've got to make the others promise not to attack us, rats or northern bats. We don't have much time, Orestes."

From inside the prison he could hear Orestes speaking hurriedly in an unrecognizable owl language. In a moment, Orestes was back at the opening.

"You have their word," Orestes called back.

Shade looked at Cortez, and he nodded.

"All the way!" the general shouted, and they rolled the stone back.

Orestes ducked through the opening. "Thank you," he said.

"No, you'll have to fight your way out," Shade told him hurriedly.

"You've given us a chance at life," said Orestes.

"We have a common enemy!" shouted General Cortez as the owls began to push their way out from the stone mound. "The cannibals have broken all laws of the jungle, they have taken more than they need for food for their dark sacrifices. They have stolen our children, our mates. Let each of us do what we can to survive!"

Shade never thought he'd be glad to see so many owls, but he was, as dozens emerged into the chamber. Though many were still downy with youth, he took some reassurance in their sheer size, their hooked beaks, and muscular chests. Now they had a fighting chance!

Shade heard the discordant creak of many wings in the distance. "They're coming," he said.

"Is that the only way out?" asked a large male owl with a brilliant white corona around each eye.

"We tunneled in from the east," said Cortez, "but our retreat has caved in. Even if we reopen it, I fear it's not big enough for you."

"So be it," said the owl. "There is only one way for us. We will fight them head-on. Let us all have luck."

Shade cast sound into the distance and sucked in his breath. A jagged thrashing of wings and teeth was moving toward them. But a slithering noise directly overhead pulled his focus back.

"Did you hear that?" he asked Marina.

She was looking overhead, puzzled.

"What is it?" Cortez demanded.

"Don't know . . ." said Shade. "I don't see anything."

But he knew, he knew they were being watched. He could practically hear the breathing now. His eyes were drawn instinctively to the rows upon rows of human skulls. Could they be alive by some infernal magic, their mouths about to shriek, their eyes ablaze?

Their eyes.

Beyond the lifeless sockets of the skulls were real eyes. Then a smudge of dark movement. Hair, a flash of leathery wing.

They've been watching us all along.

"They're in the skulls!" Shade shouted.

From the open jaws lunged long snouts and heads. Large, moist bodies dragged through. The cannibal bats unfolded themselves, clinging to the skulls' surfaces, flaring their massive wings. They lit, circling high in the chamber, their numbers growing until they were like a roiling thundercloud.

"Look, bones to add to bones," Shade heard one say in a voice thick with phlegm.

When they attacked, slashing down upon them like black lightning, it was unlike anything Shade had ever known or imagined. His whole world contracted to the inches around his body as he veered and rolled to avoid gushing jaws and flexed claws.

He heard a powerful beating of wings and knew that must be the owls, launching their assault. The noise was indescribable, the shrieking, the percussive *thud* of a thousand wings in action, screams of pain—it all seered into his head and clouded his echo vision. It was like flying half-blind.

He was alone. Where was Marina? Ariel? Wings flashed all around him. Something lashed against him and he bit it, and was rolling again.

He saw his mother being dragged through the air in the claws of a cannibal, and their eyes met for a second but there was nothing to say, nothing he could do, because there were teeth snapping at his own tail and he could only follow his body's lead and flip and tilt and dive to stay alive.

"Into the bones!" he heard someone cry, and then again, "Into the bones!"

And then he realized it was Cortez. Shade banked, could see the rats slinking down into the sea of bones for cover, making their way slowly back toward the tunnel mouth. He dove and plunged beneath the surface, wings drawn over his face for protection as bones knocked against him.

He opened his eyes, kept still, tried to get his bearings.

A set of claws clenched into the bones, lifting femurs and skulls away, trying to flush him out. He scuttled on, deeper. He saw hair, a body, in front of him. "Hey!" he hissed.

It was Caliban.

"We're going back to the tunnel," the mastiff whispered, dragging himself on. Shade saw that his right wing was badly torn. "It's the only chance. Got to dig ourselves out."

"They've got my mother!"

"Get to the tunnel!" Caliban said, refusing to meet his eyes.

"Where's Marina?"

"I don't know."

Marina trembled violently among the bones, staring at the space where, just a second before, Ariel had been. She'd seen the claws come down, plunge into Ariel's shoulders, and haul her up and away. More bones clattered nearby, and she could see the talons stabbing down all around her. She'd be next.

Where was Shade?

Her eyes fixed on a splintered thighbone, its end viciously spiked. She gritted her teeth and gripped it in her forearms. A huge hole was suddenly scooped out before her, and she recoiled. The cannibal bat thrashed its wings overhead, and then folded them, ready to drop on top of her.

Marina swung the splintered bone up just in time, and the jungle bat impaled itself on the spike, toppling onto her. Its jaws were still snapping convulsively, and Marina wrenched herself clear before the teeth sank into her wing.

"We have the tunnel!"

The voice carried through the bones. Cortez, not far away; just a few more minutes and she'd catch up.

"We have the tunnel! Retreat!"

But where was Shade?

* * * *

Shade heard Cortez call for the retreat, and he faltered, choking for breath. Retreat. Leave his father, mother. And what about the sun? Had they saved the sun, at least?

"Retreat!" Caliban hissed over his shoulder. "Come on, Silverwing, you've done all you can!"

Suddenly Ishmael was beside him. "Are you going?" Ishmael said.

"No."

"Me neither. I won't leave my brother again."

"Can we get to the top?"

"There're fissures in the stone, I know them," said Ishmael. "That's how I lived. But we need to get to the spiral steps first."

"You lead the way, I'll make sure we get there."

"How?"

"Sound. I'll make us invisible. Don't ask me how, just fly."

They locked eyes, and broke the surface of the sea of bones, wings open, beating hard.

The scene was still one of indescribable chaos, owls and bats clashing in midair, loose feathers swirling into a dense fog.

"Stay close," he told Ishmael.

Around them he sang out a shroud of darkness, a slippery weave of sound that deflected other bats' echoes. He and Ishmael were as good as invisible. It wasn't perfect: Sound leaked out through the seams of his frail shell, but in the chaos it was enough for them to veer through the aerial battlefield almost completely unnoticed.

Up and up they darted to the top of the chamber, and then skimmed along the ceiling, Shade's wingtips grazing stone. Cannibal bats streamed past them into the chamber, and Shade saw a few owls fighting their way valiantly down the long tunnel that would take them back to the jungle. He hoped fervently they made it.

Virtually all his energy, though, was concentrated on his cloak of invisibility, and he had almost no time to breathe.

"Here," said Ishmael.

They'd reached a set of steps spiraling steeply up, but their path was almost instantly blocked by more cannibals flooding down.

"This way now," Ishmael said, and led them hurtling toward the wall. Shade followed, wincing as he wedged himself into a narrow fissure between stones.

Shade exhaled, and his shroud of invisibility melted away.

"Follow," said Ishmael.

The crevice was rib-crushingly narrow, and Shade slithered through on his belly, up and up after Ishmael. Tendrils of daylight filtered down through these cracks, and he realized they must be getting close to the top of the pyramid.

"Here, here," Ishmael whispered.

The passage suddenly swelled open, and before him were two round holes through which poured dim daylight. After the darkness it was almost blinding, but his heart surged. The sun was still there. Not dead. Not eclipsed. Not yet.

He saw he was perched on a white chalky material, not stone, and with a start realized he was inside a Human skull. The holes were eye sockets, and below him were clenched teeth.

He moved his head to the eye socket and peered out.

What he first saw was a circular opening in the high ceiling, and dead center was the sun, or what was left of it. He could almost see it shriveling, being eaten up by darkness. So blighted was it, he scarcely needed to look away, though he felt he must. It was like looking at something dying, and it terrified him.

The chamber was rectangular. Feeble light played on the images carved into the stone walls. He was not at all surprised to see the feathered serpent, the jaguar, the two-headed mantis. And in each corner of the room, the slash of an eye, watching.

He looked down. Directly beneath the circular portal was a vast stone disc, its surface covered with dozens of northern bats, their wings stretched and pinned flat by the cannibals. Clustered around the stone were more bats, gripped by guards.

"My brother," he heard Ishmael whisper beside him, "I see him!"

Shade's eyes skittered across the splayed bats, ready for sacrifice. Where's Chinook, where's Ariel? Where's my father? But he had no more time to look, because

Goth soared low over the stone.

Shade recognized him instantly, the black band on his forearm, the cut of his wings, the crest of fur atop his massive skull. Another bat flew alongside him, a much older one with a crooked spine, and he seemed concerned with the sun through the portal.

"Let us begin!" roared Goth.

"Not yet," said the other. "We must wait until the sun is fully extinguished. You remember Zotz's words. One hundred *within* the darkness of the eclipse. To begin now would waste precious hearts!"

"Have they captured the intruders yet?" Goth shouted at a guard who had just flown up into the chamber from the spiraling steps in the floor.

"Not yet, King Goth. But we will have them all before long."

"If we are but one short of a hundred, you will make up for the lost offering! Bring me owls and rats now! We are about to begin!"

One hundred victims, and Zotz would be unlocked from the Underworld. Shade looked anxiously back at the sun. It was a mere sliver now, a hanging filament of light. He saw the sky darken, flocks of birds tearing back to their roosts in horror at this premature night. How long was the eclipse? If he could delay the sacrifices somehow . . .

The sun went out.

He was unprepared for this moment of total darkness. The sky was hazy; there were no stars, no moon. His eyes may as well have been plucked from his head.

In the darkness there was only sound to see by. He shut his eyes tight. He spun out a web of echoes, and the chamber painted itself silver in his head.

Goth's voice filled the humid air.

"To you, Zotz, I make this first offering, to give you the strength to enter our world and reign forever in darkness."

There was no scream, just a terrible bone-rending rip.

It had begun.

And Shade knew that now, in the total darkness, was his only chance.

SOUNDSHIFTER

He became a vulture.

Shade cleared his mind and hammered himself a new body out of sound. Feathered wings soared from his swollen chest, his neck lengthened, and his face became a vulture's face with small, vicious eyes and a short, wickedly sharp beak.

Huge, he flung himself into the chamber, every vocal chord spinning out the illusion over and over. His bat smell he couldn't cloak. A good sniff would give him away instantly, but who would come close enough? And as long as there was no light, no one could see him for what he truly was: a scared, runty Silverwing.

He swung over the chamber, his sonic wings over six feet across, and beneath him, panic broke out among the cannibal guards. He felt half-crazed, invincible. He was a vulture. He flew at the jungle bats, beak gaping. He saw things only dimly, a smear of sound in his mind's eye. He had few echoes to spare for his own vision, and so was half-blind as he careened through the chamber.

There: a cannibal guard recoiling in horror, stumbling back from his captive.

Over there: a suddenly freed northern bat wasting no time flying high, flying for the circular portal. Out, he was out, he had made it!

And there: Goth, swirling tightly in the air, stabbing sound down at him, this giant vulture.

"We are losing time!" he heard a jungle bat shout in anger. "Continue the sacrifices or we will lose the eclipse!"

Shade flew lower, strafing the cannibals around the huge circular stone, trying to scare off as many as possible. The whole chamber was winged chaos now, as bats—cannibals and northerners—churned the air in terror.

Fly! Shade screamed inwardly. All of you, fly now! Chinook, Mother, Father!

"It's sound! Just sound!"

The enraged bellow reverberated through the room, and he recognized Goth's voice at once.

"There is no vulture! A trickster is in our midst! Guards, stay on the Stone! Hold your offerings!"

Where was Goth? Shade wheeled in alarm, trying to lock on to him, and in his panic, his vulture was decaying in midair, the left wing molting and drooping pathetically, his claws crumbling like a rotting corpse.

Goth dove down on him, aiming for the vulture's neck, and flew straight through, scattering silver beads of sound.

"You see!" Goth roared. "There is nothing here!"

Shade felt his illusion falling apart and tried desperately to resolve it, but it was too late. Goth had punctured it with his claws, and now all his carefully bundled sound burst apart, and the vulture exploded across the chamber in a spray of quicksilver.

It was enough of a distraction for him to fly clear and cling to the ceiling, small again, trying to make himself even smaller. At least now he had his full vision back. He fired out echoes, and the whole chamber snapped into crystalline focus.

His heart sank. On the stone and on the ground there were still so many northern bats in the grasp of the cannibals. He saw the old jungle bat with the crooked spine rear up over one of his victims, then slash down with his claws and teeth. His movements were frenzied, desperate. When he reared again, a heart was clamped in his jaws. He trampled across the ripped, lifeless body to his next writhing victim.

The old cannibal was lifting himself to strike again, when a gaunt Silverwing hurled himself against his crooked back, knocking him over. It took Shade a moment to recognize Ishmael, now launching himself in a hissing, shrieking bundle at one of the guards who pinned the sacrificial victim.

"Fly!" Ishmael shrieked at the bat. "Fly, brother."

Ishmael's brother wrenched himself free from the guards, and flew, up and up, and Ishmael tried to launch himself after him. Only inches in the air, he was hauled back down to the stone, his tail caught in the jaws of the old cannibal. With one angry swipe of the cannibal's claw, Ishmael's chest was laid open, and he slumped lifeless.

Shade, watching in frozen horror, felt as if claws were clutching at his own heart, and he was suddenly aware he was whimpering. He shut his mouth hard, and forced his eyes away from Ishmael. But what he saw next almost made him cry out. There was Chinook, and not far from him, his mother, both on the stone, both in the cannibal's path of sacrificial victims. In less than half a minute, they'd be killed.

Then he looked up, and saw Goth dropping back toward the stone, ready to start his own dark murder.

Shade let go of his roost and plunged down after him and, as he flew, he hammered himself a new disguise, this one simpler, more familiar, and it fit him like a second skin.

He was Goth.

Scrambling madly down the rats' tunnel, Marina caught up with General Cortez.

"Shade's gone to the top! We can't leave him!"

"He's made his decision. Ours is to live!"

"You can't do this!" Marina shouted. "They've got Ariel now too! He helped you get your son. You wouldn't have that without him!"

She turned away from the rat general in disgust and started madly clawing at the roof of the tunnel, dust mixing with the tears in her eyes. She didn't even know what she was doing, only she had to get aboveground, get to the top of that pyramid—the place where they took them to kill them.

She felt a paw on her shoulder, firmly pulling her back from the tunnel roof.

"You'll start a cave-in," said Cortez with surprising gentleness.

Marina jerked away and scrambled back to the hole she was trying to make. Again Cortez dragged her back, and she saw him nod to two of his rat tunnelers, and they took over what she'd started, turning their powerful limbs to the task.

"Very well. We're going back," said Cortez.

Shade swooped before Goth and flared his wings defiantly. Goth looked up in annoyance, and then confusion convulsed his face, his flared nose spiking air as he jerked back to behold his twin. His jaws parted, but only a hot hiss escaped.

"Imposter!" Shade shouted, wracking his vocal cords to deepen his voice. "Guards, seize this trickster before he wastes more of our time!"

"No!" Goth hissed. "*You* are the lie!"

"No!" Shade roared, punching out sound with all his might. He saw the fur on Goth's chest crater with the force, and the cannibal was knocked back in the air several inches. "See my power, and how can you doubt me!" Shade shouted to the guards, who looked on in consternation. "I am king!"

The surprise on Goth's face gave way to indignant rage. "It's you . . ." he hissed. "Shade!"

"Guards," Shade shouted, "seize this imposter, and I will make him our next sacrifice!"

He saw four cannibals launch themselves into the air, their talons splayed wide to seize their king. But just as they were about to reach him, Goth lunged at Shade, jaws ready to clamp and tear. Shade was ready, and he danced clear, leading Goth higher into the chamber in a tight spiral.

He knew it was only a matter of time before Goth caught hold of his illusion and shredded it in his claws, but with every second, there was more confusion, more time for the others to escape—and less time for them to make their sacrifices in the darkness of the eclipse.

From the moment the sun was swallowed up in utter blackness, Voxzaco's mind had become a clock, counting down the seconds of the eclipse. Four hundred and fifty seconds . . . four hundred and twenty-five . . .

They had sacrificed only eight hearts before the echo vulture had frightened the guards. And now, above him, Voxzaco saw two Goths circling one another above the Stone, and dozens of guards hanging back, trying to figure out which was the true king, not daring to risk sinking their claws into either.

Time, time, the seconds ticking down, and there would not be enough time.

All was confusion in the temple. The guards were

terrified; some had deserted their posts altogether.

Voxzaco was certain of this: They would never be able to sacrifice the remaining hundred hearts to Zotz now. They had lost too much time. And too many of their offerings had escaped; he'd seen them flee as the pitiful guards cringed in terror.

All along, Voxzaco had known that Goth could never be Zotz's true servant. He knew nothing; he was vain and arrogant and unworthy of the responsibility of serving Zotz.

Goth had failed.

It was up to him now. He was old, there would not be another eclipse in his lifetime—not for three hundred more years. If he was to see Zotz reign above and below-ground, he would have to act now.

He knew what he must do.

It made such perfect sense to him.

In the center of the Stone, the metal disc. From the moment he'd first seen it, he knew its purpose. It was through the *disc* they would make the sacrifice.

And it was *themselves* who would be the most pleasing sacrifice to Zotz. What could be more pleasing to him than if they gave their own lives, their most precious possessions to him, so that he might gain power to reign? They would get their lives back a thousand times in the Underworld.

Voxzaco scuttled across the Stone, clambering over guards and northern bats to its center. With his claws he grasped the chain still fastened to the metal disc. He was old, but this he could do, his last thing in this lifetime.

He struck his wings at the air and, slowly, slowly he lifted, carrying the disc with him. Higher he flew, in all the confusion scarcely noticed.

Through the circular portal he ascended, and out into the darkness of day.

Two hundred and sixty seconds left.

He would have plenty of time. The disc was heavy, dragging him back to the earth, but he would fly high above the pyramid.

And he would make all the sacrifices himself.

Pursued by Goth, Shade streaked low over the floor and could see the confusion and terror in the guards' faces. Who was the real king, who merely a shell of sound? Many fell back as he careened toward them, and his heart leaped as he saw several more northern bats soar free.

Where were Chinook and his mother now? Free? Had they flown free? But as he skimmed once more over the stone, he caught sight of a bat with silver-tipped fur, crumpled and motionless even though no cannibals held him pinned. Why didn't he fly? Then the bat shifted awkwardly, and Shade cried out.

Around his forearm was a band.

His father.

But there was no time to do anything now. A flash of bright sound snapped his attention up to the corners of the ceiling, and with his echo vision he saw those carved pairs of eyes start to flare. And he knew those eyes for what they were now, the eyes of Cama Zotz, the eyes that had polluted his dreams for so long.

A stiff column of air burst against him, enveloping him, and he struggled against it, this dark embrace Zotz had on him. But it stuck fast, and then seemed to sprout claws and pluck at his outer shell of sound.

"Shade!" Goth roared, tilting toward him. "I see you now!"

With a howling shriek, Zotz's diabolical wind tore off a strip of Shade's fake skin, then another, and he knew that within seconds he would be flayed bare, as naked as a furless newborn, pink and quivering.

He abandoned his illusion, sloughing it off like a snakeskin and leaving it hanging in the air, collapsing in on itself. He bolted, hoping that in the confusion he would have enough time to find a hiding place.

And go back to get his father.

Enraged, Goth slashed at the shimmering carcass that still hung in the air, a grotesque double of himself. Jaws snapping, he shattered the head and let it splinter into a million tiny echoes.

He whirled in time to see the small Silverwing darting for the ceiling.

Shade!

Somehow he'd known instinctively it must be he, this same malformed troublemaker who had dogged him with bad luck since they'd first met. A world of mischief packed into a runt's body. But no longer.

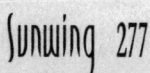

Sunwing 277

Goth stabbed at the air with sound and caught Shade in his mind's eye, there, pressing himself into a crevice in the ceiling, thinking himself hidden and safe to work more sound tricks. The Silverwing had his back to him, and Goth was upon him in three wingstrokes.

Before Shade even had time to turn his head, Goth sank his claws deep between his shoulder blades. He lunged, closing his jaws around Shade's neck, biting so deeply that his teeth smashed painfully together. He chewed furiously, waiting for the pleasure of the taste of live bat, but it didn't come.

There was no taste whatsoever.

He took a second ripping bite, and then a third before realizing he was rending air instead of flesh, filling his jaws with nothing. He reared back in disgust and outrage, and saw the dissolving remnants of another sound illusion.

"Shade!" Goth roared, whirling in fury.

With his raw throat, Shade spun himself a ragged cloak of invisibility and landed near his father. Cassiel was dragging himself painfully across the stone, toward its edge—unnoticed for the moment by the remaining guards. For just a split second, everything else in the chamber seemed blotted out as Shade gazed at his father for the first time in his life.

This was his father, this gaunt, broken creature. He shouldn't have been surprised to see him so ravaged, but he was. After all the secondhand stories, all his imaginings, he'd built his father up to be an indomitable hero.

And now to see him splayed on this stone, emaciated and helpless . . . Shade drew closer. His father's smell was pungent, of days without food or sleep, days without grooming. But beneath that was a smell as familiar and comforting as any on the earth. He smelled like home.

Shade wanted to shut his eyes and ears and lie down beside him, fold himself into his fur.

Cassiel must have sensed something close by, for he jerked round, baring his teeth, hissing. Shade took a step back in alarm and then, for just a moment, he allowed his echo illusion to evaporate and gave his father a glimpse of himself. Not that he recognized him—how could he, he'd never set eyes on him. But he saw his father frown in confusion, and close his fierce jaws.

Then Shade cloaked himself again, but this time, he threw sound over his father too, so that they were invisible to all but each other. Overhead, Shade could hear Goth thrashing around, searching for him, calling out orders to his other guards. He knew they didn't have much time. Already he could hear Zotz's wind sluicing through the room, in search of him, ready to tear away this disguise.

"You can't fly?" Shade whispered.

His father shook his head. "My wing."

Shade saw the swelling beneath the membrane, and knew that his forearm was badly sprained. Shade cursed himself. What a fool he was. He'd come up here expecting what? To save them all. And now he was without help, and they'd both die here.

"Who are you?" said his father hoarsely. "I've met you . . ."

"No."

"I know you."

"No."

"Who are you, then?"

"I'm your son."

"Shade?" said his father.

It was his turn to be taken aback. "How'd you know?"

"We named you before you were born."

And for just a second they cheated time and embraced, safe beneath the invisible shell Shade spun out for them.

"We'll crawl," Shade said. "Across to the wall, then up to the portal."

But even as he spoke the words he knew the plan was doomed. He could hear Zotz's breath moaning toward them and it lashed against them with the fury of a gale. With two shrieking, clawed hands, the sound tore apart his veil of invisibility.

"Fly!" his father told him.

"Cling to me," Shade said. "We'll fly together!"

He doubted he could ever take off with so much extra weight, but he would not leave his father.

A huge weight struck him in the chest, and he was slammed back against the stone, straddled by two powerful claws, one on each wing. Goth's searing breath poured down upon him.

"I knew it was you," said Goth. "You've stopped me

from killing the sun, but I will still eat your beating heart!"

Crouched at the rim of the circular portal, Marina peered down into the winged maelstrom of the chamber.

Beside her were Caliban and General Cortez and a dozen of his rat guards who had made the difficult climb up the face of the pyramid. All the way up they'd heard screams wafting from the summit, but occasionally Marina had caught the outlines of small northern bats in her echo vision, hurtling through the sky.

"They're getting away—some of them, anyway," she'd said excitedly to Caliban.

She'd also heard a scattered hooting of owls, and wondered if some of them too had managed to fight their way through the hordes of cannibals to the outside world.

Now they were at the top, looking down, and what she saw terrified her. It was difficult to make anything out clearly, there was so much movement. But she caught the thrashing of cannibal wings, as well as those of northern bats. She saw a huge stone directly beneath them, and for a split second had thought she'd seen Shade on it, but then he was gone, just gone. But most horrific of all was something *unseen*. It was pure sound, a kind of animated shriek that smashed its way around the chamber, slamming walls like a rabid animal in its death throes.

She didn't want to go down there, but she had to make sure Shade wasn't trapped.

Suddenly Ariel was beside her, panting, and so was Chinook.

"You got out!" Marina exclaimed. "Where's Shade?"

Ariel's face looked stricken. "I thought he'd gotten out with you. . . ."

Marina felt sick. "He must be in there."

She looked back over the rim and saw Goth plunging toward the stone, and directly below him, in the cannibal's line of flight—

Shade.

Shade writhed to free himself but it was no use. He was used up, as frail as a dried leaf. He saw Goth's jagged teeth and clamped shut his eyes and tried to send himself somewhere very far away.

He felt Goth strike him hard in the chest, knocking all the air from him, and suddenly all his instincts kicked to life and he barked out sound to see by.

Goth was sprawled on top of him, his head against the stone, and on his back were Marina and Ariel, Caliban and Chinook. They must've crashed against him with all their combined weight. Shade struggled free from under Goth's body, but could hear a low, ominous gurgle from his throat. Not dead, never dead.

"Let's go," Marina shouted at him.

"Where's my father!"

"Right here," said his mother, staring at Cassiel in disbelief. He was barely conscious now, but Shade could see a flicker of amazed delight in his eyes.

"Ariel," he breathed.

"We've got to fly him out," said Shade.

"I can do it," said Caliban. "Help him onto my back. Hurry."

Goth shuddered, and Shade looked to see one of his wings jerk convulsively as he began to revive.

"Go!" Shade urged Caliban, and watched as the mastiff leaped from the stone, wings churning, and lifted slowly into the air, carrying his father. Ariel was off beside them and Marina and Chinook too, and he leaped now, mouth opening, preparing to spin out a web of invisibility to take them into the sky.

Claws impaled his tail and dragged him back down.

It was too fast for him even to cry out. He tore free, feeling his tail rip nearly in half, and faced Goth. There was no fear left in him now, it was all used up, and all that was left was sheer determination to live. He barked sound into Goth's face, slapping him hard. Outrage exploded from Goth's eyes and lungs, and he lunged, shearing a patch of fur from Shade's shoulder.

Shade feinted and rolled, keeping Goth at bay with sound, but the cannibal was steadily driving him back toward the wall. Over Goth's shoulder, Shade could see Caliban carrying his father through the portal to freedom—and then he saw something so amazing, he thought he must be hallucinating.

Six balls of flame dropped into the pure blackness of the temple like miniature suns. Even Goth surged around to look, startled by the sudden light. Then Shade saw they were the burning ends of flaming sticks, and that could only mean one thing.

Owls.

In a thunderclap of feathered wings they exploded through the opening, and Shade saw Orestes in the forefront, his fierce eyes and beak flashing.

From the circular portal, long vines and creepers sprang over the rim, unfurling into the chamber; and running down the length of each, even as it unrolled, was a rat. He saw Cortez among them as they leaped to the walls, the floor, the backs of surprised cannibal bats, sinking their teeth deep.

Goth reared to face him once more, but before he could even part his jaws to lunge, Orestes and another owl had him in their claws.

"We've got him, Silverwing," said Orestes. "Fly now."

Shade did not hesitate. He soared up and up, and burst through the circular portal, gasping, as if it were the surface of the ocean.

"Shade, Shade, over here!" Marina called. "The owls are coming to help us! From all over the jungle!"

Shade saw more and more owls plunging down into the portal to do battle with the cannibals, and felt overwhelmed with relief.

Then, high above him in the air, he heard a faint whistling. He looked up and saw it, searing his mind's eye like a bolt of lightning.

Goth's metal disc.

Plummeting straight for all of them.

He heard Marina screaming at him to fly, but he knew

it was useless. An image ripped itself from his memory: the size of the blast created by those big discs, that towering column of fire. It would eat them all: the owls and rats still inside, everyone on the outside for hundreds of wingbeats.

Zotz would have his sacrifice after all, and it would be more than a hundred hearts—it would be thousands. He looked up into the black sky, searching for the sun.

Still eclipsed.

If the bomb fell while it was still dark, then Zotz would reign.

"Get everyone out of the pyramid!" he yelled back at Marina. "Tell them there's Human fire coming. Tell them!"

"Shade, there's no time!" Ariel cried. "Come with us!"

"I'll make time!" he shouted.

He flew straight up toward the disc, and enmeshed it in sound, studying its shape, the angle at which it fell. He was so tired now, his wings leaden, his throat raw, and where would his strength come from? For the first time in his life, he spoke to her, and called her by name and said: "Nocturna, let me be able to do this."

Falling, falling, it was shrieking now through the air, shrieking like Zotz's own breath.

He couldn't do it.

Can do it. Must do it.

An icicle was one thing; it was small, light, it was inert. This was hurtling metal, accelerated to a million wingbeats a second.

He took aim, launched a net of sound at the disc, and missed.

He closed his eyes, measured again with his echo vision, took a breath.

Please, he thought.

He opened his mouth, and sound exploded from him, raking his throat, as if something greater were speaking through him. It was like a thunderclap shattering the sky, this yell, and he watched it in his mind's eye as it streaked toward the disc and grasped it like a fist.

Hold it there.

He swirled, drenched in sweat, singing sound with all his might, pushing against the disc to hold it up.

How heavy it was!

He wished he could look down below, to see if Marina and the others were fleeing, to see if they were far enough away. He could only hope she'd done what he'd asked. He looked up into the sky, and still saw no sun. How long, how long would he have to wait? He was back in the northern forests, a newborn, huddled scared against the side of a tree with Chinook, waiting for the sunrise. Come, come, why isn't it coming?

He didn't know how much longer he could cradle this disc with his voice. He tasted blood in his throat.

"Let it fall!"

Far overhead the cannibal with the crooked spine was plunging toward the motionless disc.

"You cannot stop Zotz. Let it fall!"

He faltered and heard the disc plunge a little lower,

and had to work to slow it down. Then the cannibal bat dove onto it, locking his claws around the chain.

Shade's mind nearly buckled with the added weight.

Blearily, he saw Chinook hurl himself against the cannibal bat, trying to beat him clear of the disc, striking out with wings and jaws. He saw the jungle bat sink his teeth into Chinook's shoulder, heard his friend cry out in pain. But Chinook kept fighting, knocking, butting the cannibal, until his claws ripped free from the disc.

It dropped several feet, and Shade could barely slow it down. Hold it, hold it, just a little longer. Shade looked up and saw something shift in the great black sky, *heard* it shift.

The sun.

A slim crescent of it seared his face as it came back, blinding him.

"Fly!" he shouted out to Chinook.

The disc plunged. Shade beat his exhausted wings, hoping Marina had cleared the pyramid. Chinook was suddenly at his side, trying to nudge him along faster, but Shade's wings were unbearably heavy. He gave a quick, impatient shake of his head, but Chinook didn't fly on ahead as he'd wanted. He stayed alongside. Behind them—not far enough, not nearly—he could clearly hear the disc whistling down, first above him, then below. Any second now.

He told himself not to look.

He heard the explosion at the same moment he felt its ferocious heat, and then it was like being swallowed up by the sun itself.

SUNWING

From the high ramparts of Bridge City, Frieda looked out across the twilight sky. Her eyesight had dimmed dramatically over the past several nights, but even she could make out the massive thunderhead of owls spanning the northern horizon.

A brisk wind rustled the fur of her face, and she felt immensely old and tired. Eight nights it had been since Marina and Ariel had left in search of Shade, and she couldn't stop herself fearing the worst. Was it possible for Shade, clever as he was, gifted as he was, to survive the Human's explosives? Or the jungle with all its monstrous predators? Had she been foolish to approve of Ariel and Marina's search for him?

Questions, questions, she thought; all I do lately is ask myself questions.

She wondered too if she had been a good elder, and helped lead her colony well. In particular, her thoughts had turned to Shade, and she debated whether she was wrong to encourage in him the same passions she stoked within herself. To find the secret of the bands, to fulfill Nocturna's Promise. What was the sum of all this yearning?

Right now, as she saw the millions of owls darkening the sky, she had to fight off the grip of despair. Impossible to defeat them. Even with the huge army assembled at Bridge City, she feared they would be wiped from the earth.

"We must prepare our delegation," said Achilles Graywing, landing beside her. "King Boreal's troops will be overhead within hours."

Frieda nodded stiffly. Even such a simple movement made her tired now. "Yes," she said without much hope. "We must pray he is in a mood to talk."

"I gave up on prayer long ago," Achilles told her with a grim smile.

"Perhaps you're right," said Frieda, "but whenever I look at that horizon, I make every appeal for help I can."

Frieda looked down to see a messenger thrashing his way toward the bridge's summit. She waited patiently as the bat circled and caught his breath: Surely there could be no more bad news left to hear. And yet her ancient heart raced within her.

"General Achilles, Frieda Silverwing," the messenger panted, "bats have been sighted, coming in from the south. Silverwings, some of them. And . . . they're flying with owls."

Shade gratefully angled his aching wings, and began a slow descent toward Bridge City. Flying with his whole family was still a wonderful novelty to him: his mother and father close by on one side; Marina and Chinook on the other, all keeping pace together through the dusky air. Nearby he saw Caliban, and all the other northern bats from the jungle, streaking around them, coming home.

In arrowhead formation before them flew a dozen owls from the northern forests—a sight Shade still hadn't gotten used to, even after several days and nights of traveling together. Owls and bats within wingbeats. True, they kept mostly to themselves, roosting and hunting separately, and speaking little with the other group. But Shade sensed this was more from awkwardness than suspicion. He saw Orestes in the vanguard and smiled to himself. It was because of the owl prince that the other birds had agreed to form a convoy with them. And Shade was right about what good protection they would be. They'd made it out of the jungle safely and, able to fly day and night, they'd made good time heading home.

Alive: It still made Shade shake his head in amazement. He was alive.

After hearing the huge metal disc explode, and feeling the terrible heat engulf him, he remembered nothing until he groggily woke in the full blaze of day, splayed on the topmost branches of a tree. His whole body sang with pain. Patches of fur had been vaporized on his belly and back, and sections of his wing membrane had been badly seared. He felt as if he'd been pummeled by some giant beast. He was mangy and scarred, but he was alive. And so, miraculously, was Chinook.

And the sun was still shining.

Strange, for a bat to be so happy to see the sun. After millions of years fearing it, staying away from it, he'd tried to save it. Looking at it gratefully, he supposed he'd succeeded.

It wasn't long before Marina and his mother had found him and Chinook, and helped them limp back to Statue Haven. A huge circle had been scorched from the jungle by the explosion, and trees burned still. At the center of all this he could make out a smoldering pile of stone—the remnants of the pyramid. He wondered if Goth had been destroyed in the blast, and couldn't quite make himself believe it.

He was amazed at how many had survived. Marina had flown back inside the pyramid and warned the others. The owls had helped Cortez and most of his remaining rat soldiers escape by carrying them out on their backs. But there were so many losses too. Ishmael had not returned, though his brother had. And dozens more had died inside the pyramid: owls, rats, and bats. More lost lives to add to the thousands who'd already died when their discs had exploded over the Human city.

Shade glanced over at Chinook. He'd lost both his parents, but at least he wasn't an orphan anymore, not really. Three nights ago, Shade had secretly asked his mother and father if Chinook could join their family, and they had instantly agreed. And so had Chinook when they'd asked him.

"Hey, Shade, we're brothers now!" Chinook had said, digging his thumb playfully into Shade's ribs.

Shade winced, shifting away. "I tried to stop them, Chinook, honestly, but my parents had their hearts set on it." Chinook didn't know it was all Shade's idea, and Shade wasn't about to tell him. With a sigh, he knew he'd be getting a lot more snow dumped on his head now. Still, he didn't regret it. Not yet, anyway.

Now, as they neared Bridge City, he turned to his father. Already, it seemed impossible that Shade had ever been without him. And he realized that in some ways he hadn't, not really. Even in his absence Cassiel had been such a presence in his daily thoughts, it was as if his father must, one day, materialize to answer all his son's questions, to explain himself.

Over the journey, Shade had heard all about Cassiel's terrible adventure. Last spring, he'd been one of the first to find the Human building and the forest inside, and he'd spent months there as it slowly filled with other bats. At first he'd been hopeful, but then the Humans started experimenting with them, trying to perfect their metal discs, and Cassiel had known many bats who'd had their wings burned off—or worse.

"You have no idea how badly I wanted to escape, to get back to you, warn you all," he told Shade and Ariel. "But I couldn't. The stream never occurred to me," he added, looking admiringly at his son. "And then, once they took me in the flying machine to the jungle, I almost lost hope of ever getting back. It was all we could do to survive night by night. I never thought of rescue, and certainly not by my own son."

"He's even crazier than you," Ariel said with a smile.

"Certainly braver," Cassiel said, and Shade burned with pleasure at this compliment. But he quickly looked over at Marina.

"I did a lot of stupid things," he said, shaking his head. "If it weren't for Marina and you too, Mom, I'd have died in the jungle probably. All of us."

"You have a way of dragging me into things," said Marina wryly. "I'll give you that."

"You're like me," Cassiel told his son. "Both of us greedy for knowledge. I wanted to take the sun back for all of us. I wanted to know the secret of the bands."

"There was no secret," said Shade bitterly. "We were all wrong about the Humans helping us, Nocturna's Promise." For a moment his happiness at finally being reunited with his family paled, and he remembered that their journey north was hardly a triumphant homecoming. It was a preparation for war. He'd heard all about King Boreal raising his armies to fight at Bridge City.

"I mean, we saved the sun," said Shade indignantly. "You'd think the owls would be grateful for that, but somehow, I doubt they'll be impressed." He felt weary. "Now we've just got another fight ahead of us."

"They might help us," Marina reminded him, nodding at Orestes and the other owls.

Shade nodded. It was the one hope he harbored too. But at the same time, he worried that once they all reached Bridge City safely, everything good they'd shared in the jungle would somehow be forgotten: The whole convoy north would simply be a matter of convenience, and they'd go back to their own warring sides. Orestes too.

Soon he would find out.

As Shade neared the glittering peaks of Bridge City, he saw a small group of bats flickering toward them as they made their descent.

"It's Achilles Graywing," Marina said.

Shade watched as the famous general drew warily closer and then called out, "Are you flying with these owls of your own free will?"

Shade knew the general must think they were all prisoners of the owls, perhaps held hostage in exchange for safe passage over Bridge City.

"Yes," Cassiel called back loudly, "we're with them freely. They are friends."

Shade could hear mutters of amazement pass among the other bats.

"This is hard to imagine," said Achilles Graywing, "when our northern horizon is blackened by an owl army, less than an hour away."

"Is my father among them?" Orestes called out impulsively.

Achilles looked at the owl warily. "Your father?"

"King Boreal."

"It is King Boreal who leads them," the general replied coolly.

"Then I must speak to him at once," Orestes said.

"Our delegation has already departed to do so," Achilles replied.

Orestes circled back to Shade. "Let's hurry, then," he said.

"You're going to help us?" Shade asked.

"Of course," replied the owl, "with all my heart. Wasn't it obvious?"

"Father, I'd be grateful if you'd let me speak," Orestes told King Boreal.

High above Bridge City, the leaders of the bat and owl kingdoms circled warily around one another. Shade felt distinctly out of place among Halo Freetail, Achilles Graywing, and the other bat elders. And he felt particularly uneasy flying so close to the massive King Boreal with his magnificent silver head and the lightning-streaked plumage he shared with his son. Shade knew that this was to be the last talk before the battle began, and he watched Orestes anxiously as he addressed his fierce father.

"Are you on good terms with your father?" he'd asked hopefully as they'd sped to the aerial meeting place.

"Not particularly," Orestes had said.

And in fact, their meeting was far from what Shade would have expected, a stiff nod between father and son. But maybe, Shade thought, that was just because of the situation. This was not the time for emotional reunions.

King Boreal looked irritated at his son's request to speak. "Has this any bearing on the matter at hand?" he said in a bone-rattling thunder.

"Yes."

"Be brief."

"We cannot go to war with the bats," said Orestes nervously, looking around at the other owls as they tried to suppress their contemptuous laughter.

"I think your son needs more tutoring in such matters," muttered one of the owl ambassadors.

King Boreal turned his baleful eyes on the speaker, and needed to do no more in rebuke.

"Why do you say this?" he asked his son sternly.

"Shade Silverwing saved my life," Orestes began falteringly. "Not once but twice. Last fall when we closed the night skies to the bats, we thought they'd been murdering birds. But these northern bats weren't the murderers. They were jungle bats from the south."

"We have already heard these lies," snapped King Boreal.

"I have seen them myself," insisted Orestes. "And I would have been killed if it weren't for Shade. He risked his own life to do it, even though we've declared war on him and his fellow bats."

"An unusual act of bravery, perhaps," said King Boreal coolly, fixing his moonlike eyes on Shade, "but irrelevant. What does this have to do with the larger issue at hand?"

"The Humans have been taking owls and bats south

to help them wage war," Orestes pressed on, and waited for a moment for the surprised exclamations of his elders to die down. "I can explain more later, but this is what I wanted to say. The south is home to thousands of cannibals, and they took owls prisoner there, and if it weren't for Shade, we would have been eaten alive by these monsters. Because of him, we escaped and returned home."

"Again, I ask you, why should this make us change our course of action?"

"Because we don't want war," Shade blurted impetuously, and received a glare from Halo Freetail.

King Boreal laughed scornfully. "You have waged war on us before," he said. "Fifteen years ago, as I recall. But you're not old enough to remember such things, young Silverwing."

"We waged war, yes, but in rebellion," Achilles told King Boreal. "We wanted the sun back. We wanted to be free of your tyranny, the risk of death should we see so much as a splinter of sunrise!"

"But you have lost the sun, all of you," thundered King Boreal, "for your treachery at the Great Battle of the Birds and the Beasts."

"Because we didn't take sides!" Achilles said hotly.

"No, because you switched sides," King Boreal retorted.

"You are mistaken, King Boreal," Achilles said. "As you have been for millions of years."

"It is tragic that you can believe your own lies," said the owl king.

"What does it matter?" Shade blurted out angrily

"Silence," Halo Freetail hissed at him. "Your place is not to speak here."

"Why shouldn't he?" Orestes said.

"Because he knows nothing," said King Boreal, "like you."

"Let him speak," said Achilles calmly. "One of our greatest elders, Frieda Silverwing, has had much confidence in this young bat."

"It happened so long ago," said Shade haltingly, more nervous now that everyone was listening to him in hostile silence. "It's over, even if we can't agree on what the truth is."

"The truth is *everything*," said King Boreal.

"I thought so too," said Shade. "I thought the sun was stolen from us, and I wanted to get it back, and I thought the Humans would help us somehow. I thought we would beat the owls in war, I really did." He faltered, wondering if he should've said that. But it was too late to stop now. He just had to go on before what he wanted to say slipped away from him. "I thought that was the truth, but it wasn't. The Humans didn't help us fight a war with you. They didn't bring us back the sun. They just wanted to use us, all of us, owls and bats. That's how I met Orestes, in one of their indoor forests. Maybe he wanted to kill me; I guess I wanted to kill him too. But there was something else in there that wanted to kill both of us."

"The cannibal bat," Orestes said.

"Yeah," said Shade. "And I don't even know why I

helped Orestes that first time, maybe just because he was being attacked and I didn't like to see it. And then he helped me. And that seemed important, I guess. More important than what happened at the Great Battle, a million years ago. . . ."

He'd lost hold of what he was trying to say, and trailed off. He didn't even remember what he'd just said; probably a babbling mess.

"We were always taught bats were traitors," Orestes said to his father, "that you couldn't trust them. But Shade isn't like that, and neither are the others I met. We fought together for our lives. We trusted each other."

"There might be other Human buildings," Shade said, "where they're keeping bats and owls prisoner. We should be using our energy to free them, not fighting each other."

King Boreal looked from Shade to his son in one slow blink.

"I find all this youthful naïveté trying," an owl ambassador said.

Achilles Graywing sighed and looked at the stars overhead. "We would be wise to heed it more carefully," he said.

"Perhaps so," said King Boreal, and for the first time, Shade thought he looked tenderly at his own son. "I had given you up for lost, and I missed you sorely."

"Me too," said Orestes, flying closer.

"My appetite for war is dulled," said King Boreal. "Let us agree to a truce, if that is acceptable to you. We can meet this summer in the northern forests and talk more of this, in the hopes of coming to a better understanding."

"Yes," said Halo Freetail, "let us do that, King Boreal."

"The night skies are no longer closed to you. You have them once again in peace."

"The sun," Shade breathed, before he could stop himself.

He swallowed as King Boreal's head swiveled back to him, eyes flashing. Oh no, I've ruined everything, he thought.

"The sun?" said the owl king, eyebrows lifting. "Are the nights not enough for you?"

All he could do was shake his head.

"That must be a matter of discussion when we next meet. Until then, I can consent to an interim measure. You have given me back my son, Silverwing. So in return I give you your sun."

When Shade landed beside Frieda on the sheltered ledge beneath the bridge, she was so still, he feared he was too late.

"Is she breathing?" he whispered anxiously to Marina, who'd flown down with him.

"I believe I am." The Silverwing elder opened her eyes and looked at Shade with some amusement. But her words whistled faintly with effort. "Your mother told me all about your meeting with King Boreal."

"We can all go home now," said Shade excitedly. "They're freeing all the Hibernaculums. We can go back to our forest! In the sunlight! I want to help make a new Tree Haven. I mean, it's the least I can do since I got the first one burned down, right?" He knew he was rattling on, but he was afraid not to talk, afraid what he might see, might hear.

Frieda just smiled. "I told you there was a brightness to you. It's always so satisfying to be proven right. Not something that happens very often when you're an elder." She coughed. "You did what *I* wanted to do. You fulfilled the Promise."

With great difficulty she raised her wing to reveal the silver band on her forearm. The sight of it made Shade wince. It used to be such a powerful image for him, a sign of hope, of strength. He'd wanted one so badly. Now it would always be a hideous reminder of what the Humans had done to all of them—and of a horrible delusion that had falsely raised their hopes for centuries. He hated the sight of the bands now.

"No," Frieda wheezed, seeing it in his face, "the bands were important."

Shade didn't know what to say. How could he contradict her now, when she was so sick?

"I think I understand," said Marina with surprise. "They did play a part."

"How?" Shade demanded angrily. How could anyone say that now?

"The bands set us on the path," Marina said. "They made us seek the Humans out."

"And look where it took us," said Shade.

"Oh, he's not as smart as he thinks!" said Marina gleefully to Frieda. "Yeah, they took us to the Human building, and the fake forest. And that's where the owls were too."

Shade looked from her to Frieda, mystified. But Frieda nodded, her eyes sparkling.

"Go on," she urged Marina.

"What if you hadn't met Orestes, if you hadn't saved his life? You won each other's trust. I doubt King Boreal would've called a truce if that hadn't happened."

Shade nodded sheepishly, finally realizing.

"The Humans brought us together," he said.

"United us," said Frieda. "We didn't win the sun through war. We won it through peace."

As Shade watched, Frieda smiled, as though she'd just caught a glimpse of a favorable future. She rustled her wings, folded them comfortably against her body, and shut her eyes for the last time.

TREE HAVEN

It was a good tree, a massive silver maple with a broad trunk and a multitude of strong, high branches. As the sky paled with the coming dawn, thousands of Silverwings, male and female, were at work, hollowing out the insides of the great tree, turning it into a nursery roost for the colony. Just a few hundred wingbeats to the east were the charred remains of the old Tree Haven, the place where Shade had been born, and which he'd seen burned down by the owls last fall.

Beneath the tree, among the buckled roots, Shade was working alongside his father, carving out the walls of the new echo chamber. Every colony had one, a perfectly circular stone chamber, whose walls were so smooth that a bat's voice could bounce between them for centuries. It was here that all a colony's stories were spoken, and contained as echoes within the walls, so that nothing would be forgotten. Last fall, when Tree Haven burned, its echo chamber was breached, and all the stories of the colony had fled like ghostly bats, dissolving in the air. Now they would tell the stories again.

As he polished the wall with a small rock, Shade remembered how Frieda had taken him to the echo chamber for the first time. There, he hadn't simply heard the stories, he'd *seen* them as the echoes flooded his head with silvery pictures. As if he'd been there, he saw the Great Battle of the Birds and the Beasts, the Banishment, and heard Nocturna's voice make the bats a Promise, that one day they would regain the light of day. But Frieda had died before she could see a sunrise—not one of those fake ones from inside the Human forest, but a real one in the outside world.

"I wish she were still alive," he said.

His father nodded, knowing instinctively who Shade was talking about. "She would've been happy that your mother took her place, though."

"Yeah," said Shade. "Mom's a good choice. I mean, she didn't blow up the cannibals' pyramid, or save the sun or anything, but she'll be good." He saw his father looking at him humorously. "What?"

"I know you wanted to be an elder."

"I didn't," said Shade, looking away, embarrassed.

"You did," laughed Cassiel. "Hardly a year old, and you expected to be made an elder! You've done some amazing things, but you've got some years to go yet, my son."

"Come on, you wanted to be asked too," said Shade with a grin.

His father shook his head and started to say something, but then just looked back at him. They both smiled.

"Probably best neither of us were," said Shade.

"Better for the entire colony," his father agreed. "Hotheads like us don't make good leaders."

He grinned and went back to polishing. It was such a simple thing, talking to his father, but still a novelty, and every so often he'd feel a pulse of tremendous happiness. For the first time in his life he felt complete.

Almost, anyway. He sighed inwardly.

"What do you think of Marina?" he asked his father casually.

"Fine young bat."

Since returning to the northern forest a few weeks ago, lots of the young bats had been choosing mates. He'd watched it all with a feeling of acute discomfort. The truth was he still felt ridiculous, especially around female bats. And even, lately, around Marina, which rankled him most of all. They'd been such good friends; she'd risked her life for him, and he used to feel so completely at home with her. But now everything was different, and he just couldn't believe she'd take him seriously as a potential mate. It wasn't so long ago he'd first met her: He was a runty newborn, lost, scared, and she was a full year older than him—something she *never* let him forget. She always seemed so colossally unimpressed by him. Sure, he was supposed to be a hero. Then how come he never felt like one?

"Yeah, she's pretty great," he said. He put down his

polishing stone with a sigh. "I'm not much to look at, especially after half my fur got burned off."

"It'll grow back. Anyway, let's have a look at you." His father pulled back, tilting his head from side to side. "You're not so bad, no uglier than your father."

"I'm not big like the others. Not . . . handsome. Like Chinook."

"No, you're not as handsome as Chinook."

"No," said Shade, put out that his father had agreed so readily.

"You know what?" his father said. "I don't think Marina cares."

"You don't?"

"No. She's smarter than that."

"I'm going to stretch my wings," said Shade abruptly.

"Take your time," said his father.

Shade shot out of the echo chamber, spiraled up through a larger cave, then hurried on all fours through the undulating tunnel that led up into the base of the new Tree Haven.

All around him, Silverwings were at work, chipping away ledges and roosts for themselves from the soft wood. He flew up through the hollow trunk, seeking out Marina with sound. Near the top of the tree, he saw his mother overseeing the work on the elders' roosts, which would be at the very summit.

"Shade," she greeted him, nuzzling his cheek.

"Have you seen Marina?"

"She went out to hunt, I think."

Without waiting, he hurled himself through a knot-hole in the trunk, and was out in the night. How he'd missed all this over the months. It was early spring, and the air was still crisp, a hint of frost glinting from the branches and grass. But everything was starting to live again, leaves beginning to unfurl, buds opening. He wondered if he would ever feel the same about the day as the night, and decided he never would. The night would always be special somehow.

"Marina!" he called out, snapping up a few midges as he flew. He thought he saw her up ahead, and veered after her, calling out her name again. "Hey, wait up, will you!"

"Race you to the stream!" he heard her call back over her shoulder.

"Do we have to?" he shouted, but she showed no signs of stopping, and he hated the idea of her beating him. He trimmed his wings and darted after her, through the branches of a big chestnut—a shortcut he knew. He blasted out from the trees and swirled over the stream, dipping low to skim some water into his mouth. It was so cold, it burned.

"Beat you!" he cried out, settling on an overhanging branch.

"No you didn't."

He jumped. She was hanging just several inches away, folded up in her bright wings, and looking for all the world like an autumn leaf that hadn't fallen. He smiled. It was just the way he'd first met her, on the island, long ago.

"How's your roost going?" he asked her, suddenly awkward.

"I finished it a few hours ago."

"I'm glad you're staying with us."

"Hmmmm," she said lazily. "I couldn't pass up the novelty of being the only Brightwing in your colony. Oh, by the way, Chinook just asked me to be his mate."

Shade nearly choked on his mosquito. "What?"

"Yeah, just an hour ago."

"Oh," said Shade stiffly. "Well, he's a handsome bat, like you said."

"Everyone's choosing mates now. You've noticed that, right, Shade?"

"Yes," he said through gritted teeth.

"You know it's something I've really wanted, don't you?" she said, looking at him intently. "I mean, I'm older than you, I know that. It's not the same for you yet. But for me, I have to have a home. Ariel's been so good to me, but I want my very own family now. You understand, right?"

"Yes," he said, looking away.

"So you'll be my mate, then," Marina said, grinning.

"Be your . . . what about Chinook?"

"I told him no thanks. I did the right thing, didn't I?"

"You're not allowed to be anyone's mate but mine," said Shade, curving his wing around her and drawing her close.

"Good," she said, her voice muffled against his fur. "It worked out just right, then."

"I thought I heard your voices," said Ariel, landing on the branch.

"Marina's going to be my mate!" Shade exclaimed.

"I know; she already told me."

"You did?" he asked, looking at Marina.

"Well, come on, Shade, it was obvious. Who else would put up with you?"

"I'm sure you'll both be very . . . competitive," said Ariel with a smile, "and happy too." She looked at Shade. "Your father says the echo chamber's almost finished."

Shade nodded.

"I was talking with the elders, and we agreed that you should tell our most recent story."

"Me?" Shade said. He'd never even imagined such an honor. His voice telling a story to the walls of the echo chamber, living on for centuries, long after he was dead. Always there for the Silverwing colony.

His mother nodded. "It's what Frieda would have wanted. It's your story, Shade."

"I'd love to do it," he said.

"We'll begin after dawn," said Ariel, and flew off.

Shade looked up through the branches of the tree into the brightening sky. All around them, birds were beginning their dawn chorus from their nests, and he could even hear an owl, hooting in the distance. And the sound no longer made him feel afraid.

"Come on," he said to Marina, "I'll show you the best place in the forest to see the sun rise."

AUTHOR'S NOTE

During the Second World War, the United States military initiated Project X-Ray, a top secret program in which bats were trained to carry and deliver explosive devices. Ultimately the project was scrapped after hundreds of bats escaped from the test range, incinerated several army buildings, and took up residence beneath a large fuel tank.

This historical incident was the inspiration for one of the main story lines in *Sunwing*. Aztec and Mayan mythology were also rich sources of ideas for me when it came to writing about Goth and the Vampyrum Spectrum. The Aztecs really did have a huge, beautiful calendar stone that was more accurate than anything in Europe at the time—and this became, in my story, the stone that predicts the total eclipse and eternal night. (The Aztecs had a very profound fear of the sun being extinguished forever on certain dates.)

Bridge City is based on the real city of Austin, Texas, where the underside of the Congress Avenue Bridge is home to a million free-tailed bats, which can be seen flooding into the sky at twilight. Finally, I got the idea for Statue Haven from the giant statue of Christ the Redeemer, on Corcovado Mountain, overlooking the city of Rio de Janeiro.

Coming soon, the next book in the *Silverwing* sequence:

FIREWING

He woke to the enormous weight of stone, crushing down on him. The stench of seared rock and dust clogged his nostrils. Sluggishly at first, and then with increasing panic, he dredged his mind for memories. He could not remember what he was, or whether he had a name. He tried to lift a shoulder, dig in with a hind leg.

Push.

Exhausted by the effort, he wheezed, coughing dust from his mouth and nostrils.

What happened?

Who am I?

Fight, he told himself. *Fight this.*

Shoulders hunched, claws digging in, he pulled. His legs found purchase and he felt the leaden weight above him shift, allowing him a few precious inches. His head was aching with molten pain, fire raging in all his joints. His left wing was still extended, pinned flat by stone. He tried to pull it in, feeling as though he were dragging it inch by inch through the serrated jaws of some giant beast. He bellowed to dull the pain, and finally had his wing folded tight against him. Shuddering, he took a few moments to recover. He made the mistake of trying to open his eyes, only to have silt pour into them. Shutting them tight again, he cracked open his mouth, and sang out sound. Almost instantly his echoes were slammed back to him, painting an unintelligible silver mess of rock in his mind's eye. Buried alive.

He had a sudden image of himself, hundreds of feet below the earth, unable to reach the surface, the air slowly being forced from his lungs. Roaring with terror and rage, he flexed and thrashed, shoulders and back buckling against the stone. He felt it give, tumble down around him. Again and again he heaved himself upwards, his rear claws pushing against anything they touched.

Slashing up through the rubble, his snout broke the surface first. He pushed the rest of his head out, greedily sucking back air. Slowly he opened his eyes, all a blur with tears and dust, and saw before him in the gloom a barren plain of rubble and mud, stretching to all horizons. He cast out sound, and heard no trees or vegetation or life of any kind. Just earth and sky and a hot gritty wind that assumed its own ghostly silver shape in his echo vision.

Is this normal?

No, he was expecting something else—but what?

Think, he urged himself. *Remember.*

He hauled the rest of his body free from the rock and mud, and shivered, though it was not cold, his wings drawn tight, chin pressed into his chest. His mind throbbed, trying to unlock itself. And then a few images flared in his mind's eye—

Trees that soared to the sky and formed a canopy.

Below, a world of lush vegetation. Creepers and vines and mosses and flowers.

A pyramid of stone, with other creatures like him, swirling around it.

Home.

He looked around at the rubble strewn in all directions. This was not home. Then how had he come to be here? Again he thought of that stone pyramid, stared at it in his memory, urging it to show him more.

A flash of light, the beginnings of some cataclysmic noise—and nothing more.

An explosion? Some kind of disaster? And this . . . was this all there was left, everything flattened to a rocky plain? Tilting his aching neck, he squinted up at the heavens and saw, through the swirling dust, stars.

Instinctively he spread his wings to fly, but the earth would not release him. He felt immeasurably heavy and tired. After a bit of rest, he told himself. After a rest, you will be able to fly. Instead, he began a slow crawl, moving with the wind, opening his wings a little and angling them so he was driven along by it.

He didn't know where he was, or where he was going, but sooner or later he would have to meet another living thing who could tell him.

Then he stopped. His nose twitched, as if trying to catch a scent. Hunching forward, head cocked, he listened. Something was wrong. Very, very wrong. Not outside, but inside.

He tried to breathe calmly, to listen, to think.

Then it came to him.

His heart wasn't beating.

In a panic, he coughed and thrashed about, hoping to force his heart into action. He pounded his chest against the rocky ground. Beat! Beat! Desperate for air, his vision flared and swam—then suddenly cleared.

And he realized he wasn't dying.

He was already dead.

At the same moment, his name came surging back to him. He opened his mouth to speak it and his voice sounded alien to him, saturated with grime and exhaustion.

"Goth."

F **DATE DUE** Ani

FOLLETT